1/23

AWKWARD

Marni Bates

KENSINGTON PUBLISHING CORP.

www.kensingtonbooks.com

This book is dedicated to everyone who
has felt awkward and / or invisible.
So . . . pretty much everyone.
It gets better.

ACKNOWLEDGMENTS

My mother, Karen Bates, encouraged me, inspired me, supported me and spent countless hours editing with me over frozen yogurt. She also laughed with me about all my embarrassing moments, then suggested I work them into a novel, thus creating my current way of life. Best of all, she loves me, awkwardness included. Thanks, Mom! And to the rest of my family: I'm still not picking up the tab. Deal with it.

I'd also like to thank my super agent, Laurie McLean, my fantastic editor, Megan Records, and all the great people at Kensington Teen. Thanks for your support!

Chapter 1

You probably think you know me . . . and I understand why. You've probably read about me on AOL or heard Conan O'Brien or Jon Stewart reference me for the punch line of some joke. It's okay if you haven't. In fact, I prefer it that way. But let's be honest: the whole world knows about Mackenzie Wellesley and her social awkwardness. Except maybe some people in Burma and Sudan . . . but you get my point.

The thing is, despite all that's been said about me (and there has been a lot), only a handful of people actually understand how I was able to go from a boring high school student to a pop culture reference in the space of a week. That's why I am even bothering to explain. Don't worry: this won't be one of those stupid celebrity autobiographies where I describe my sordid past and complain a lot—my past isn't all that sordid, and that's just lame.

Let me start by saying that I've never hungered for the spotlight. My younger brother, Dylan, was always the one who craved The Big Moment. You know: catch the football in overtime with a few seconds left on the clock to score the winning touchdown. The very idea of a stadium full of people watching me makes me want to hurl. That's probably due to my elementary school ballet recital. I remember every detail perfectly. My mom was in the audience cradling a baby Dylan in her lap as I leaped across the stage. I was craning my neck, searching for my dad in the crowd, and worried that he wouldn't show up. That's when I glanced into the wings and spotted him right behind the curtains . . . making out with my dance instructor.

We have the recital on tape. You can tell when my world imploded by the way my brown eyes expanded and my shoulder-length brown hair whipped my face as I looked from my dad to my happily waving mom. But it gets worse— so much worse. I was frozen while all the other little girls twirled and flounced around me. I stumbled out of formation and—blinded by the stage lights—I tripped on the sound system cable and went flying right into the curtains, which promptly fell down and revealed my dad sucking face. That's when I decided it was better to be invisible than to fall on your face in a ridiculous pink tutu.

Freud would probably say that's why I suffer from a fear of crowds and attention. And in this specific case I think Freud might have a point. I've been paranoid ever since that damn recital—and the divorce. I avoid the spotlight. I guess you could say that I strive for anonymity. But I'm fine with my geekdom—totally cool with the fact that I never get invited to parties. I fill a certain niche at my school, the local nerd, and it's a role that I've gone to a lot of effort to create for myself. And while, yes, a normal day for me means three AP classes, it really isn't so bad. Definitely stressful, but I like it—especially because it'll look great to financial aid committees who decide on college scholarships.

So, yeah, I'm happy with my life. I've got friends, a job, and an awesome GPA to propel me into a solid university . . . or at least I *did*, until I became famous.

Chapter 2

"Hey, Kenzie. You'll never guess what happened!"
My best friend, Jane Smith, has been saying that to me almost every morning on the school bus for the past eleven years. Yes, she has the unfortunate distinction of having the most boring name of all time. She is also the only person who can call me anything besides Mackenzie. You have to make some concessions for friends who have stood by you since elementary school. But not even Jane is allowed to call me Mack. That's one nickname I've placed off limits.

"Okay, what happened, Jane," I responded, rolling my eyes.

Jane grinned and tucked a strand of her dark auburn hair behind an ear. "So I was sitting in the library."

"I'm shocked." Jane made Hermione Granger look like a slacker in the studying department. If she didn't have her head in a book at the school library, then she was shelving them at Fiction Addiction Used Bookstore.

"Funny. So I was in the library finishing my AP Calc homework when Josh asked if I'd seen *Battlestar Galactica*." She sighed. I kid you not, *sighed*. "That means he's into me, right?"

I rolled my eyes again and tried to ignore that my best

friend was practically swooning over a boy who wanted to live inside the World of Warcraft. After all, she can't help being a hopeless romantic . . . just like I can't help being a cynic.

"Uh-huh."

"Then we had this long discussion about the greatest sci-fi television shows of all time."

"Right."

"And this means . . ."

"That he's definitely into you." I know all my lines as a supportive best friend. Although I must not have said them with the required amount of enthusiasm, since Jane then rolled her eyes.

"I can't wait for Corey to get back from his Speech and Debate tournament."

Corey's been our mutual best friend since sixth grade. So when he told us he was gay, we just went to more sports events to scope out guys. And since Jane and I both have study schedules instead of social lives, I guess it made sense for her to want Corey's opinion.

I just laughed as we pulled up to Smith High School. No, it wasn't named after Jane—it was both an unfortunate coincidence and an incredibly boring name. Then again, boring is the best adjective for Forest Grove, Oregon, a suburb outside of Portland and my hometown. The school was actually named after Alvin and Abigail Smith, who wanted to be missionaries until they found out that European diseases had killed off the native population. Nothing like having "the Missionaries" as a school mascot, especially since they represent the destruction of an entire culture. I kept that to myself, though. I've noticed that saying stuff like that out loud generally doesn't go over real well in Forest Grove.

Anyway, Jane and I strolled over to our lockers, careful to avoid the courtyard area between the academic buildings where the Notables reigned. See, my school is divided into two main social classes: the Notables (who exist in a sphere of coolness) and the Invisibles (like, well . . . you get the picture). Jane and I weren't stupid enough to linger on Notable turf. When you're a member of the geek squad, you learn to make yourself scarce and to travel in herds. So I was pretending I hadn't heard Jane moan about the cancellation of Joss Whedon's show *Firefly* five hundred times before when the most notable of the Notable girls, Chelsea Halloway, effortlessly tossed her long, dirty blond hair and made eye contact.

At Smith High School, one look from Chelsea is the only forewarning of impending doom. Chelsea has a knack for subtly and skillfully turning girls into social lepers. Still, when you have a connection to someone like Logan Beckett (the most notable Notable guy at school), you're usually free from the nastiest bouts of dweeb hazing. So as his history tutor I was fairly safe. Chelsea usually ignored me. This sudden eye contact was unprecedented.

"Um," Jane said uncomfortably, "I think Chelsea is looking at you."

So it wasn't just me.

"What should I do?" I hissed.

"I don't know. . . . Talk to her, I guess."

We traded nervous looks.

"You'll walk over with me, right?" I whispered. Then I laughed desperately as if she had just said something terribly funny.

"Um . . . you'll be fine, Kenzie. I'll be waiting just a few feet away by the lockers. Breathe . . . find your inner vampire slayer or something."

"Thanks, way to be helpful," I told her sarcastically. We were getting closer and closer to Chelsea. It was time to forge ahead and talk to her . . . or to flee. For some reason my mind flashed to the phrase "innocent until proven guilty," and I thought, *Wouldn't it be great if I could be "cool until proven geeky."* Then I remembered that:

1. High school doesn't work that way.
2. I'd already proven myself to be a geek a billion times before.
3. Even with the tutoring, my social standing couldn't get much worse.

All I could think was, *oh, crap,* when Jane ditched me only a few feet away from Chelsea. I couldn't blame her for not wanting to get involved. There's only so much you can ask of a friend, even a best friend.

I jerked my head in a neurotic sort of nod at Chelsea and was about to say something classy (like "hi") when my mouth inexplicably went into overload.

"So." My voice came out an octave higher than normal. "How's it going? What's new with you guys? Any exciting plans for the weekend?"

The Notables stared at me in disgust.

"Right," Chelsea said smoothly. "Looking forward to the weekend. Listen, I need help on an essay. I'll stop by Logan's house with it on Saturday . . . *if* you don't have any other plans, of course."

I hate how some girls can keep their words totally civil while they're slicing away at someone's self-esteem. She was *really* saying, "You're such a loser, I'm positive you've got nothing else planned. So I'm ordering you to be at my beck and call. Bye-e!"

She was right too. I had no social life—just homework.

"That sounds great!" I said enthusiastically. Then I realized only losers get excited at the prospect of doing someone else's homework. "I mean, it'll be . . . convenient at his house. Kill two birds with one stone." I winced—lame cliché. "As long as Logan's cool with it."

Okay, I was lying. It wouldn't be freaking convenient to have her around when Logan needed to concentrate on the American Revolution. She'd probably distract him with her hair tosses and her cleavage . . . and I'm not just saying that because I have boob envy and a complete lack of curves.

Chelsea turned to face someone with her lips puckered into a pout. I looked and felt my stomach drop. *Of course* Logan Beckett would be right there silently watching his history tutor get flustered over a simple request. Because that's how my life works.

"Your house around two?" Chelsea all but purred. "How's that for you?"

Logan eyed Chelsea as though he could see right through the seductive little come-ons with one look. Which was weird since I knew they had dated back in middle school. Everyone had been really surprised when the Notable royalty broke up in seventh grade. Of course, that decision made a lot more sense when Chelsea's new boyfriend—a high school sophomore—took her to homecoming.

There had been rumors since Chelsea's boyfriend had left for college that she and Logan would reunite. Corey and Jane had even bet on the outcome.

So I was standing there like an idiot while Logan's mouth curved into a half smirk. I should've been relieved he was too preoccupied with Chelsea's flirting to pay attention to me, but it was more than a little insulting. I'd been pulled away from my friend, removed from my comfort zone, and coerced into a free tutoring session (yes, it was coercion. Chelsea and I both knew the rumors she could spread if I didn't agree), only to be studiously ignored.

That sort of inconsideration is why I viewed Logan Beckett only as a tool for social safety and a regular paycheck. Not that it mattered. Guys like Logan don't notice girls like me—and if they do it's a fleeting interest that lasts only until they spot someone with longer legs or deeper cleavage. Depressing, but true. On the other hand, I didn't have to try to decipher his lopsided grins. I'd have felt sorry for Chelsea if she didn't have the personality of a barracuda with none of its niceties.

Logan Beckett, on the other hand, had it all: classic good looks, money, social standing, and the captaincy of the high school hockey team. But you'll have to forgive me for not being impressed. Being born rich with killer genetics isn't exactly a personal accomplishment. And the only thing that the hockey stuff proves is that he can hit a puck. Insert eye-roll here. Not that I've mentioned any of this to Logan. Freud would probably say I'm repressed.

But in this case it pays, quite literally, to be repressed. I needed the tutoring job. At the rate we were going, his doctor parents were financing my college laptop and textbooks. So I was determined not to mess it up.

"That'll work," Logan said with that half smile still in place.

Chelsea turned her eyes up at him prettily. The move made her eyelashes look even longer, a trick I'd never master. "You don't mind the interruption?"

I thought I caught a small grin of amusement from Logan, as if Chelsea had unwittingly stumbled upon something very entertaining.

"I think I can bear it."

"Okay, then." I felt like I was getting lamer by the second. "I'll tutor Logan on Saturday, from noon till . . . three?" Chelsea nodded regally, so I backed away, nearly tripping as I made my hasty exit. "Great! I'll write it down in my planner. See you guys then."

That's when I saw Patrick listening in. I could practically hear my system switching into overdrive. Logan might not do much for me, but I've been secretly in love with Patrick Bradford for years—ever since the day in middle school when he shyly asked to borrow twelve dollars to pay a library fine. I didn't even care that he'd never paid me back—not when he looked at me with those melty chocolate eyes.

Seeing Patrick so close, I panicked. As I turned abruptly, my backpack smacked *hard* into a burley member of the high school football team. Alex Thompson was invested in the appearance of manliness—an appearance that was greatly diminished when a gawky girl of five feet seven and a half inches knocked him down. For the record, it was the weight from all my AP textbooks that propelled him off the cement steps that separated the Notables from the Invisibles. But I sincerely doubt he was thinking about his tough-guy reputation when I sent him flying and he landed with a sickening crunch.

I completely freaked out.

I scrambled, stumbled, and nearly fell on top of him. I didn't see any blood, but he was pale and still. All I could think was, *Oh, my god! I have to DO something!* I didn't realize the words were coming out of my mouth.

I threw a leg over, straddling him, and started doing timed chest compressions. I couldn't remember if that was exclusively for heart attacks, but I kept hammering away. I alternated between shouting for the nurse and yelling, "Does ANYONE know if I'm doing this right? AM I KILLING HIM RIGHT NOW? Can SOMEONE make sure I'M NOT KILLING HIM RIGHT NOW?!"

I was fully hysterical when two strong hands grabbed my shoulders and forcibly removed me from Alex. The world had gone fuzzy around the edges, like a camera out of focus, and I had trouble breathing. I barely noticed when someone shoved my head between my knees, like some weak, quivering heroine from a sappy romance novel who might faint at any moment. Normally, this kind of assistance would irritate the hell out of me. I'm quite self-sufficient, thank-you-very-much. But this wasn't exactly the most normal of situations.

Alex Thompson wasn't moving. He didn't appear to be breathing. *I killed him*, I thought numbly. *I killed him with my awkwardness!* My organs felt like they'd just been pulverized in a masher as I hoped for some small sign of life.

So I was shocked when he pulled himself up to a sitting position. I guess it's rather difficult to move when approximately one hundred and forty pounds of female launches herself onto you and starts pounding your chest. I might not look like much, but I'm deceptively strong. Something Alex Thompson discovered the hard way . . . and did not exactly appreciate.

"What the hell is wrong with you?" he exploded when he got his breath back. "Jesus, you're insane!"

I was so relieved to hear him speak that his words bounced right off me.

"I am so sorry. I am so incredibly sorry. Really. Are you all right? I'm sorry. It was an accident. I didn't see you until I knocked you over . . . in front of everyone. Which really was a poor choice of locations. Not that there is a *right* place to knock somebody over." I shut up when it became painfully clear I wasn't about to say anything smart. "Do you need any help? Or should I just go? I should probably leave, right?"

Alex just ignored me, stood, and turned to Logan, who must have been the mystery hands that had terminated my first attempt at CPR.

"How'd you get stuck with a spaz like that for a tutor, man?"

Which made me wish he hadn't recovered, but before I could say anything my eyes connected with Jane's. She was standing right by the lockers, a hand clutched over her mouth, and I knew exactly what she muttered, because it's the same thing she says every time I make a fool of myself.

"Oh, Kenzie."

Somehow Jane managed to marinate those two simple words in pity, disbelief, sympathy, and indulgence, like she couldn't believe what I had just done and yet she had seen the whole thing coming.

Ouch.

Chapter 3

I didn't stick around. Listening to Logan and Alex insult me wasn't my idea of fun . . . so I fled the scene. The warning bell for class jangled as I replayed the last five minutes in my head. I had managed to babble, knock down (then straddle) a football player, poorly attempt CPR, then babble some more—an impressive amount of social damage . . . even for me.

Class was a welcome distraction from my image of Alex's expression—shocked and pained—when he smacked the pavement. Although after his "spaz" comment, I was feeling decidedly less guilty. I kept wondering how Logan had responded. Maybe he said something like, "She's useful, man." Or maybe he blamed his parents for the situation—told everyone it was just to get them off his back. *Or maybe,* I thought bitterly, *he just shrugged.*

It was Logan who had asked me to be his tutor, the first week of this school year. He was already behind on the reading and had stood there with his rumpled, dark brown hair flopping into his gray-blue eyes, waiting for me to finish stuffing my backpack. Which confused the hell out of me since it's not a normal occurrence for the hottest guy at school to wait *for me.*

"Um . . . can I help you?" I sounded like the reference librarian—like I ought to ask if he had any overdue books.

"Maybe," he said. I scanned our surroundings warily, wondering if other Notables were watching. They tend to travel in packs.

"Okay. Right now? Because I have another class after this . . . and I'm guessing you do too. So . . . is it something that'll take a while? Because if so, maybe now really isn't the best time . . ."

"Can you tutor me?" he interrupted, much to my relief.

"Right now? Because American history can't be that reduced. I mean, sure, it might not be as extensive as, say, European history, but . . ."

He looked at me as if I were a complete idiot, which was understandable given the circumstances.

"My parents are willing to pay you to tutor me . . . if you want the job."

My mouth dropped open, not really the most attractive of expressions.

"Your parents will pay *me* to teach *you* the same subject that *I'm* taking?" I said incredulously.

"That's right." He gave me one of his sweeping dismissive glances. "Can you walk and stare at the same time?"

I stood up mutely and shouldered my backpack. I had the uncomfortable feeling that I must have been missing something. I suspected a trap. Seriously, what was the catch? Ordinary-looking girls like me (brown straight hair, brown eyes, brown stains on garage sale shirts) do not get invited to hang out with the Notables. Used and dismissed by them, sure, but not hired for a semipermanent job.

"So I just teach you history," I clarified. "And get money for it?"

"Were you hoping for some other form of payment?" His casual manner didn't mask his amusement. "Because if so . . ."

"Money's good," I interrupted, wishing that my Irish / Italian gene pool didn't make it so obvious that I was blushing. "But why do you need a tutor? You seem reasonably in-telligent."

"And only really stupid jocks need tutors, right?" His amusement solidified back into disgust. I felt like slime.

"That's not what I said," I muttered, although the thought had crossed my mind. "Why do you want a tutor?"

Logan's face became brittle. "I don't want one. But it'll make sense if you take the job. So, are you in?"

Okay, I know you might be wondering why I ever took him up on the offer. But a paying tutoring gig meant that I could stop babysitting. And, for all his flaws, at least Logan Beckett was potty trained.

"Above minimum wage?"

"Yes."

"How often?"

"We work around my hockey schedule. Every other day and Saturdays."

I couldn't help staring again. "Seriously?"

He sighed, and his mouth settled in a grim line. "Do I look like I'm kidding?"

I shook my head and felt even more self-conscious. I mean, Logan Beckett is a Notable. And a guy. I don't exactly hang out with a lot of people who fall into either one of those demo-graphics.

"You've got yourself a deal." Maybe I shouldn't have been so hasty, but I knew Corey and Jane would flip out if I turned down Logan freaking Beckett for tutoring. That kind of thing can rescue social lives at Smith High School.

That'd been about two months ago. Not a bad streak for a geek like me, all things considered. But I'd hoped I would last even longer before Notables were pointing me out. And things were about to get so much worse.

Chapter 4

I tried to catch up with Logan after the bell released us from AP US. Not to discuss what had happened with Alex, or to escort him down the hallway, but because of Mr. Helm's stupid diagnostic test—the one that supposedly showed us how ready we'd be for the national exam if we took it tomorrow. If Logan had done well on it, I wouldn't have to freak out about Chelsea crashing our next study session. If, on the other hand, he didn't get the material, I needed to come up with a solution—fast.

Logan moved a lot faster than me, probably because he wasn't gawky, or clumsy, and he didn't lug around textbooks. Actually, he rarely showed up with a backpack, preferring to carry a spiral notebook with a pen tucked inside. Occasionally the pen would be misplaced and he would have to ask someone nearby for a loaner—which was probably the subject of many a nerdy girl's diary entry. There'd probably be a whole page of: *OMG! My hand touched his! They touched!*

Lame.

Anyhow, he was already moving down the packed hallway when I stepped out of the classroom, forcing me to yell, "Hey!" to get his attention. Maybe I should have been more specific because a dozen kids turned to look at me and none of them were Logan.

"Um . . . Logan!" I tried again. He stiffened at the sound of my voice, like he'd been moving extrafast in an attempt to avoid me. Which just made me feel terrific. Not.

"Hey," I said lamely when I reached him. "So, um, how'd you do on the diagnostic test?" I could feel the eyes of other students send my blood pressure up. "I thought it was pretty rough. The multiple-choice section in particular wasn't easy. I guess it's a good thing the real exam isn't for a while and . . ."

Yeah, I know. I babble. I'm working on it.

Logan didn't interrupt me though. He seemed to find it vaguely entertaining—like I was some walking science experiment that struggled to control motor functions. I cut myself off instead.

"So . . . um, how was your test?" I repeated awkwardly.

He shrugged and started walking down the hall again.

"Wait, does that mean it went well? Is a shrug good?" I didn't think so, but it rarely hurts to ask.

"It was a diagnostic test. I'm diagnosed."

"Sure, but I need to see the diagnosis."

Logan nodded in the direction of the now-empty classroom. "Mr. Helm told us not to feel pressured to share our results." His voice was mockingly solemn.

"Right. No pressure to share with classmates. Except I'm your tutor. Which makes it my job to know how you're doing. So if I could just see the test?"

I didn't mean to make the last part sound like a question, but telling Logan Beckett what to do didn't come naturally to me. Something else I had to work on.

Logan held his test out of reach. I'm tall for a girl, but he still had a good few inches and a lot of muscle on me. There was no way I'd see it unless he handed it over or I kicked him really hard in the shin. I figured I should save that particular move for something more important than a diagnostic test.

"Or what?" he asked childishly. Great, it was like preschool all over again.

"Or I tell your parents?"

Damn.

Logan grinned at the note of indecision in my voice. "Right. You can hardly speak at school but you're going to tell my parents everything."

"Okay, so I probably wouldn't do that." I decided to try out a slippery slope fallacy on him. "But if you don't show me, I won't know what you need help on, which means that I wouldn't be a good tutor. Which means the AP test will be harder for you. And the consequences of *that* . . ."

"Okay," Logan said, probably just to get me to shut up. "I'll show you mine if you show me yours." Great, we had graduated to elementary school.

"Why don't you just show me your test?"

Logan just shook his head, making his bangs fall attractively over his eyes.

"Nope. Why don't you want to show me? Not able to ace it?" His eyes danced at the idea.

There was no point in stalling. I opened my backpack, pulled out the test, and held it tightly in front of me. "All right, on the count of three."

Logan ignored me and effortlessly swapped the tests. Logan had scored 29 percent. I had clocked in at 98 percent. I'm not sure which one of us felt more uncomfortable with the results.

"Ninety-eight percent." Logan didn't sound surprised, just impressed and half-amused. "How the hell did you do that?"

I examined the tops of my black Converse shoes. "Um . . . I studied?" God, could I sound like a bigger dork? "A lot. I studied a lot. History has always been my best subject, so . . ." I turned my attention to the test in my hands. "I think we should have an extra study session, maybe try a new studying technique or . . ."

He handed my test back and nodded in agreement.

"How about Sunday?" There was no trace of a smile on his face now.

I usually tried to keep my Sundays clear, so I wasn't exactly psyched about spending it discussing the Colonists . . . again.

"Great!" I told him. Stupid, stupid, Mackenzie. "Sounds totally . . . um . . . great. So study sessions on Saturday and Sunday. A history-packed weekend."

Throughout our conversation the two of us moved in the general direction of the lockers. The nearer we came to the scene of my most recent embarrassment, the more gawky I felt—like a mini–growth spurt was shooting me up several more inches. And trust me, I'm plenty tall already.

People had started noticing us too. Well, not me so much, but certainly Logan. Notables kept greeting him in passing, and he nodded back casually while I tried not to freeze or trip.

My enthusiasm over studying earned me another one of his "you are an amusing freak of nature" looks. I felt myself go redder. Not an attractive flush either. My face gets ruddier, which makes it more difficult to see my freckles but does not create any other positive changes.

"Well"—I tried to undo some dork damage—"I mean, no one actually looks forward to homework on the weekend. But I should be able to squeeze you in . . ."

Why is it that popular kids magically show up just when something can be taken out of context to sound sexual? Spencer, another hockey-playing Notable, strolled over just in time to cut me off mid-babble by saying, "That's what she said."

Which I admit was a little funny—juvenile and overused, but still, funny. My face turned another shade of tomato while Logan grinned and went into guy mode.

"Hey, Spence, how's it going?"

I instantly felt like a third wheel. I couldn't talk about hockey or partying or anything else Notable. It was better for me just to keep my mouth shut.

"Just bombed a Geometry test," Spencer said, unperturbed. "Maybe next time, I'll borrow her."

Spencer grinned good-naturedly while he gave me an appraising once-over.

"I doubt she's your type," Logan said as if I weren't standing *right there*. "You really don't want Mack here nagging about your grades. That's what your parents are for. Besides, I'm not sure how well you'd handle the pressure. We just got your Woodshop grade up to a B so you can stay on the team."

I could really learn to hate Logan Beckett. For the record: more like "you're not *her* type." Spencer was the straight-C student, and if he hadn't been such a great athlete, he would have been booted out. Well, that, and if his parents hadn't donated a building to the school. Private schools aren't the only ones that respond to lots of money. Even in Oregon, bribery can get you anything from a discreet nose job to higher test scores. Not that I would know about either, but I've heard stories . . . and watch cable.

Spencer's stroll became noticeably more slouched. "You know I hate waking up early for class. Eight a.m.—it's just not right."

"Not when you've got a hangover from the night before."

"Damn straight. You going to Kyle's party tomorrow? The weekend starts on Thursday, man."

"Today is Thursday," I corrected helpfully. *And no, it doesn't.*

"That's great! All the more reason for you to come. Are you down?"

I waited, hoping that he would say, "Sorry, man, but I've got too much studying to do."

No such luck.

"I'll be there."

I reached my next classroom (AP Gov) and had to make a polite departure, which is hard to do when the Notables barely recognized your presence in the first place.

"So I'll see you Saturday," I said to Logan.

"See you, Mack," he said without so much as a glance, disappearing around a corner with Spencer before I could protest the nickname. I hate it when people call me Mack. Really, *really* hate it. I was left standing Notable-less with all the other AP nerds, muttering, "Mackenzie, not Mack," to myself.

Lame.

Chapter 5

Dinner at the Wellesley house that night was not pleasant. It didn't matter that I managed to survive the rest of the day without any awkward encounters with Notables—the damage was done. When I got home, tired from a full day of academic activity and social humiliation, I found an irate brother waiting.

"What the hell were you thinking?" Dylan bellowed.

"Hi to you too, *baby* brother," I said, emphasizing the "baby" just to piss him off. That's my job as the older sister. He was already so mad that my latest offense didn't even register.

"Why were you talking to Chelsea Halloway? Don't you know she's out of your league?"

"Don't you mean out of *your* league, Dylan? I have no interest in joining her ranks. Of course, *you* might have to hit the gym and drop a few IQ points to really fit in. I'd also recommend steroids. I'm sure your future BFF Alex Thompson can get you a prescription."

"Alex Thompson does NOT use steroids!" he yelled defensively. "Just—don't screw this up for me. Your actions reflect on me. So why don't you hang out with Jane and Corey, okay? Leave popularity to people who can actually formulate sentences in public. And for God's sake, don't jump football players!"

Okay, I admit that stung. Getting reprimanded for my lack of social skills by my middle school brother was flat-out embarrassing.

"How did you find out about that anyway?" I asked, pretending to be nonchalant about the whole thing.

He looked completely disgusted with me. "You're kidding, right? Every time you humiliate yourself, I get a text about it. Do you have any idea how expensive you are? I owe Mom fifteen bucks a month for unlimited texting, thanks to you."

"You just wanted it so you and your little friends could discuss Chelsea Halloway's miniskirts. Not that you have a shot in hell with her." I ruffled his hair. "I don't think she's looking for a younger man right now. Middle school isn't exactly what she wants in a boy toy."

He shoved my hand away and glowered. "I've got a better chance with her than you've got with Logan Beckett."

I nodded in agreement. "Right, again. But here's the difference: I'm not interested in Logan Beckett. Or anyone in the Notable crowd." Except for Patrick, but my little brother *really* didn't need to know that. "Which means I can humiliate myself—or you—in front of them whenever."

Dylan stared at me in horror. "You won't say a word about me, understand? Not one word!"

My mom picked that moment to enter the room. Our yelling at each other (well, more Dylan's yelling at me) had gotten her attention.

"What's going on?" she asked tentatively, as if she didn't really want to know. In all honesty, she probably didn't.

"Nothing new. Mackenzie humiliated herself in public. Again. Can't you make her stop or ship her off somewhere? Or *something!*"

"There's nothing wrong with your sister, Dylan," Mom said firmly. "She's just special."

That was not what I wanted to hear.

"Special Ed, maybe," Dylan muttered nastily.

The two of us glared at him.

"Well, it's true!" he said defensively. "That's why she's taking so many AP classes. Too bad socially, she has the IQ of a . . ."

But my mom didn't let him finish that sentence. "Let's all calm down before dinner. Dylan, your sister is not going anywhere—get used to it. And Mackenzie—" My mother paused. "Why don't you try a little harder to . . . um . . . blend in at school."

You know you're awkward when your *mother* points out your ineptitude.

"Gee thanks, Mom," I said sarcastically. "Blend, huh? You know what? Why don't I practice 'blending' and disappear right now." I headed up the stairs to my room, hollering behind me, "Now you see me," and slamming the door to signify the "now you don't." But I couldn't hold a grudge against my mom. So I sulked over my homework for an hour before I went downstairs to set the table, empty the recycling, sweep the kitchen floor, and wipe down the counters. That's how life works in a single-parent home—you pull your weight. My mom really didn't need to come home from work to deal with stupid bickering matches.

She wasn't entirely wrong either. I did "blend in" more at school the next day. I just happened to flee for the school library whenever someone asked about the whole Alex Thompson / CPR debacle. The librarian was pretty cool about letting me camp out in the back with the latest arrivals. I thought the whole thing would blow over. I figured if nothing major happened on Friday, then by Monday I wouldn't have to try to be invisible. People would just naturally ignore me again.

Saturday morning and everything seemed perfect. I woke up early, grabbed my Rollerblades, and skated until my mind was beautifully blank. The only time my brain ever really slowed down was when I slept or skated. That's why I made a point of visiting the local elementary school blacktop at least once a week. If I didn't, I'd never be able to maintain my well-ordered, superstructured lifestyle.

Then I had to get myself ready for an encounter of the Notable kind. I tried out a pep talk as I tugged on my most comfortable pair of jeans. I told myself it didn't matter if Logan Beckett was a smug, arrogant, annoying jock, because I was a strong, confident, capable woman who could tutor the hell out of him. That I'd never be stuck as a waitress in a crappy suburb in Oregon, trying to raise two kids on my own . . . like my mom. I'd figure everything out in college, and someday I'd look back at high school and think, *God I hated tutoring Logan Beckett. Paid off though.*

That's what I told myself as I stood outside the Hamilton house and waited for Logan to pick me up. *Not because I'm embarrassed of my own house,* I assured myself as I paced the edge of the sidewalk like walking a balance beam. But if Logan Beckett happened to think that the Hamilton's Victorian-style home were mine . . . there was no harm in it. I didn't want his pity at the sight of my own weed-riddled, paint-peeling, aesthetically unappealing house. If there was one thing I couldn't stand, it was the cloying sympathy everyone poured on after the divorce. It was all, "Oh, isn't that awful! Up and left with the ballet teacher! Whatever will you do? You poor, poor dears." I had very nearly screamed when elderly ladies pinched my cheeks and assured me that "Daddy'll be back, darling." He wasn't, and I needed him as much as I needed a black eye.

I could've used a car though. That way I wouldn't have had to wait for Logan to pick me up—late—looking like the party had just ended. Even exhausted, he still looked attractive—just sort of sexily rumpled. I'd have looked like death warmed over. The few all-nighters I pulled cramming for AP tests last year taught me that if I didn't want people suggesting I see the nurse, I would need a minimum of six hours' sleep a night. Less than that and people ask if I'm ill.

"Want anything?" Logan asked as he pulled into the Starbucks parking lot. I was a little impressed that he'd been polite enough to ask.

I fumbled in my backpack for my wallet. "A mocha Frappuccino would be great."

"What size?"

"Um . . . a small?" Okay, so I didn't really understand how Starbucks sizes worked. It's not my fault they all sound enormous.

I had just gotten my wallet in hand when Logan opened his car door.

"Wait a second!" I ordered, as I rifled for the cash to foot my bill.

He looked caught between amusement and annoyance as I fumbled for quarters. "Don't worry about it."

Shows how much he knew about me. I always pay my own way.

But before I could protest, Logan was striding away. I considered following him and shoving my crumpled one-dollar bills, quarters, and dimes onto the counter when the time came, but paying him back later seemed like a less embarrassing plan. Then I saw Patrick Bradford walking in my direction and stopped thinking altogether.

Patrick. He was heading right toward me, and I hoped with every pathetic fiber of my being that the two of us could talk so he'd finally realize how perfect we'd be together. It was an opportunity I couldn't miss. Mustering up my courage, I opened Logan's car door and stepped out onto the curb.

"Hey, Patrick!"

No, I wasn't the one who called out to him.

I turned to see Chelsea Halloway sitting with her two best friends outside the Starbucks. Jane and I had nicknamed the duo Fake and Bake, since Steffani Larson was a product of Clairol Blonde, MAC cosmetics, and (rumor had it) a very discreet plastic surgeon, and Ashley McGrady has been hitting the tanning beds ever since sixth grade. I wondered if Starbucks was a Notable postparty tradition to counteract the alcohol consumed the night before.

I didn't know what to say. No guy would rather spend time with me than bask in the glow of their attention—not even Patrick. Not that Chelsea and Steffani would gush over him the way they did over other Notable boys (cough, Logan), but that was only to be expected. After all, Patrick was still on the Popularity Fringe between Notable and Not able. Which explains why he just nodded at me and kept walking without saying a word. Or maybe he thought it'd be best for me not to come to Notable attention.

The girls giggled at something Patrick said, and I couldn't help wishing they would choke on their lattes or get massive brain freezes. I felt like such an idiot plastered against the side of Logan's shiny black car while I stared slack-jawed at the Notables. There was no way the Evil Trio had missed me. And yet none of them so much as waved in my direction. I was still standing there when Logan walked out holding our drinks.

"Logan!"

Again, not me. The squeal came from Chelsea, and since she was bringing over her essay in a few hours I thought she was overdoing it. Not that Logan seemed to mind. He just raised an eyebrow at her enthusiastic greeting. Maybe that's how girls like Chelsea got boyfriends: by showing lots of enthusiasm and cleavage.

"Hey, man." That came from Patrick. I tried not to laugh.

It just seemed so . . . forced, like he had wanted to say, "Yo, dude. What's up?" but knew he would sound like a moron, so he was settling for moron lite. Which, in my opinion, was totally adorable.

I took a deep breath. *Okay,* I ordered myself, *time to stop being such a wimp.* Any second Logan was going to hand me my drink and the other Notables wouldn't be able to pretend they hadn't seen me.

So I made the first move. I walked right over to the group of them, keeping my eyes on the mocha Frappuccino the whole time so I could act cool. That didn't work so well when it was in my hands.

"Um, thanks," I muttered. "I'll pay you back later."

"Don't worry about it," Logan said easily. I guess when your college tuition is squared away, you don't have to be stingy about money. I couldn't help being a little envious. It seemed so nice to spend money without wondering how much each item would set back your timetable for a college laptop.

"I'll pay you back later," I insisted.

"Hey, are the two of you dating or something?" Patrick said uncertainly. I choked on my drink, but it had nothing to do with laughter.

"Good one," tittered Chelsea. "Like the two of them would be dating!"

She was a darling. Really.

"Um, no. No, no, no." Maybe I should've stopped after just one "no."

Patrick grinned and I felt my knees weaken. He just looked so sweet with his chocolatey brown eyes all melty—like the mocha Frappuccino I was holding in my hands. I inched a little closer to him. I just couldn't resist—the smile pulled me in.

"Just getting some coffee," said Logan.

"Yeah," I confirmed. "Because it increases alertness and is a great study agent. Did you know that coffee has been used as currency before?"

Patrick shook his head slowly to silently communicate that I was committing a huge faux pas. The girls stared at me in disbelief while Logan sipped his drink and looked amused.

"Why would we want to know that?" Chelsea asked snarkily.

"Um . . . because it's interesting?"

I kept my eyes on Patrick so that my insides would stay soft and gooey. I'd freeze up instantly if I met one of the Evil Trio's cool-eyed gazes. Logan put his hand on my shoulder (shutting me up instantly) and said, "I'll see you guys later." Then he steered me to the car. I waited until we were both buckled before I turned to him.

"It would be cool, right?"

"Yeah, it'd be cool."

I hadn't expected him to agree with me. He was looking at me intently, evaluating with his suspicious gray eyes, and I tried not to squirm in my seat.

Sometimes it felt like he was the tutor and I was the one failing the tests.

Chapter 6

"I had no idea you were into Patrick." Logan's voice was bland with just a hint of amusement.

"Wh-What makes you think *that?*" I managed to stutter.

"The way you were drooling over him was kind of a hint."

I stared but failed to read his expression. He had grossly exaggerated one little moment of awkwardness and yet he looked so complacent. A seduction attempt? *Me?* What was he talking about?

I wasn't above setting the record straight.

At a red light, I looked Logan dead in the eyes. "I don't flirt that way. I have better things to do with my time." I hoped this sounded cutting and smart. "Now, do you want to use your brain or just let it atrophy?"

Silence ruled in the car. And I admit it: I took it personally . . . and then I got pissed. It wasn't the joking teasing of friends because we were NOT FRIENDS. He's a Notable and I'm an Invisible, and if I'd somehow managed to forget that, his Starbucks analysis had done the trick of reminding me.

"Okay, what's going on?" I couldn't take the quiet anymore.

He shrugged. How much more noncommunicative can you get.

"What is wrong with you?"

"I'm fine," he said gruffly.

"Look, I don't know what your problem is, but deal with it! I can't tutor you if you don't speak to me. And I need this job so that I can buy a MacBook."

"That's what you're doing this for?" he asked in disbelief. "A laptop."

"Um . . . yeah," I said. "Why'd you think I was tutoring you, for a Nobel Prize?"

He ignored my question and just looked thoughtful. "Makes sense. It has your name written all over it." He grinned at my obvious confusion. "Mac-kenzie saving for a MacBook."

I felt my hands tighten instinctively and had to order myself to relax. "Very clever. I've never heard that one before. . . . Oh, wait, yes I have. And I don't go by Mack."

I don't think he was listening as we pulled into his driveway. A few minutes later, we were settled in his kitchen with our textbooks open.

"So the French and Indian War," I tried again, "was between . . ."

Logan ran one hand through his hair in frustration and looked down at the ornate doodle he had created in his notebook. "The French and the Indians?"

"Not quite."

Exasperation was written all over his face. "Then why is it called the French and Indian War?"

"Well, because the winners are the ones who pick the name."

"So who won, the French or the Indians?"

"Neither." The disgusted glint in Logan's eye made me quickly add, "The British and the Colonists won. It'd be pretty long if it were the British and Colonists Against the French and Indians War."

That got an almost-smile, so I kept going. "The British won with the Colonists. They just named it the French and Indian War because that was who they were fighting against."

Logan was about to say something when his parents entered the room.

"Hello, Mackenzie," his mom greeted me warmly. "How's the studying going?"

"Hi, Mr. and Mrs. Beckett," I said, wondering if I should refer to them both as Dr. Beckett or whether that would just make things confusing. "I think it's going pretty well. Just covering the highlights right now." I tried to make it sound like everything was under control when clearly it wasn't. Logan had gotten 29 percent on his diagnostic test. That wasn't "fine" by any stretch of the word. Nothing from class seemed to be sticking. All Logan had done was create a binder full of drawings. I saw sketches of classmates, ships in peril, and long-necked giraffes all jumbled in the margins. Great.

"And how are the two of you?" I asked in an attempt to deflect attention.

"Oh, just fine," his mom replied as she pulled out sliced turkey from the refrigerator and began making a sandwich. The Beckett house was nothing if not pristine, expensive, and classy. Which is what you get, I guess, when you have two doctors and one child instead of one waitress raising two kids and depending on child support from her cheating ex.

"Any excitement at the hospital?"

"Nothing too interesting. A few kids with alcohol poisoning needed their stomachs pumped. Apparently there was quite a party last night."

Even the adults were more clued into the party scene than me.

"I wouldn't know," I replied honestly, like the studious good-girl type I am. "I'm not a drinker. Not really my style."

Logan looked me squarely in the eyes. "No kidding. I never would have guessed."

Jerk.

"Well, isn't that refreshing," his mom said chipperly. "That you know your limitations and stay within them." She turned to her son. "Isn't that nice."

"Yeah." He looked like he was stifling the urge to laugh. "Very nice."

We both knew why I didn't drink—you can't if you aren't invited to those kinds of parties.

I almost said something when the doorbell rang.

"I'll get that," said Logan's dad, who popped open a can of Diet Coke and strolled to the door.

"Hi, Mr. Beckett." I recognized the voice as one of pure evil—a girly tone accustomed to treachery and debauchery. I'm lying. All I could tell was that it belonged to Chelsea Halloway. The rest was merely a well-informed hypothesis.

"Logan, you have a *friend* here to see you." The emphasis his dad placed implied that maybe "friend" wasn't the best term to describe their relationship. Not that it was any of my business.

I closed the AP US textbook and mentally psyched myself to deal with Chelsea. I don't know what it is about the girl (maybe her perfectly coiffed hair or her impeccable makeup), but she always intimidated me. It didn't matter if I saw her at school, or Starbucks, or in Logan Beckett's kitchen, the girl reeked of Superiority. Or whatever the latest fragrance was from Victoria's Secret.

"Hey, Chelsea," I said casually when she finally entered the kitchen. I stood up and moved toward the banana bread muffins. The Dr. Becketts had told me to make myself at home on my first day of tutoring, which meant I didn't have to ask every time I wanted to raid their refrigerator. I get a mean case of the afternoon munchies.

"Hey," she replied before abruptly turning to Mrs. Beckett

with a dazzling smile that said, *I am beautiful and just the type of girl you want your son to date.*

Suck-up.

"How have you been, Mrs. Beckett?" Chelsea asked sweetly.

"I'm doing well, Chelsea. And you?"

Chelsea flicked her hair back over her shoulder. It moved like a freaking Pantene commercial. "I'm great."

"Do you and Logan have plans later—once Mackenzie is done tutoring?"

I was surprised to hear my name mentioned. I was blending in with the refrigerator as I snagged a Diet Coke. Still, Mrs. Beckett didn't seem the type to forget the geek when a popular girl entered the premises.

"Actually, Mackenzie is helping me with an essay," Chelsea replied confidently. She did everything confidently. She and Logan would probably go on to produce very confident offspring.

"Are you up for that, Mackenzie?" Mrs. Beckett asked me kindly. "You're not too overworked?"

"I'm fine," I said. What else could I say? The truth?

"Sorry, Chelsea, but my brain is fried. You're on your own with the essay. I guess that means you'll start a nasty rumor about me in the girls' locker room. I should have called to cancel, but you don't give Invisibles like me your phone number."

Yeah. That'd go over real well.

"I'm fine. Logan can take a break, maybe flip through some flashcards, while I help Chelsea. Then we'll attack the textbook again," I said instead.

Mrs. Beckett nodded as she put the finishing touches on her sandwich. "All right, well, good luck." And with that she pulled her husband out to the pool, leaving me on my own with two Notables. I needed all the luck I could get.

Chapter 7

"I'm not sure I can help you with this."

Which, as far as realizations go, totally sucked. It's just not fair when the prettiest, most popular girl at school is also intelligent. I mean, *come on!* The girl had to have some flaws (besides her tendency toward evil), otherwise I'd have to suspect that she was secretly a cyborg from another planet. But so far . . . nothing. I didn't even know why Chelsea wanted me to look at it, unless it was all some ploy to spend time with Logan.

"What's wrong with it?" Chelsea asked defensively. She sat up straighter in her chair, breaking the clear view of her cleavage that Logan appeared to have been enjoying.

I could have told her, "Nothing is wrong with it! It's a solid essay. No worries, Chelsea, your English teacher will love it." But that wouldn't be the whole truth.

"Well." I pointed to the book in front of me. "You think the main character, Janie, in *Their Eyes Were Watching God* found true love, right?"

"Right."

"Well, when I read the book, I didn't think it was about love at all."

That definitely got her attention. "What are you talking about?" she asked disgustedly. "It's about how she turns to the wrong men before she finds the right one." That last part was clearly delivered for Logan's benefit, beneath lowered lashes. Even I could tell it was a come-on.

"I thought she was pathetic." That got a scowl from Chelsea and an amused grin from Logan. "She jumps into abusive relationships until she has to shoot her rabid husband. I thought the real message was . . . guys are dogs."

Logan raised his eyebrows at the last part of my critique.

"Hey," he said calmly. "Not true."

"Sometimes it's true. Not all guys, obviously, although present company might not be an exception." Chelsea's eyes bored holes into me, but Logan grinned.

"Well, thanks," Chelsea said, leaving the words "for nothing" lingering unspoken in the air.

"Sorry, I can't be more helpful. So, Logan, how's the French and Indian War?"

"Thrilling," he told me straight-faced. "I wonder how it's going to turn out."

I grinned. "I'm betting the Colonists win."

"Way to spoil the ending." He closed his textbook, so I had to flip mine to the right section.

"It's actually pretty cool. If you look at the Battle of . . ." But Logan wasn't listening to me. Chelsea had leaned forward while pretending to concentrate on her essay. Yeah, guys aren't dogs. Right.

The rest of the tutoring session was pretty uneventful. Mainly because every time Logan started paying attention to either me or the textbook, Chelsea dropped her pencil and had to lean *way* over to pick it up. Or she tossed her long hair behind her so it swung softly right back to the front. It was pretty clear her essay was the last thing on her mind and that Logan didn't mind the show.

With Logan having the attention span of a guppie as Chelsea pretended to be an extra on *90210*, the study session fizzled out. I felt like a failure. It was pretty obvious that the stuff just wasn't sticking. So it was really fortunate that I was tutoring Logan again on Sunday.

He dropped me off in front of the Hamilton house, and I headed home once the sleek black car disappeared. Dylan was waiting for me outside.

He looked like someone had died. Really. I took in his ashen expression and I burst into a full on sprint, ignoring the *thud, thud, thud* as my textbook slammed against my back.

"Dylan, what's wrong? Is Mom okay?" I called out.

He didn't say anything until I reached him, and then he merely grabbed my arm and yanked me into the house.

"You've got to see this." Dylan led me straight to our family computer. It was about a billion years old and took forever to start up again. Dylan brushed the mouse aside, and the screen saver of Dylan, my mom, and me happily laughing at the beach dissolved. What I saw behind it made me want to throw up all the banana bread I'd eaten.

A YouTube video with a blaring caption that announced:

Mackenzie Wellesley: Most Socially Awkward Girl Ever!

That alone made me want to curl into a little ball until my mind numbed. The video below made me feel even worse. It was the whole scene, right there, recorded for the enjoyment of millions. All Dylan had to do was click and I could relive it frame by frame, watching myself smack Alex Thompson with my backpack, look horrified when he didn't respond, and then sling my leg over his stomach so I could try to do CPR. Worst of all, while I had been pounding on his chest, Alex was staring with undiluted horror and surprise . . . and weakly trying to fend me off.

How had I not seen that? I must have been so intent on my CPR that I didn't notice him trying to swat me off. Every time he moved to unseat me, the force of one of my timed compressions sent him right back to the cement. The speakers played my desperate apology loud and clear.

"Are you all right? I'm sorry. It was an accident. I didn't see you until I knocked you over . . . in front of everyone."

I blanched. I hadn't realized just how badly I'd screwed everything up. I never wanted to go within fifteen feet of Alex again.

And beneath the video was a whole set of comments. The very first one read simply: *Ha! LOL! What a freak.*

I stared at the screen in silence as the words began ringing in my head. Whatafreak, whatafreak, whatafreak. I was having a hard time breathing, and I knew that any second I would start to cry.

"There's only one solution," Dylan said hoarsely. "You have to move. Maybe you could stay with . . . someone."

I didn't stick around to hear anything else. I went straight to my room, crawled into bed, pulled the covers over my head, and pretended I was far away. It didn't really help. If I'd had any idea what was in store for me, I never would have left my room again.

Chapter 8

My mom told me it wasn't a big deal. I don't know if she actually believed it, but she said that the popular kids just felt intimidated by my intellectual prowess and not to take it personally. Right. That's why people were laughing at me on the Internet.

My mom had just finished telling me that no one looked at YouTube when Jane called to give me a heads-up. Not that she had to, because I kept running downstairs every couple of hours to see how many more people had viewed it. When I saw the number shoot to around thirty thousand I stopped. Every time I saw the number or scrolled down to see new comments, I could feel my blood pressure skyrocket.

It was good to hear Jane's calm voice.

"Um, Kenzie," she said when I picked up. "Listen, we have to talk."

"Let me guess. I'm already the high school laughing-stock?"

She paused, weighing her words carefully. "Well, yeah. . . ."

I could always count on Jane to be honest.

"So what do I do?" I asked, cutting to the point.

Another pause. "Do a better job finding your inner vampire slayer?"

I stared at the phone. "That's it? That's your advice? You're supposed to figure out a way to fix everything! Get with the program."

She laughed. "Sorry, Kenzie." Her voice became serious. "How are you handling this?"

"I've been hiding in bed. I'll be fine—just one more moment of humiliation to add to the list."

Jane started laughing again. "Oh, Kenzie. It's not even the worst one. Remember in elementary school when you farted during yoga?"

That's the problem with having friends who have known you forever: they know every single slipup.

"Or two years ago when you got nervous talking to the exchange student and ended up spraying his face with spit?"

"Yes," I said dryly. "But thanks for that lovely walk down memory lane."

"I'm just saying, this too shall pass."

I smiled. "Thanks."

"So how did the tutoring session go today? None of the Notables mentioned the video, did they?"

"Nope." I grinned. "I saw Patrick at Starbucks."

"Oh, God. Gag me with a spoon."

Which wasn't really fair, since I listen to her talk about her crushes all the time. I keep asking Jane what she has against Patrick, but she just says, "Oh, nothing."

So I chose to ignore that little comment. "Then I went and studied with Logan. Which was . . . weird."

"A conversation between you and a Notable felt awkward! No way!"

I laughed. "Point taken. But this time it was different. . . . Okay let me back up. He made this snarky comment about me throwing myself at Patrick." Jane let out a small gasp of surprise. "I didn't! But here's the weird thing: I totally snapped."

"How so?" she asked seriously. "You okay?"

"Yeah. I just let him have it. I momentarily forgot he was a Notable and acted more like I do around you."

"Oh, so like a general pain in the ass?"

I grinned. "Thanks. That's so sweet of you to say. Really."

"So was he surprised?"

I thought it over. "Sort of. He seemed kind of amused. I think it actually shattered some of the tension."

There was silence from the other end of the line.

"I don't know what that means," Jane said finally.

I laughed. "It doesn't mean anything."

"Just be careful, 'k, Kenzie? Because you are not allowed to transfer schools. Corey and I can't survive high school without you."

And that's why Jane and I have been best friends since elementary school.

"Don't worry. I'll be fine. Unless Dylan kills me in my sleep. . . ."

This actually didn't strike me as unfeasible. Dylan had refused to speak to me. The only reason my mom gave him space was because he'd refrained from swearing. He said I was humiliating and a blight on his social life, but no actual swear words were uttered.

So I gave him Sunday to cool off. I did my homework, tutored Logan, and waited for Dylan to calm down. But on Monday he wouldn't meet my eyes over breakfast.

"Morning," I said to him, just to break the ice.

Dylan grunted back noncommittally.

"Look, it's not like I had anything to do with this mess. So you can act like a petulant five-year-old or grow up and cut me some slack."

He glared at me fiercely, unaware of just how much he looked like our dad when his face contorted. Dylan had been so young when we'd been ditched that he didn't recognize how many mannerisms they shared. And in our family there was no greater insult than a Dad comparison. I remember the one time I promised Dylan to see his soccer game and didn't make it. His expression had conveyed anger and hurt, and he'd brushed his sweaty bangs out of his face and said, "Way to pull a dad, *Mack*." It had made me feel like crap for a month.

So I didn't tell Dylan that he looked like Dad. I just noticed the resemblance and bit my tongue.

"Of course you had nothing to do with it, because you're so perfect," Dylan snapped. "You know what I want? FOR YOU TO LEAVE ME THE HELL ALONE!"

Nothing like a supportive, loving family in times of crisis. I let him storm out of the kitchen. It couldn't be easy having the high school laughingstock for an older sister, and I was a laughingstock. I found that out at school that day. The YouTube video followed me down the halls, buzzing like a nasty swarm of flies. Some jerk even grabbed his friend while I was walking by and shouted, "Oh. My. God! Am I, like, killing him?" in a falsetto voice. I didn't think it was a particularly good characterization of me. I just ducked my head and considered homeschooling—at least until I was no longer the school's most recognizable dweeb.

The only upside was that Corey had returned from his Speech and Debate tournament. Jane had clearly brought him up to speed about my latest (and largest) embarrassment, and the two of them were determined to distract me over lunch.

"They're not looking at you," Jane said irritably when I once again scanned the cafeteria.

I stared at her. "Um, yeah, they are."

"Well, only a little." Corey shrugged with fake nonchalance. "It's not a big deal."

I slumped back in my chair. "Easy for you to say. No one keeps offering to teach you CPR."

Corey just shrugged again. "Could be worse."

"Oh yeah?" I challenged. "How?"

"They could write nasty comments about you in the bathroom. Or haze you in the locker room. Or dump a slushy on you or something."

Corey has seen way too many television shows featuring geek abuse. But I decided not to contradict him and concentrated on eating my sandwich.

By the time I got home, I was exhausted. Tired of alternately straining to hear the whispers and trying to block them out entirely. I was on edge even during my AP classes, and I continuously felt like a bug being examined under a microscope. At least I didn't have to tutor Logan.

It was nice being home alone. Dylan was busy with football practice and my mom was at work, so I made myself a snack, cranked up my music in the kitchen, did a few chores, and started in on my homework. I couldn't resist creating a nice little fantasy.

It started with me graduating from the hellhole that is Smith High School. Then I'd leave for college on a wonderful scholarship and return without my social awkwardness for the ten-year reunion. That's when I'd find Chelsea Halloway still taking undergraduate courses at the local community college. That was the fantasy anyway. At the reunion I'd be chatting agreeably with everyone, and Patrick would realize just how much he missed me. Then he'd sidle over with a drink and those melty eyes and whisper an invitation for a walk. I'd smile beatifically and we'd leave the crowd holding hands. And later that night . . . well, it wouldn't be awkward then either.

My mom came home when I was about an hour into my AP Gov work. She was exhausted, but she started making an enormous casserole that would provide enough leftovers to last a week. She hated to cook, and I tried to escape to my room, knowing that in under five minutes ABBA would be blaring, ingredients would be everywhere, and if I were spotted, my help would be requested. Since I'm an even bigger disaster in the kitchen than my mom, I tried to make a hasty retreat.

"Mackenzie," my mom called out, "would you mind cutting up the . . ."

The ringing of the phone interrupted us.

"I'll get it." I leaped for any excuse not to get drafted into kitchen duty. "Hello?"

"Is Mackenzie Wellesley available?"

I stared at the phone in disbelief. It was almost never for me.

"Um, that's me."

"Hi. I'm calling from AOL News. We want to get your thoughts on your YouTube video."

"Um," I replied, "I don't know what to say about it."

"Did you find it embarrassing?"

"Of course." What a stupid question. Like I could possibly watch my attempt at CPR without wishing I could just sink into the floor. The reminder of the video had my stomach feeling queasy all over again.

"What, specifically, embarrassed you the most?"

I started pacing. "I don't know. Probably the way Alex started twitching when I—" The sound of muffled laughter shut me up.

"Sorry." He coughed. "Just a few more questions. How do you feel about being the new poster child of social awkwardness?"

"Sorry, I'm the *what?* I don't think I'm the poster child of anything."

I heard a chuckle on the other end. "All right, then what's it like knowing your video has been viewed a million times?"

I stared at the phone, certain that I had misheard. "Pardon me," I said politely. "Did you just say a *million* times?"

"Of course. Ever since the video hit YouTube, FAIL Blog, Facebook, and Twitter, it's been getting a lot of attention."

I sucked in my breath. *Oxygen,* I thought weakly, *is a good thing.* I just had to make sure I kept getting it.

I paced faster. "I'm not sure I'm comfortable with this."

"Just a few more questions." This time it didn't feel like a request, but I didn't know how to extricate myself from the conversation.

"How does it feel to be famous?"

My mouth fell open in disbelief. "I wouldn't know. It's never happened to me."

"Well, you are."

"No," I insisted, "I'm not."

"Fine," he said soothingly. "Then how does it feel to have Ashton Kutcher twittering about you."

"ASHTON KUTCHER DID WHAT?"

I didn't mean to yell it. And I especially didn't mean to give Dylan a reason to come running into our miniscule office.

"Am I being Punk'd right now?"

"You didn't know?" The AOL guy sounded shocked but recovered quickly. "How does it feel to be the next unexpected sensation on a par with Susan Boyle?"

"I am NOT Susan Boyle. I'm not British."

I turned on the computer to double-check the Twitter thing, and while I waited for the computer to load my mouth worked overtime.

"I am NOTHING like Susan Boyle. She has an undeniable talent. Anyone can knock over a football player." I clicked on Internet Explorer. "So I am NOT famous or important. This is all one big joke, and I'm not going to fall for it."

"Mackenzie, what is going on?" Dylan shouted.

The only sound I could hear on the other end of the phone was the *rat-a-tat* of fingers pounding furiously on a keyboard to record my quotes. I typed, "Ashton Kutcher, twitter" into Google and then I was frozen staring at the words: *Wow this video is hilarious. Wifey and I can't get enough.* And with it was a link to . . . me.

"Oh, my God." The phone slipped out of my hands and I lurched to the bathroom. I was so upset I almost threw up. Thankfully, Dylan didn't follow me. He hung up on the AOL guy and waited for me with a cup of water in his hand.

"You okay?" he asked nervously. I checked out my reflection in the bathroom mirror and could confidently say that I looked like death warmed over. My face was so pale and drawn that I made Evan Rachel Wood in her Marilyn Manson / Goth phase look healthy. There was panicked screaming in my head and nothing made sense. I tried to break it down, analyze it, and come up with a plan but wound up gripping onto the toilet. My panic response seemed to be connected to my stomach.

I took the glass from Dylan, sloshing half of it on myself, but I managed a long gulp before sinking to the bathroom floor. I couldn't meet Dylan's eyes.

"I'm. What am I going to . . . is there any. No. I'm dead." I couldn't even finish sentences. Dylan hesitated, then sat down and held one of my hands.

"It's going to be okay, Mackenzie."

"No. It's not."

So he stayed on the floor, holding my hand, and saying the one thing that neither of us believed: everything is going to be fine.

Chapter 9

The whole thing exploded from there. My mom found us still sitting on the floor when she called us to dinner. We were studiously ignoring the ringing phone. She reached out to answer it, but Dylan stopped her, took her aside, and explained the situation. The whole thing was so ridiculous, so impossible, that if I hadn't still looked like I had both feet in the grave she wouldn't have believed it. I was still having trouble mentally processing. Apparently, I'd become famous.

I didn't want to move. Ever. I didn't want to eat, or sleep, or breathe. But I knew that I couldn't stay in the bathroom forever—certainly not without freaking out my mom, and she had enough to deal with already. So I joined Dylan and my mom for dinner, choked down some noodles, and pretended to be fine. Then I trudged up to my room, kicked off my shoes, and climbed under the covers fully clothed.

I didn't scream the next morning when it all came crashing back. I decided to pretend like nothing had happened. I dressed normally in my jeans, black Converse, and plain brown shirt. I was going to keep everything nice and normal. That lasted until I boarded the bus and found Corey waiting for me. I instantly felt guilty about not answering my cell phone the night before, which was the only reason Corey would come within five feet of the bus. Ever since he had learned to drive, he didn't deal with public transportation.

"Why didn't you call me?!" Corey demanded. "Were you too busy giving interviews and becoming FAMOUS?"

I really wish he hadn't yelled that last bit.

"What interview?" I asked him.

"Mackenzie, you're all over AOL. Something about not being like Susan Boyle. I just skimmed it. You're also all over Facebook, Twitter, and YouTube. Everyone in the U.S. has now seen that video. My *grandma* thought it was hilarious."

I slunk down lower in my seat. "Great."

"The fame is not the point," Corey said, his voice filled with exasperation. "Why didn't you call me?"

"Because I really wish none of this was happening."

Corey let that sink in, and nodded. "Right. I guess it does screw up the whole low-profile thing."

Jane boarded the bus and handed me a baseball cap. "Here." She thrust it at me. "No one notices people in a UCLA hat and jeans. It should help."

"Help with what?" asked Corey.

"Staying invisible." I could tell she wanted to add, "Duh!" but checked herself. Because who really says that anymore?

"Why should Mackenzie stay hidden?"

Jane and I just stared at Corey in confusion.

"Okay, just hear me out," he continued. "I know that Mackenzie is used to being invisible, but what if she weren't. What if she used this instead?"

"Used it how?" asked Jane skeptically.

Corey smiled his I've-got-a-plan smile. "Okay, so ideally Mackenzie would remain invisible, but since this video is the hottest thing on YouTube, things won't just return to normal. The media are going to pursue you, Mackenzie. So you need to hide in plain sight. Blend in with the Notables, for real this time, and people will stop paying attention. Otherwise, let's face it, you're going to end up on national Worst Dressed lists."

I looked down at my jeans, which were sort of worn and relaxed. "What's wrong with what I wear?"

Corey grinned. "Nothing. The baggy sexless jeans and plain shirt combo is all the rage in Milan."

"Shut up."

"Look, the point is," Corey continued, pointedly ignoring me, "that you need to change. If you stay ordinary it's going to get bad, Mackenzie. Remember when we watched *She's All That*? After the popular guy expressed interest in the geeky artist, she had to improve her style to blend in."

"You cannot seriously be taking your advice from a Freddie Prinze Jr. movie made in the nineties," Jane protested. "Think *Devil Wears Prada*. Nice girl becomes materialistic and awful and tosses aside the people most important to her."

"Yeah, but how awesome did Anne Hathaway look once she started wearing cute clothes? That could be Mackenzie!"

"I'll think about it," I told Corey noncommittally, because it was the only way to shut him up.

The bus pulled up to the high school, and it was there that I got my first shock of the morning. The place was swarming with reporters holding microphones and examining the student body for one particular face—mine.

"Yeah, I think you should do that," said Corey as the three of us disembarked. "I don't think the baseball hat is going to get you out of this."

Okay, wading through reporters isn't easy. Now I understand why celebrities are always scowling and flipping off the paparazzi. It's distracting when people are all over you snapping photos and asking stuff like, "Mackenzie, will you take a CPR class?" "Mackenzie, how does it feel to be famous?" and even "Mackenzie, what's your favorite television show?"

I know in the movies when the president is being hassled by the press he always keeps walking with his head down, saying, "No comment. No comment," but that looked stupid to me. Why not just answer the questions and get it over with? Except I was learning quickly that the press aren't easy to deal with. So I tried to get through the mass of reporters and answer at the same time.

"Um, no CPR class," I mumbled, which just got them more riled up.

"What about your love life?" someone shouted.

"What love life?" I asked.

"NO COMMENT!" screeched Jane, and she promptly put the entire football team to shame with the way she ran interference. Bookended by my friends, we were able to scurry into the high school, leaving a royal mess in our wake. Everyone was staring and snapping photos of my encounter with the paparazzi on their cell phones. Great.

I turned to Corey, who was panting next to me. "How am I going to survive this?"

He grinned. "Come on, that was fun!"

"Yeah," I grumbled. "I've always wanted to be mobbed into buildings."

Jane elbowed me. "Um, Mackenzie. Mr. Taylor is coming toward us."

Mr. Taylor, the school principal, is something of a joke. He's large, thick-necked, and has a booming laugh that reverberates around the hall. His pride for the school sports teams knows no bounds, which is why guys like Spencer can stay on the hockey team despite their grades. I'd never needed to form an opinion of him before, since he had completely ignored me.

He turned to Jane. "Mackenzie, we need to have a talk."

Corey snickered. "Then you should probably be talking to

Mackenzie." He pointed at me. "You know, the famous one."

"Mackenzie, of course," he blustered. "Come with me."

Corey saluted. He's never been good at dealing with authority figures, especially ones that valued the football team over the debate team. "Yes, sir," he said sarcastically. Then he whispered, "Good luck," in my ear before dragging Jane away.

Yeah, this was not how I wanted my day to go.

Mr. Taylor walked me to his office in silence while the whole student body watched. People kept snapping photos on their cell phones while I flinched. Mr. Taylor boomed at his secretary, "Hold all my calls."

"Well, Mackenzie. It appears we have an, ahem, situation here."

I wanted to say, "No shit, Sherlock," but I kept my mouth shut.

"Frankly I'm a little concerned about your safety." He dropped a copy of *The Oregonian* in my lap. The headline read: **Can You Say Awkward, Mackenzie Wellesley?** I started reading the article.

> Seventeen-year old Mackenzie Wellesley had no idea that when she tried to resuscitate a fellow high school student she'd be infusing life back into news cycles. The video of her accident has received millions of hits online ever since it first appeared on YouTube. Ms. Wellesley's climb into the national spotlight was helped along by Twitter postings from celebrities that range from Ashton Kutcher to The Office comedian Rainn Wilson. And don't expect this girl to disappear anytime soon. "I'm not Susan freaking Boyle," says Ms. Wellesley, asserting her individuality.

> Sounds like we'll be hearing about her and her
> video for a long time to come.

Most of this information wasn't all that new. Still, reading about myself in the newspaper made me feel lightheaded. I tried not to freak out, I really did. I reminded myself to breathe and sucked in a lung full of air.

"So what do you want to do about it?" I asked Mr. Taylor. I expected him to say, "Well, in cases like these we have a procedure set in place to minimize the disruption of your daily life." But he didn't, because there is no procedure. There is no plan in place, no just-in-case scenario for a student becoming ridiculously famous over a single weekend. That stuff just doesn't happen.

Until it happened to me, I suppose.

Mr. Taylor leaned back in his chair importantly. Which was ludicrous because he obviously had absolutely no control over the situation. "Your mother is going to be here soon so the three of us can chat."

I instantly felt guilty. My mom works at this cute little restaurant and puts in long hours to make ends meet. I always feel guilty when she's interrupted at work.

"You don't have to do that," I told him. "I'm going to be fine. We'll just work something out and I'll fill her in later."

No sooner had the words left my mouth than my mom burst into the office in her black suit and heels.

"Are you okay, honey?" she asked, ignoring Mr. Taylor entirely. My mom has always been like that. Her first priority isn't soothing ruffled egos—it's keeping Dylan and me safe.

"Fine, Mom."

Mr. Taylor cleared his throat. "Mrs. Wellesley."

"Ms. Wellesley, actually," my mom corrected.

Mr. Taylor decided to take that in stride. "Well, your daughter is in quite the predicament, Ms. Wellesley."

I thought that was the understatement of the century.

"Yes, she is," Mom agreed calmly. "What are we going to do about it?"

Mr. Taylor puffed himself up like a blowfish. "Well, I believe that the most important issue at stake is Mackenzie's safety. Then we have to consider the quality of her education. Now, I will look into restricting the press from school grounds, but we need to look at our options."

My mom nodded in agreement and let Mr. Taylor continue.

"Due to, ahem, recent events, it might be for the best if Mackenzie altered her schedule a little. She can stay in the same classes but do her work privately in the school library, where she won't be distracted . . . or a distraction."

I stared at him. "No way!" I blurted. "Do you have any idea how many AP classes I am taking this year? Three. If you want to pull me out of P.E. that's fine, but there is no way I can miss my other classes. I'll never be able to catch up. And then I won't ace the national exams. And then I won't be as attractive for college scholarships. And then . . ."

Mr. Taylor interrupted me. "I can see you feel very passionately about this. However, I'm not sure you understand what you are getting into. It's a lot of attention, Mackenzie. Are you sure you wouldn't rather be in the library?"

I straightened in my seat. I knew what was in store for me. People sneaking photos of me on their iPhones. People whispering about my love life and my wardrobe. People asking about the stupid video. But college would be worth it, and those AP tests were my way in.

"I'm sure," I said firmly. "This . . . predicament is not going to stop me from living a normal life. Same friends, same job, and the same classes." I heard the tardy bell ring and rose from the chair. "I'll call you after school on my cell,

Mom. And thanks for the suggestions, Mr. Taylor, but I have class now."

And with that, I left. I marched down the empty hallways determined to act as though nothing had changed. I wasn't fooling anyone. That much was obvious when every single head in my class swiveled and gaped at me—including one Logan Beckett.

Chapter 10

Everything felt off in class that day, mainly because everyone was looking at me instead of Mr. Helm. They seemed to be *waiting* for something, maybe expecting me to burst into tears. And since my life goal was to fly under the radar, I wasn't thrilled about being on everyone's monitor. My every movement was evaluated and analyzed. By the time class was over, I was exhausted. I'd been pretending so hard that all of my energy had leached out of my body. I wanted to tell Principal Taylor that he was right—it was way too much attention—and chow down on some ice cream at home.

But I couldn't. I didn't want to admit defeat. So I didn't try to evade when I saw Logan waiting outside the classroom for me.

"Hey," he said. Not, "Are you all right?" or "So tell me, Mackenzie, how does it feel knowing Ashton Kutcher finds you funny?" Just "Hey."

"Hi," I mumbled. We never talked at school—or rarely. Why would we? I ruled the classroom and he was the reigning king of the hallways. Not much common ground. "What's going on?"

"Is our study session still on today?" He asked it casually as we started walking with the herd of students.

"Of course it is." I momentarily stopped moving. "I can't lose this job. And really it's not going to . . . let's talk about it later." I cut myself off as we separated for different class-rooms.

"All right. Outside Helm's room."

And with that he was gone. His dark brown hair and jean-clad body were swallowed up among other similarly dressed guys, leaving me to obsess over what he might say at our study session. "Sorry, Mackenzie, it's not you . . . wait, never mind, yes it is. I don't want my tutor to be the awkward girl on YouTube."

I was still thinking about it an hour and a half later during lunch. I poked at my burrito and hoped it would taste better than it looked—not a particularly difficult feat, since it looked inedible. Corey and Jane slid into their customary seats beside me, and it was as if our conversation had been unfrozen as soon as we were together.

"Okay, so the first thing we have to do is update your clothes," said Corey. He pulled out his notebook. "I sketched a few things during Chemistry. Now in this one I have you wearing jeans that show off that adorable butt of yours, a scoop-necked shirt, note the detail on it, with your hair down."

I fingered my ponytail. "What's wrong with having my hair up?"

"Messes up the look," Corey explained, flipping the pages to another sketch. "Now, here I picture the dress in a deep blue."

Jane snorted. "Because Mackenzie is really going to wear a dress like that to school . . . or anywhere else, for that mat-ter." She looked at it a little more closely. "Although it would be really pretty."

"The Old Mackenzie wouldn't. But the New Mackenzie might get club invites or something." Corey gestured broadly at the window. "We live fifteen minutes away from Portland—a city with culture and clubs. Already we've missed out on tons of concerts because we're under twenty-one. Well, now we can get in." Corey was so excited he was practically squeaking. "Do you think Miley Cyrus has any trouble getting into clubs? No. She can always walk in like it's no big deal."

"And in this equation, I'm Miley Cyrus?" I said in disbelief.

"It's a Party in the U.S.A., Mackenzie. My point is that we should be prepared for anything."

"Well, I'm prepared to ditch this," I said after a bite of my burrito. "I'm getting a muffin. Anyone want one?"

"Yep," said Jane. "Oatmeal cinnamon for me."

"I'll add it to your tab," I told her with a sidelong grin. Jane and I had alternated muffin runs for the better part of two years, making it impossible to keep track of a debt.

I was grinning all the way to the food line and then smiling as I pulled out my money. The cafeteria muffins are ridiculously tasty, and it's hard to be depressed with a bundle of deliciousness in each hand. Which is why I didn't notice the spilled soda on the cafeteria floor. I never would have noticed it at all if I hadn't been jostled out of line—*hard*—just as I was fumbling to pay the cashier.

It all happened in slow motion. My feet slipped, my body lurched, and I tumbled to the floor. Instinctively, my hands shot out to catch myself but only succeeded in demolishing the muffins. My wallet exploded on impact and showered the sticky floor around me with pennies, nickels, dimes, and a handful of quarters mixed in for good measure. I didn't get up right away. My head had smacked the floor hard on my way down, and the world was spinning. For a moment all I could think about was the pain. God, it hurt. My brain felt like it had been tossed around in a washer on spin cycle. I felt arms tugging me off the ground and slowly became aware of Corey and Jane.

"What?" I began, but Jane cut me off.

"Let's get you to the nurse."

But Corey wasn't going anywhere without a fight.

"You assholes!" he yelled at the small clump of snickering football players who surrounded Alex Thompson.

Which is when I realized that I hadn't just had a random embarrassing cafeteria experience: I'd been set up. And judging by the satisfied smile on Chelsea's face, she'd seen the whole thing coming and hadn't said a word. Not so much as an "Oh no! Mackenzie, look out!" For all I knew Alex Thompson and the other Notables plotted it together. My eyes scanned the expressions of the Notables around her while I tried to think past the pain. Most of the table was laughing and probably thinking, *There goes that Awkward Girl again. What a loser.*

I rubbed the back of my head tentatively, and for the first time my eyes met Logan's. He was already halfway across the cafeteria and moving steadily toward me. It registered briefly as weird that Logan didn't sit at the Notable table. I wasn't sure I'd ever seen him sit there, actually. I could feel the migraine pounding with the rhythm of Logan's feet as he stalked across the cafeteria.

I panicked . . . again. I'll admit that now. I saw him and I was *positive* he was going to fire me. Let's look at the facts, shall we?

1. He's a Notable
2. I humiliated myself in public again.
3. He had a reputation to maintain.
4. I didn't fit into that reputation . . . at all.

I couldn't let him fire me. I had to escape before I was out of a job or a best friend who looked intent on fighting with a football player. I grabbed Corey's shoulder.

"It doesn't matter," I said lamely. "Let's get out of here."

"What the hell do you mean it doesn't matter?" he seethed. "They think they can body check you and get away with it?" He swore loudly and rather eloquently to my way of thinking.

Alex Thompson just grinned. "Payback. Although maybe I have to spend some time on top of her for us to be even."

I felt sick, and not just because my head was ringing and my every movement was probably being filmed. Alex actually thought it was fine to knock me down and joke about forcing himself on top of me . . . and all because of a minor accident. This was his way of proving his manliness.

I stepped toward him carefully.

"Don't you *ever* think about touching me or my friends ever again," I told him in a voice that I managed to keep both cool and even—barely.

"Or what?" he sneered.

"Or I'll show you just how much damage a good girl can do." I smiled. "Believe me, I can hurt you without laying a finger on your skin."

I turned back to Corey and Jane, who were staring at me with open-mouthed amazement. "You guys ready to go?"

They nodded and the three of us made our exit. For the first time in the past two years I'd spent in high school, I felt vaguely cool.

Too bad the feeling didn't last.

Chapter 11

"You handled it well."

I tried to figure out what the hell Logan was talking about as we walked from Mr. Helm's classroom, where we had agreed to meet, to the parking lot at the end of the day.

"Handled what well?" I asked, rubbing my temple to fight back the rager of a headache that had kicked up a notch as I'd left the cafeteria.

"Alex and his friends."

I noticed he didn't say "my friends" and wondered what to make of it. Had my brain not felt diced, strained, and broiled, I definitely would have analyzed that for deeper social significance. Instead, I just shrugged.

"Could've done worse."

He grinned, much to my surprise. "No kidding."

I couldn't help smiling back. "I got the last word. Did you notice that? And I actually made a pretty convincing threat." I tried not to notice the way his dark hair flopped in his eyes as he unlocked the car and I slid in. "It sounded credible to you, right?"

He pulled out of the lot. "Sure, but I doubt you could really hurt the guy."

I leaned back against the seat. "It was the first thing that came to mind. But I suppose I could do *something* and get away with it. It's hard to believe the valedictorian, or future valedictorian," I corrected myself, "was the catalyst for anything."

He tapped the steering wheel in time to his music. "I guess."

"The reason it worked was because I left the threat to his imagination. Will I mess with his locker, or his report card, or his college transcript? Impossible to know. What we imagine is usually far more intimidating than reality. Psychological warfare."

"So you psyched him out. Personally I prefer just going at it."

"What?" My head jerked up and I leaned forward. I'd been distracted by idly wondering what it might be like to have his hands on the back of my neck, or lifting my chin to angle for a kiss. Thoughts I had no business thinking about a Notable, particularly one who was going to date Chelsea (again), marry her, and show up to the ten-year reunion with their perfect six-month-old baby.

"Fighting," he clarified. "A few good hits on the ice and I feel much better."

I imagined launching myself at Alex in the cafeteria, fists clenched. I bet I could have done some damage . . . before I was dragged to the infirmary.

"I'm a pretty good fighter," I commented. "I had to learn to throw a punch or I'd always be stuck watching Monday Night Football."

"Older siblings?" Logan asked, and it hit me just how little we actually knew about each other.

"Younger brother. Dylan. Plays quarterback at the middle school and idolizes any guy who wears pads."

Logan considered that for a second. "Skinny? Reddish hair?"

I stared at him. "Yeah."

He shrugged. "Good kid. I coached him at a sports camp over the summer. Listens to instructions."

"Your instructions, maybe," I said. "He doesn't exactly fall over himself to do me any favors. Although, he was pretty great last night when I got the call from . . ."

I let my sentence dribble out as it finally hit me what was missing: the press. I had spent the entire day fearing the questions of doggedly persistent reporters, but there wasn't anyone around. I'd had literally fifteen minutes of fame before becoming old news.

"They're gone!" I could have floated the rest of the way to Logan's house.

"Who is?"

"The newspaper and television people. They all cleared out." I leaned back in my seat with a sigh of relief. "I can go back to being a nobody. Wonderful." I wasn't even being sarcastic.

Logan pulled into his long, elegant driveway—his whole life was surreally perfect. "You want to be ignored?" he asked incredulously.

"Well, yeah," I said, stating the obvious. "If the choice is between being ignored or being ridiculed and body checked in the cafeteria line, it's not exactly a tough call."

"What about a third option?"

I just stared at him. "We go to the same high school, right? For me, there is no third option, which is why I'm studying so hard for college." Logan didn't say anything as we got out of the car. "What are your plans?" I asked curiously.

"College. Somewhere. My parents want me to check out their alma mater, USC, but I'm not sure it's for me."

I nodded. "It's weird, isn't it? The way adults expect us to have it all figured out. Once I get into college, that's it. I have to become a history major, then a historian. When, for all I know, I might end up loving sociology and moving to Australia to study aboriginal culture."

"Aboriginal culture, huh?" he said. "Well, you don't think small."

"Nope," I agreed as we walked into his house. I pulled out my textbook and laid it in front of us on the kitchen table. "Now, where did we leave off?"

Chapter 12

I woke up the next morning exhausted. Working with Logan on AP US cut into the homework time for my other classes. I had a boatload of work due for AP Gov and was operating on five hours of sleep. I'm not a morning person. I wake up early physically, but I'm always close to snapping at someone. So when I came downstairs and found that Dylan had finished off the milk, my bad mood darkened. I pulled out some Eggos and shoved them into the toaster.

Then I heard the scream.

It sounded like Dylan had broken a leg, pulled a tendon, and smashed every metatarsal in his foot—all at the same time.

"Dylan?" I hollered. All my stupid big sister instincts had jumped into overdrive. "Dylan, what's wrong?"

When I found him sitting in the computer room, pointing to the screen, I could have killed him.

"Are you kidding? You scared the crap out of me, you jerk."

Dylan just stared blankly oblivious to my outrage and kept pointing to the screen.

"I don't care what it says about me, okay? It's over. After today I'll be old news. Got it?"

But Dylan shook his head and clicked the screen.

For a second I was confused. Dylan was watching YouTube, but instead of me, the screen showed the latest music video from the rock band ReadySet.

I'm guessing you already know about them. I mean, *come on,* it's ReadySet we're talking about here. Their songs have been *huge* ever since the band used inventive music videos to launch themselves into popularity. At the very least you've heard of their lead singer, Timothy Goff, the eighteen-year-old taking the music industry by storm.

I'm still impressed with how they handled the footage—the brilliant way they worked me into the music video for their high-energy song "Going Down." The camera slowed with Alex midair before the drums burst into action the instant he connected with the ground. It was all so artistic: the changing background colors, the splicing, the close-ups . . . everything. It looked like my CPR Incident had been choreographed for the song. Really, the lyrics fit that well. Especially the lines:

> You fell like a girl from a looking glass.
> You swore that you'd always come back.
> But I've got a scribbled-up document.
> It says that you've gone away.

My expression, the naked panic on my face, gave the song depth as well as humor. A perfect blend and an instant hit.

I was so screwed.

"Th-That doesn't mean anything," I told Dylan. But I knew I was wrong. They had even incorporated my "AM I KILLING HIM RIGHT NOW?" into the song. And it sounded great.

Dylan met my eyes. Maybe it was the sisterly protective thing again, but he looked so small—just a scrawny runt with a mop of reddish hair and a sprinkling of freckles. And I was systematically screwing up his life.

"Mackenzie." He said my name slowly, as if testing each syllable. "One YouTube clip can go away, but this . . . it's a different story."

I wanted to say that I'd already handled the press, thank-you-very-much. But as much as I hated to admit it, he was right. My life was already chaotic before America's biggest rock sensation used me as some kind of muse. Now anyone who'd missed my moment of extreme embarrassment could catch it repeating endlessly on MTV-2.

And people would want to know about me. You don't watch a great music video without wondering about the people in it. That's why that wedding couple dancing down the aisle became so famous. First it went on YouTube, then AOL, until suddenly *The Office* was doing a spoof, and the couple was under fire for using a Chris Brown song after he famously beat his ex-girlfriend Rihanna. So then the newlyweds had to go on *Good Morning America* and donate money to the prevention of spousal abuse. All because someone filmed their nuptials and posted it online. Crazy, but true.

"I-I have to go to school," I said flatly. I squared my shoulders and walked straight to the kitchen to fix my mom's coffee. The whole time I told myself that soon I'd be a regular teenager going to a normal high school outside Portland, Oregon. So what if my fifteen minutes of fame weren't over yet? I could survive another fifteen.

Probably.

I played it cool. I handed my mom the mug and told her I needed her to drop me off at school. She sipped and nodded. But even though she never said, "Mackenzie, I don't have time to play chauffeur!" I felt like crap. The last thing she needed was more stress in her life. I'd have to make it up to her with more than a cup of coffee. She downed her drink while I ran through my schedule, searching for time I could spend vacuuming, sweeping, and Windexing—after school, tutoring, and homework, but before dinner.

My mom's eyes cleared with the coffee, sloughing off the gray mist that comes when she's only half awake. I wish I had inherited my mom's eyes, a clear blue, instead of my dad's boring brown ones. Her flame red hair made me think of leprechauns dancing on gold.

"Let's go, then," she said.

There were no reporters lingering on our driveway or ankle deep in the lawn that was a continuous clump of weeds. Maybe the ReadySet thing wouldn't be a big deal after all. That thought lasted until we pulled up to school.

It was like the day before . . . only a billion times worse.

"What the—"

I didn't let my mom finish. If I looked at the veritable sea of reporters, I might lose my nerve. I opened the door to make a run for it. Five feet from the car I was swallowed up in the jumble of business suits, cameras, and sound equipment. I spun in circles, desperately looking for someone I knew—someone to help me. I was panicky, naïve, and unprepared. A microphone was thrown in my face, and I clutched it as I searched for my exit.

"Mackenzie, what size are you?"

"Are you a ReadySet fan?"

"Are you going to their concert Thursday night?"

"Um." *Too many questions!* "Size, uh, twelve, I think? Yeah, I like ReadySet. Who doesn't? But I don't have tickets. It's probably sold out."

"Is it true you're dating the lead singer, Timothy Goff?"

"I've, uh, never even met the guy." I was tempted to just drop the microphone and bolt, but I was afraid of being charged for any damages.

"Mackenzie, what are you wearing?"

I looked down at myself uncertainly. "Um, jeans?"

"Do you have a favorite designer?"

I stared at the reporter in disbelief. She looked so polished in a dark blue silk blouse and tailored suit pants. And she was asking *me* about fashion.

"It's from a garage sale," I mumbled. "I don't—"

But there was a whole new set of questions.

"Where do you want to go to college?"

"Who's your favorite celebrity?"

"How does it feel to be 'America's Most Awkward Girl'?"

"Are you seeing anyone right now?"

I couldn't process what I was hearing.

"I'm sorry," I said politely. "Really. I know you guys are just trying to do your jobs, but I need to get to class. And you're freaking me out." I blushed and focused on the microphone. "I'm sorry," I repeated. "But you want one of the Notables, not me." I could have bitten my tongue off at the slip. "I don't do designer clothes. I'll never afford them. And with AP tests, tutoring, and high school, I can't deal with all this *attention*." I made it sound like the plague. "So thanks for your time, but I need to go now."

I was relieved to see a determined police officer wade her way through the cameras. She looked like a hero on a cop show, with her brisk, no-nonsense walk. She'd probably spent her career proving herself until she was the toughest cop in the area.

She snaked out an arm to grasp my shoulder as we headed for one of the buildings. "Ignore them," she instructed me as reporters kept yelling, "Mackenzie, who are the Notables?" and "Is it hard living in a single-parent home?" I saw her nod as other police officers moved in to enforce a media perimeter. A quick glance over my shoulder told me the media weren't finished with their interviews. A whole circle of reporters listened to the Evil Trio. From the corner of my eye, I saw Chelsea toss her hair into a cascade of gold down her back. She'd look like a goddess while I looked like a geek. Not for the first time I wished Chelsea was famous instead of me.

The policewoman kept her hand firmly clamped on my shoulder until I was safe from the paparazzi. Even inside the English building, she didn't ditch me. She steered me over to the nearest drinking fountain.

"Drink," she ordered. I obeyed her instinctively. My mouth must have become dry during my impromptu interview—something I'd failed to notice. Just like I hadn't realized my hands were shaking like hummingbird wings.

"Feel better?" she asked, once I gulped my fill.

I didn't trust my voice, so I just nodded.

"Good." She looked at me appraisingly and then shook her head. I thought I caught pity in her eyes. "Next time: head down, shoulders back, no eye contact, no faltering, and you'll be just fine. Now get to class."

I was following her instructions when she called out, "Ms. Wellesley."

I turned around.

"Good luck."

She had no idea just how much I needed it.

Chapter 13

There were eyes everywhere. No matter where I turned, I met half a dozen stares. Every single movement I made was analyzed—my nervous habit of tucking my brown hair behind my ears was documented. I could hear the persistent clicking of cell phone cameras, and I tried my hardest not to flinch, hide my face, or flee into the girls' bathroom.

In all my time at Smith High School, I'd never felt more isolated and alone.

At least no one made fun of me anymore. The same jerk who had imitated me in a falsetto voice now eyed me speculatively without saying a word. I was definitely no longer an Invisible. It was like a new category had been created just for me: the Spectacle. Everyone observed but nobody spoke to me. Great.

Even Jane and Corey were affected. They pretended things were normal, but they were clearly rattled by this new level of visibility. Jane kept scanning the other lunch tables as if expecting an attack. Like some kid was going to scream, "ReadySet should have used *me* in their music video!" before opening fire on our table. Teenagers had done stupider things for worse reasons.

"So . . ." Corey said conversationally. "Are you going?"

I looked up from the muffin I was systematically mangling into a pile of crumbs. "Huh?"

"The ReadySet concert tomorrow. Are you going?"

"Are they playing nearby?" I asked blankly.

"Portland, Rose Garden, tomorrow night, seven-thirty."

I glanced at Jane. She was still staring at the kids who were staring at us.

Great.

"O-kay," I said slowly. "Cool. But even if it hasn't sold out, I couldn't afford a ticket."

"I was hoping you could use your, er, connections to score us some seats."

I nearly choked on my Diet Coke. "Connections? I don't have any *connections.*"

"Since you're in the music video, it's only right that you are invited to the show." He flashed his slightly wicked grin. "Maybe you could bring some friends who would *kill* to go to a ReadySet concert. Friends who wouldn't mind driving into Portland for the show or footing the gas bill."

"I get it," I said, laughing. It's pretty hard to be offended by Corey—maybe because his ploys are always so obvious. "I'll let you know if anything turns up, I promise."

He leaned back in his chair, pleased with himself. He was wearing a plaid shirt and skinny jeans that somehow didn't look creepy on him, which was impressive since most guys can't pull off the look. Corey jerked his head and his bangs swished to one side. Seriously, they *swished.* My hair never obeys me like that.

"What about you, Jane," I asked. "Anything you want me to score?"

"What?" She jerked back into the conversation. "Sorry, I was distracted by the fact that *everyone in the school is staring at us!*"

"Look, there's nothing I can do about the attention. A few days from now this will all be over."

"In the meantime, have you considered hiring a stylist?"

Before I could answer Corey, Logan slid into an empty seat next to Jane. The cafeteria went silent before a hum of mass whispering began. Jane's mouth dropped open, not attractively I might add, as she stared at him in shock. Notables are always a shock on the system. I felt like I'd just consumed another shot of caffeine.

Corey sat up in his chair but pretended as if a Notable visit was an everyday occurrence. I could practically hear Corey's gaydar beeping, as he tried to decipher Logan's sexuality. I was guessing straight since he'd been distracted by Chelsea's cleavage, but I've got notoriously bad gaydar.

"Hey," said Logan smoothly, as if eating a hamburger and fries with a pair of Invisibles and the Spectacle was no big deal.

"Um, hey," I managed. Jane needed more time to untangle her tongue. "How's it going?"

"Fine." He picked up a fry and turned to see everyone in the cafeteria watching the four of us. "That's a little intense."

"No, really?" I couldn't help saying. "I hadn't noticed."

Corey elbowed me in the ribs, but Logan just grinned. Slowly Jane and Corey began to relax.

"So . . . has Alex given you any more trouble?" Logan asked casually.

This time I really smiled. The one time I'd seen Alex in the cafeteria he'd given me a wide berth. Just the way I wanted it.

"I guess my threat yesterday worked!" I elbowed Corey back, a little harder than necessary as payback. "Told you I could handle it."

"Yeah, way to deliver an empty threat," Jane said weakly.

"I could probably tell *Teen People* about him or something." I considered it for a moment. "But I don't think I've got the nerve."

Corey paused midbite of his pizza. He can scarf down twice the amount of junk food I can and fit into size 4 skinny jeans. Boys and their stupid metabolisms. "He just better leave you alone, Mackenzie."

Jane and Logan nodded in agreement—which was weird. Why would Logan Beckett care whether a football player harassed me? Unless . . . maybe he wanted more friends. But that couldn't be it. He didn't need Invisible friends—he probably had too many invites for keggers and parties already. Plus, I couldn't picture him looking forward to a movie night with the three of us.

"How's AP US going?" I asked him, to take the attention off me.

God, I'm a geek.

"I didn't get what Helm was talking about today."

"Well," I said. "Remember in the chapter how . . ."

"Study session after school?" he interrupted. "I could use the extra time."

"Um, sure." The answer was automatic.

"Great," Logan said simply. "I'll meet you after class." Then he turned to Corey and asked him something about Woodshop. While the two of them discussed cherrywood and sanding techniques, Jane and I carried on a nonverbal conversation.

A small shake of the head meant she couldn't believe what was happening.

My answering shrug confirmed I didn't get it either.

Then Jane flicked a glance at Logan before letting her eyes linger meaningfully at me.

I shook my head deliberately. I am so not Logan's type, which is (of course) tall, willowy, blond, and generously endowed. That's why he and Chelsea are obviously suited for each other. Just like I'm perfect for Patrick.

Jane raised an eyebrow, and it was a good thing the boys missed my derisive little snort.

The world's social order would have to implode before Logan Beckett and I ever became an item. I couldn't see that happening either.

Chapter 14

I didn't know where I was supposed to meet him.

He'd said "after class," but that didn't really tell me any-thing. I mean, was I supposed to stand outside AP Lit and wait for him to appear? I didn't like that idea. I may fear the spotlight, but I am no Cinderella waiting around. I learned a long time ago that when you depend on people, they usually let you down. Not that I believed all guys wanted to make out with ballet instructors—I'm not that damaged. I just knew that the only person I could rely on was myself.

But none of that gave me any insight into where I should meet Logan . . . or what I should say to him.

"Hey, long time no see."

Yeah, probably not.

"So that was an interesting meal."

Not that either.

"Were you on something when you sat down at my table? Because hanging out with Invisibles is going to affect your social status. You get that, right?"

Mental head slap.

I was still searching for a conversation starter when Logan appeared, looking as unconcerned as ever.

"Hey." He smiled like I wasn't just the pain-in-the-ass

tutor he put up with to get his parents off his back. I wondered why he was meeting up with me in the first place. I had yet to really make a difference as his tutor.

However, a smile, even a fleeting one, was far from his standard disinterested shrug. Maybe he was looking for an in with Corey—we'd have to discuss his gaydar later.

"So about tutoring today . . . I'm not sure that's the best idea."

He studied me. "Are you backing out?"

"No-o." Mentally I was screaming, *Yes! The paparazzi might be waiting for me! Are you INSANE?*

"Good." He nodded his head toward the exit. "Let's go."

I hoped that the press wouldn't be there. That they'd left before school ended like they'd done the day before. That we could walk over to his car without *Teen People* snapping photos of me in my ratty jeans and sweatshirt.

"So did you hear about—"

Logan never got the chance to finish his sentence. The paparazzi should have left. I mean, hello, I'd already said way too much. What were the vultures hoping for . . . another scene, maybe? I could practically see it:

ME: (blinded by the flashing of cameras) Wh-what?

REPORTER ONE: Mackenzie, do you blame anyone for your fame?

REPORTER TWO: Mackenzie, do you regret your attempt at CPR?

REPORTER THREE: Mackenzie, how does it feel to be famous?

ME: I—ACK!

Tripping over my own feet, I tumbled into Logan who, prompted by the new chant of "Kiss her!" grinned and obliged.

* * *

Wait, what?

Where had that come from? I needed more sleep—that was the only explanation for it. The only one I'd consider. Freud would have a field day, but the first part of my imagined script was dead-on. The press moved in, and I found myself under siege with questions hurled like grenades. I grabbed Logan's arm to steady myself when a cameraman jostled into me hard.

"Let's run for it," I hollered, to be heard over the questions. Without waiting for a response I bolted toward the parking lot and pulled him behind me.

I completely impressed myself with my imitation of a badass if-you-don't-move-you-will-be-crushed policewoman. I used my speed to propel me through the crowd.

Still, the questions were so much worse than I'd imagined.

"Mackenzie! Who's your friend?"

"Are the two of you dating?"

"What do you think of *Twilight*?"

This time I didn't respond. I just ran as fast as I could, grateful that I was wearing my black Converse. Logan's longer legs pushed him ahead and left me struggling to keep up. Which burned my ego, since I'm no slouch when it comes to running the presidential fitness mile.

It's a good thing we grabbed hands or we'd have been separated. A cheesy romance lover might think it was romantic, but there's nothing "romantic" about getting smacked in the face by a stranger's elbow.

Still, we made it to his car without any major injuries. Logan didn't waste any time getting the hell out of there. He drove carefully, just to make sure no photographers became speed bumps, but he drove fast. I used my arms to obstruct my face while Logan swerved and barreled down streets to lose the entourage tailing us.

"Do you know what you're doing?" I demanded. "Because my knowledge of car chases is limited to *The Bourne Identity*. Let's think this through before we make a mistake."

Logan shook his head. "I know exactly where we're going."

"Okay." I waited for him to say more. He didn't. "And where would that be?"

"It's a surprise." He turned sharply, and I got a newfound appreciation for my seat belt.

"Not a big fan of surprises. I've had enough of those to last me a lifetime." I gestured at the paparazzi tailing us to make my point.

"I think you could use a few more." He cut smoothly onto the freeway. "You can pick the music."

"Gee, thanks." I dug into my backpack, plugged my iPod into Logan's speaker adaptor, flipped to a playlist, and let the music flow.

"Wilco?" he asked, and I nodded in surprise. Maybe he was more rock and less jock than I'd originally assumed.

"Good stuff."

I was about to ask about his music taste when I realized we'd left Forest Grove behind us. Far behind us, actually. We were headed into the city.

"Portland?" I gaped at him. "You want us to lose them in *Portland?*"

"Do you have a better idea?"

"I—I guess, well . . . I—no," I stuttered.

"Then there you go, Mack."

I was too distracted by the situation to object to the nickname.

"But . . . the gas money. We should've just—"

Logan cut me off. "My idea, my money."

Which was a huge relief, because I couldn't afford the gas, especially when I still owed him for that cup of coffee. But it also completely sucked. I didn't *ever* want to be the type of girl who does stupid stuff like mooch off of guys. I had no idea what to do about Logan Beckett's habit of shelling out money. *I'll just have to keep a running tab,* I decided. *And pay him back as soon as possible.*

"Almost there." He pulled into a parking garage.

"You're kidding, right? A mall! *You* are taking *me* to the *mall!* Do you have any idea how weird this is?"

"Yeah." That was all I got. Just "yeah." I hate boys and their stupid monosyllabic answers sometimes. "Run!"

I took his advice, and the two of us raced into the Lloyd Center with the paparazzi right on our heels. That's when I started seeing the genius in his plan. Outside we would have been sitting ducks, but inside it was easier to blend and disappear. I was surprised the idea had not occurred to me.

"Come on." I followed Logan until I saw the store and put on the brakes.

"No," I said flatly. "No way."

"Look," Logan said quietly. "It's either this"—he gestured to Victoria's Secret's unbearably pink sign—"or that." I looked behind me and saw the press scanning the area.

"Fine." I ducked inside with him. "But I resent this."

He laughed but checked himself quickly.

"Don't you think this is a tad, um . . . conspicuous?" Logan ignored me, reached into a hot pink drawer, and pulled out a dark purple bra.

"Act natural," he muttered, and handed me the bra. Then, looking like he did this every day, he pulled me into one of the dressing room stalls. He settled himself on the minisofa looking pleased while I stared in shock.

I was in Victoria's Secret, with Logan Beckett, holding a purple bra, and being chased by the press.

My life had officially become stranger than a Tim Burton movie.

"They won't think to look in here," Logan informed me as I sank to the floor.

I nodded and stared at my feet. "So do you come here often?"

He laughed again, and I was struck by the niceness of the moment. It was weird, but I was actually having fun. Not something I had expected to happen.

"Oh yeah. I take all my dates here. Cozy, isn't it?"

"Nice . . . ambiance," I said, looking pointedly at the bra and hot pink couch.

"Pink is the new blue," he replied. "Or so I've been told. . . ."

I pulled my boring, straight brown hair out of my ponytail and let it fall around my face. "Oh, my god!" I channeled my inner Notable. "I heard that too! That's total whatchimacallit!"

"Completely," he said, playing along.

"So you think it's safe to leave yet?"

Logan shrugged. "Probably, but we should have a plan."

"A plan?"

"Yeah, those reporters know what we look like. We'll need a disguise." He was having way too much fun with this.

I stared at him in disbelief. "Of course. Stupid me, I packed my superhero suit in my other backpack with my bundle of cash."

Logan pulled out his wallet, but I didn't give him the chance to speak.

"You're kidding me, right? You *cannot* keep spending money on me like some kind of sugar daddy." Yes. I said the phrase "sugar daddy" to Logan Beckett.

Kill me now.

Logan's mouth twitched into a grin. "I was thinking of a loan."

"A loan?" I repeated.

"Yeah. My parents pay you ten bucks an hour, right?" I

nodded as he handed me a fifty-dollar bill. "Well, now you owe me five hours of your time."

I sighed. "Five and a half hours, actually. I still owe you for Starbucks from a few days ago."

He smiled. "You remembered."

"Of course. So five and half hours . . ." I did some mental calculations. "If we start studying soon, I should be out of debt by the end of this week." I nodded approvingly. "I can live with that."

"You know we could chalk up the coffee as a tutoring expense."

"A tutoring expense?" I repeated skeptically.

"Yeah, caffeine is a study agent that was once used as a form of currency."

"You remembered." I was shocked that anything I said stuck with him. Maybe I wasn't the worst tutor after all.

"Of course," he repeated, mimicking me to perfection. I laughed.

"Five and a half hours and we're square." I couldn't owe Logan money. "I pay my own way."

Just fingering the fifty-dollar bill was making me nervous. Or maybe it was the casual way he handed it over. Both sort of freaked me out.

"This probably isn't necessary." I tried to hand it back. "Really. I can just . . ."

Logan ran his hand through his hair in frustration, something I had only seen him do while staring blankly at a history textbook.

"Look, just take it so we can leave. If we stay in here too long the store people will wonder what we're up to." He raised his eyebrows suggestively.

"Okay," I said quickly. "Let's go."

"Let's meet up at the ice skating rink in forty-five minutes." We stepped out of the dressing room as he added in a louder voice, "I don't think that bra is really you. Black is more your speed, Mack."

I glared but only saw his back as he left me alone in Victoria's Secret with a bra in one hand and a fifty-dollar bill in the other. Just when I thought things couldn't get any weirder . . . well, I guess they did.

Chapter 15

Okay, so I took Corey's advice. The press were searching for the Mackenzie they had seen earlier—the one with no makeup and no fashion sense. I had to look trendy, which isn't easy for a girl on a tight budget. I bought a clingy, deep purple shirt that made my jeans look way less "baggy and sexless," as Corey had put it earlier. In fact, I looked sexy in an I-could-do-martial-arts-and-then-go-on-a-date kind of way. A thin coat of mascara, eye shadow, and lip gloss from testers on display and I was a whole different girl. It's crazy what a little makeup can do when someone's desperate for a disguise.

Having gunk on my face felt strange but made it easier to leave the safety of the store. I decided to think of it as feminine war paint or a Halloween mask. I did my best to stroll casually to the rink and pretend I was a Notable. Really. I imagined that instead of Mackenzie Wellesley, Queen of Awkward, I was Chelsea Halloway, Queen of Smith High School. Would Chelsea ever slump or scuttle over to the mall ice skating area? No. So neither did I.

Even Logan had trouble recognizing me. His big disguise was a soft-looking gray cardigan, which was probably supposed to make him look preppy except it totally failed. He still looked like a rumpled Notable, what with his nicely fitting jeans and tousled dark brown hair. The sweater just made his gray eyes look smokier.

"Well," he said when he saw me. "You look . . . different."

"And you look the same."

"Yeah, well, I blend."

I tried not to snort. Sure, he didn't raise attention—except for every teenage girl's hormonal, hot guy radar within a forty-foot radius.

"So let's get our skates."

The Portland Lloyd Center has a small crowded rink, which I've always thought was part of its charm. Couples and families skate endless circles together while little kids topple over everywhere.

"All right."

Fifteen minutes later I was laced up and wondering what I'd gotten myself into. If I didn't tutor him soon I'd feel guilty about the loan. I'd never done history on ice before.

"Are you sure this is a good plan?" I asked skeptically. "Why don't we just sit somewhere and discuss the American Revolution?"

"Scared?" His voice held a challenge.

I marched deliberately to the ice (as much as I could march in ice skates) and swiveled jerkily to face him. "You coming or not? We have studying to do."

Logan was on the ice in a matter of seconds. I thought he looked comfortable in the school hallways, but on ice it was like his whole body became an extension of the skates. He cut in front of me and turned in one fluid gesture so that we were face to face.

"Okay. Shoot."

"Who was the second president of the United States?" I asked, looking over his shoulder to make sure he wouldn't accidentally crush a toddler.

"John Adams. Relax, I know what I'm doing."

"The third president?"

"Thomas Jefferson."

I wobbled on my skates. "Good."

"Are you done with the easy stuff?"

Now, that caught me by surprise.

"I thought you preferred the easy stuff."

He paused to consider. "I think I'm up for a challenge."

"Okay, I'll give you a name, date, or event. You tell me everything you know about it."

I sensed him nod since my main focus was on finding my equilibrium. My Rollerblading prowess didn't cross over, although I'd been careful to get hockey skates. Logan had raised an eyebrow when I rented them, but all I had to say was "no toe pick" and he understood. Figure skating toe picks and I don't get along.

"Samuel Adams."

"Beer," he replied promptly.

"What?" My head jerked up too quickly and I lost my balance. The stupid skates sent me hurtling toward the ground, which was exactly what I deserved for thinking that I could tutor and skate at the same time. The Greeks had a word for that type of pride: hubris. And it usually came before a very long and painful fall.

"Oof!" I crashed into something solid but not cold enough to be the rink. When I realized I was gripping Logan's new sweater for all I was worth I quickly apologized. "Sorry. It takes me a while to adjust to these things. I'd be fine on Rollerblades but ice skates . . ."

"It's a different type of motion," he said, but his eyes seemed wary.

"Yeah." I loosened my grip on his sweater and straightened.

"So you Rollerblade." He tilted his head and looked me over. "How long have you done that?"

"Twelve years and . . ." I did some quick math. "Five months."

Logan looked half-amused. "That's precise."

"It was memorable." I wasn't smiling.

"What happened?"

"Well, my dad left. Twelve years and five months ago. Right after my . . ." I clamped my mouth shut.

"Your what?"

I looked at him with my most intense you-don't-want-to-mess-with-me face. "This goes nowhere."

"Fine."

"And no laughing."

"Done."

"Myballetrecital" I mumbled, hoping it would be too slurred for him to catch.

"You did ballet!" He choked. "Seriously?"

"We said no laughing! And it was just for a few months. My mom thought it might help my dad, well . . . accept that I'm a girl."

Logan raised his eyebrows at that. "He had trouble understanding the concept?"

I smiled, but it felt a tad forced. "He was convinced I'd be a boy. He didn't look at the sonogram because he was sure I'd be a boy named Mack. They had to extend my name to Mackenzie. I guess I'm just lucky that it works."

"Yeah, if they'd picked out Todd, that'd have been rough."

I laughed. "Yeah. Anyhow, I had a blue room and all these baseballs and stuff."

"Which you never used?"

"Lots of kids aren't into sports. I just happened to be one of them. My dad tried to play catch with me, but it wasn't my thing. My hand–eye coordination has always been zilch. So my mom thought it would be good for me to try ballet."

"Okay," Logan said slowly. "I don't see where the Rollerblading fits in."

"Well, after the recital, my dad left." I conveniently edited out the part about him sucking face with my instructor. "I didn't say anything for a week. My mom was freaking out, trying to get me to verbalize my emotions. And then I said I'd rather be eaten by an elephant than ever do ballet again."

"An elephant?"

"I liked the visual. So I asked her to take me to a sports store, and I grabbed the only thing that didn't include flying objects."

"The Rollerblades."

"Yep. That's how I got started."

The whole time I told him this, I became more comfortable with the gliding movement of the skates.

"What about your dad?"

"What about him?" I looked up from the ice.

"Did he ever see you skate?"

"Nope. He started a new family. Occasionally we get holiday cards, two kids—both boys. Sounds like he's happy."

"Sounds like he's a moron."

That caught me by surprise. "That too." I laughed.

"I'm still going to call you Mack."

I rolled my eyes. "Of course you will."

"But I don't wish you were a boy." His grin made my pulse kick up a notch.

"So, um, your parents seem cool." I had to say something to break the flirty mood. Or was I just imagining it? Hard to know for sure.

He nodded. "Yeah, they are. It'd be nice to have a sibling though. Sometimes they push too hard."

"You mean they'll do stuff like hire tutors for you?" I

slapped a hand over my mouth in mock horror. "How awful!"

He grinned. "You should see the freak they stuck me with. This one girl with a guy's name was such a . . ."

I whacked him on the arm before he could finish the sentence.

"Back to studying. Now, Sam Adams." He opened his mouth, but I cut him off. "And don't say beer!"

Chapter 16

Yes, we studied. I did an excellent job grilling him, then filling him in when he didn't know an important fact. He actually seemed to be paying attention—a welcome change from his typically bored expression and doodling. It felt like an elementary school birthday party—everything seemed simple for a minute. No press, no staring eyes, and no pressure. I think Logan enjoyed himself too. He laughed at me when I slipped, but he still offered me a hand up. And when he grinned, grabbed my hand, and whipped me around a curve, it kind of felt like a date—the type where a boy wants to spend time with a girl who isn't paid to be there. But of course it wasn't. Because, no matter what the press did, I would still be geeky Mackenzie Wellesley.

It lasted only until we went to the food court—the whole wow-this-almost-feels-like-a-date thing. That's when I screwed it up. We were superrelaxed, talking about our favorite movies, and standing in line for greasy Chinese food, when I said we should pull out our textbooks. I swear, that's all I said, but he tensed up instantly and his jaw stiffened.

It shouldn't have been a big deal. His parents were paying me to tutor, not to imagine I was on a date with their son. No way could I accept their money if I hadn't earned it. Finances might be tight in my family, but I'd never stoop to accepting money I didn't deserve. I'd become very financially savvy. My middle school graduation dress? Seventy-five cents from a garage sale. Beat that, Chelsea Halloway. Well, I guess she had, in a supergorgeous off-white strapless dress . . . but I bet it cost a fortune.

Anyway, I take money seriously. So after I stretched my fifty-buck loan to include some beef and broccoli, I pulled out my textbook. I also did a quick sweep of the area and didn't see any press, so I figured we were clear.

"Okay," I said. "We left off with the British advantages for war." After much page turning, I found the spot. "You read them off while I eat."

I tried to get back the good-natured friendliness because a very small table and a mound of kung pao chicken and rice was all that separated me from an irritated-looking Notable.

"Look, we can stop the clock," Logan said easily. "Let's just eat and go over it later."

"Five more minutes," I pressed. At the rink he really seemed to be getting it. If he was on the verge of a breakthrough, I wasn't going to let Chinese food get in the way. "Here, 'Britain had over three times the population of the colonies.' "

My voice trailed off as I watched Logan glare at the words with his mouth firmly shut. His gaze crawled slowly from the spot I'd pointed to last.

"C-Can you read?" I blurted the question without thinking.

The pure annoyance in his eyes made me instinctively jerk back in my chair.

"I can read," he said defiantly. But he forcibly shut the textbook.

"Okay." I stabbed a piece of broccoli. "But . . ."

"But what?" Clearly he wasn't going to be up-front with an explanation.

"You tell me." I forced myself to meet his eyes and was relieved to see that he looked more frustrated than anything else. "You're obviously not telling me something that as your tutor I should know."

I said that last part in a rush before I lost my nerve. Then I watched in surprise as Logan slouched back in his chair.

"I'm dyslexic." He said it calmly but with an obvious trace of bitterness. "Is that what you wanted to hear?"

"Oh." Well, that made sense.

"Yeah. Oh." He laughed. "I fit perfectly into that dumb jock cliché of yours now, don't I?"

"Because you've got dyslexia or because you stare at Chelsea Halloway's boobs?"

Oh, God. Did I really just say that?

He stared at me and then started laughing for real.

"Um, what I *meant* to say," I corrected myself, "is that dyslexia doesn't make you stupid. In fact, people with dyslexia often have above-average physical coordination, artistic talent, and empathy." I nodded toward his doodle-filled notebook. "Judging the whole hockey thing and your drawings, you're at least two out of three."

Logan stared at me in disbelief. "You know all that off the top of your head?"

"Sure," I replied evenly. "Near photographic memory. Steven Spielberg, John Lennon, Walt Disney, Steve Jobs—all dyslexic. Not to mention . . ."

"I get the picture," Logan interrupted.

"Right. Well, then, you see it's nothing to be embarrassed about."

"Yeah?" There was just a hint of a question in the one-word response.

"Yeah." I met his eyes head-on, determined not to screw this up. "But we're going to need a whole new plan of attack." I opened my notebook, uncapped my pen, and started scribbling down notes. "Let's ditch the textbook and check out some more auditory or visual learning techniques." I unthinkingly began to tap the pen against my lower lip. "There's a miniseries on John Adams that might help. We can always raid the library's history movies." I paused, struck by what those videos would effectively do: replace me. "I can help you pick them out, if you want," I offered. "You can call me after each one and we'll discuss it."

"Or you could watch them with me."

"I can't let your parents pay me to watch movies," I blurted out.

"Mack, it's not a big deal."

"Yes, it is. You're just used to tossing money around. Not everyone has that luxury, and I like your parents too much to fleece them."

"Fine. We'll renegotiate the pay when we watch the movies. Problem solved."

He made it sound so reasonable, like there wasn't a huge, gaping social chasm between us that made it weird for me to see movies at his house.

"Um, I guess that could work," I said awkwardly. What else could I say? "Logan, the other Notables, Chelsea in particular, will make life uncomfortable if they think we're hanging out. You'll get jokes about 'slumming it' and I'll get snide comments in the girls' locker room. Just warning you."

How stupid would that sound? It was *high school,* not the Hindu caste system, where the Untouchables have to avoid "polluting" the upper classes. Okay . . . maybe the two weren't that different, but all of this stress over the Notable / Invisible divide was just stupid. We were two teenagers in the same AP history class. End of story.

Logan didn't seem to notice my hesitancy and took a big bite of kung pao chicken. Ravenous, I attacked my own dish as I jotted down study ideas.

"We should pull some kids' books at the library."

Logan raised an eyebrow. "I really do know how to read."

"Kids' books generally do a better job highlighting material, so I like to use them for review."

He grinned. "You've got a photographic memory but you read kids' books before AP tests."

"*Nearly* photographic memory, and it's good to review the basics. You still work on your hockey stance, right? Same principle."

"You're one strange girl."

I stared at him uncertainly with a forkful of broccoli raised to my lips. "How so?"

"You list off people with dyslexia, read kids books, and practically inhale Chinese food."

I shrugged. "None of that's so strange. I thought you meant my balance issues and my tendency to babble around your friends."

"Now that you mention it . . . why is that?"

"Why is what?"

"Why are you so nervous around people? When you actually relax, you're not nearly as, hmm . . ."

"Awkward?" I supplied.

"Intimidating."

My mouth fell open. "Me? Intimidating. Yeah, right. And Chelsea Halloway secretly volunteers her time at a homeless shelter."

Logan laughed, then sobered. "Seriously, you can be intimidating."

"Really?" It was the most outrageous thing I'd heard since I had found out that I had become famous.

"Yeah. Especially in class." Logan deepened his voice in a dead-on impersonation of Mr. Helm. "Ah, yes, Mackenzie, would you like to explain the Stamp Tax to the rest of the class?"

I blushed. "Okay, *maybe* in class I can be a bit intense. But that doesn't make me intimidating!"

"Oh, yeah?" Logan was really warming to the subject. "What about when you yelled at the substitute teacher?"

"I did not!" I protested. "And even if I had, the guy deserved it. He was flat-out *wrong,* but he stood there and said one of us had gone to college and one of us hadn't. As if that changed anything." I paused. "You weren't in that class. How'd you hear about it?"

"Spencer mentioned it," he told me with a smug half smile. "He said you were pretty hard on the guy."

"He was a jerk with *misinformation.*" I shook my head in disgust.

"And you don't think you're intimidating."

"Yeah, well it's not like I'm a Notable!"

"What?" he asked, and I felt like an idiot. Because rule number one about secret nicknames—they have to remain a secret.

"You, Notable." I gestured with my fork. "Me, Invisible." I ate another piece of broccoli. "Or at least I was. Now Dr. Phil wants to talk to me."

Logan nearly choked on his Coke. "Dr. Phil called you?"

"Something like that. I'm a little fuzzy on the details. Dylan texted me something about going on *Dr. Phil* or *The View.*" I put down my fork. My appetite vanished at the thought of appearing on national television.

"But you don't want to do it?" Logan asked.

"Of course not!" I stared at him. "I'm already enough of a freak without officially becoming America's Most Awkward."

"You're not a freak," Logan told me. His appetite remained unaffected, and I watched enviously as he speared his last piece of chicken. "Strange, but not a freak."

"Gee, thanks," I said sarcastically, but I couldn't help feeling flattered. Logan Beckett didn't think I was a freak.

Chapter 17

I should have known that the media wouldn't leave me alone. I was so glad there were no photographers around Logan's car that I climbed in without a second thought. It was hard for me to concentrate on the paparazzi when I was with Logan—not because of his looks but because I never knew what to expect. He kept making dry, sarcastic comments that might have irritated me if they hadn't been so damn funny.

It felt good to hang out with him, which is why I didn't notice the trouble until Logan was idling outside the Hamilton house—while thirty feet away my home was under siege. My lawn was coated with reporters the way my mom slathered peanut butter on my PB and J sandwiches.

My jaw fell open. "Oh, my . . . keep driving!" I ordered Logan as I slid down to the floor. "Just . . . go!"

I didn't have to tell him again. Logan didn't peel out, leaving a layer of rubber or anything obvious. He just drove past my house and didn't stop until we reached the basketball court where I usually Rollerblade.

"Interesting." His bangs flopped into his eyes. "So that's your house."

I hauled myself back onto the seat. "Listen, I can explain."

"And I'm sure your explanation will be stupid."

"Oh yeah?" I retorted, sticking my chin up defiantly. "And why's that?"

"Because there is no good reason to lie about where you live."

"No good reason to lie about dyslexia either."

He swiveled to glare at me. "That's not the same thing at all."

"Sure it is," I argued. "We both don't want anyone's pity. Of course, I also wanted to avoid a hockey team panty raid, but other than that . . . same situation."

His lips twitched, and I could tell he was trying not to laugh at me. Oh, he was still annoyed, but his sense of humor hadn't ditched him.

"Panty raid?"

I shrugged. "I watch cable."

"And way too many lame high school movies."

"Look, I should have pointed out my house earlier. But people do stupid things. So if we could just go back and you could drop me off, that'd be great."

Logan started the engine. "You want me to just drop you off and drive away."

"Um, yeah."

"When your house is crawling with reporters."

"I can handle it," I told him exasperatedly. I was starting to get really sick of feeling weak. Okay, yes, ordinarily I'm a wimp, but I was handling the situation. I hadn't let the reporters, or Alex Thompson, or Chelsea Halloway, or *anyone* keep me from living my life, which meant that I had to be a hell of a lot stronger than everyone thought. "I'll be just fine on my own."

"Of course." Logan nodded his head curtly. "You don't need any help. My bad."

I knew I was being insulted, but I didn't know how to object. So I just looked at him and said, "You should really just drop me off. I don't want the press snapping pictures of us and speculating about my love life."

He nodded as the car turned onto my street.

"Okay, so just a little bit closer," I directed. "And . . . stop!"

I sprinted toward my door, using my backpack as a shield from the press, before Logan could say another word. My focus was centered on making it the thirty feet in one piece. I was bombarded with aggressively demanded questions until I felt like my head would never stop buzzing.

"Mackenzie, who was that?"

"Were you on a date?"

"Are you sure he's not just interested in your fame?"

That last question nearly made me laugh. The idea of Logan Beckett using me to get his face in the papers was patently ridiculous. Logan probably liked the exposure as much as I did. I tend to trust my gut instincts on stuff like that.

Dylan pulled me inside—no easy feat with a throng of reporters and a hallway crammed with packages. It looked like the contents of an entire UPS truck had been dumped in our house. The labels all said the same thing: Special Delivery for Mackenzie Wellesley. Things had gotten beyond weird.

Dylan shoved one of the boxes into my arms, and I struggled not to drop it.

"What the hell?"

"It belongs in your room." He lifted a package himself. "You can show all this stuff, whatever it is, to Mom later. We need to get it cleared up before she gets home."

Sometimes it was too easy to think of him as an annoying kid brother and forget that he cared about our family as strongly as I did.

"Come on." His voice held a large dose of irritation. "She'll be home soon."

Hefting the box, I followed Dylan. I gawked when I saw

my bed transformed into a swampland of letters, messages, and Post-its. Dylan didn't give me time to obsess. He just dropped his box, then snapped at me to follow suit.

It took us over forty-five minutes to transport everything upstairs, and that's excluding a five-minute water break where I rubbed my aching arms. After all my hauling, I never wanted to see another box again. I'd been stabbed and poked by boxes until I felt like one extended bruise. I tried not to whimper every time my body expressed its displeasure with me. Running from the paparazzi, ice skating, and now weight lifting with my boxes was way too much physical exertion for one day.

I couldn't resist checking out my pile of mystery packages. I grabbed a pair of scissors and attacked a box with a few deliberate swipes. Then all I could do was stare in openmouthed disbelief.

Shakily, my hand reached in and the smooth texture of silk slithered provocatively over my fingers. It was without a doubt the most gorgeous, subtly sexy thing I'd ever seen. It looked like a dress that would render the wearer invincible. I could picture Helen of Troy wearing it, although the dress could probably launch a thousand ships on its own. It was cute, fun, daring enough to show some leg—and it was mine.

I kept stroking the material, fighting the urge to both laugh and cry. The label revealed it was a BCBG Max Azria creation. Setting aside the dress, I pulled out the pair of heels left in the box. I examined them like I was Cinderella getting her first look at the glass slippers.

"Oh, my God"—was all I could say as I stripped off my Converse sneakers and slid my feet into the sexy, black, open toe heels. I had no idea how the reporters were able to figure out my shoe size, but they fit perfectly.

There I was in my new designer shoes and I couldn't stand up. Not because I didn't trust the thin, spindly heel but because I knew there'd be no going back. The shoes were incontrovertible proof that my life had changed—that after years of digging at garage sales I owned something wonderful and luxurious. Finally I had something that was just for fun.

So when I finally stood and swiveled in front of my cheap floor-length mirror, it was quite a jolt. For the first time, I couldn't quite recognize myself. I was left wondering what type of person this new girl might be . . . and whether I'd like her.

Chapter 18

I showed my Mom my now-overflowing closet, but I didn't call Corey or Jane that night. I wanted to personally gauge their reactions. I expected them to be stunned—shocked to see their best friend, Mackenzie Wellesley, show up to school clad in designer labels. Really, really cute designer labels. Oscar de la Renta flats, Calvin Klein jeans, and tops from Anthropologie. My textbooks? Yeah, they were lovingly cradled in the folds of an oversized Hobo bag. I'd even applied some makeup that morning—just simple lip gloss and eye shadow, but there was no way I'd land on anyone's Worst Dressed list. I'd woken up an hour and a half earlier than usual to ensure it.

And I'll admit it—it was cool showing up to school looking like a million bucks. Hell, I might have been *wearing* a million bucks. Well, more like five hundred dollars' worth, but compared to my favorite jeans (a steal at twenty-five cents) it certainly felt like a million. The clothes and makeup made the media attention seem more like a game of make-believe than real life. When the cameras were on me, I pretended that I was effortlessly chic and didn't notice the fawning.

The crazy thing was . . . I think I pulled it off.

Other things were definitely different. Guys paid attention

to me in the hallways, and most of it seemed centered on my new casually sexy look. Either that or I had botched up the eyeliner and everyone thought: *Hey, look at Raccoon Girl!* But if the slow, appreciative once-overs were any indication, I didn't resemble any nocturnal creatures.

By the time I had purchased my cheeseburger and fries at lunch, my two best friends had processed my un-Mackenzie-like ensemble.

"You look great!" Jane declared easily when I sat down. I grinned at her before turning to Corey.

"What do you think? Too much? Don't hold back on me now."

He pursed his lips thoughtfully.

"Jane's right: hot but not slutty. Just don't rub your eyes or you'll look like a hot mess. And ditch the ponytail."

I pulled out my hair tie and let my shoulder-length hair frame my face as I popped a French fry into my mouth. "You guys have any plans for tonight?"

Jane shook her head with her mouth full of muffin.

"No," Corey said sadly. "Homework as usual."

"Oh, okay. You guys wouldn't be interested in going to the ReadySet concert with me, would you?"

Corey's mouth dropped open. "You got tickets? *Shut up!*"

Jane pulled out a textbook. "I'll earn it as a study break. I won't stop studying until the concert, starting . . . now!"

I couldn't stop grinning like an idiot. "You can still give us a ride tonight, right, Corey?"

He nodded, speechless after his initial explosion.

"Good." I snagged another two fries. "It'd be a shame to waste backstage passes."

Corey's delighted shriek rang through the cafeteria. He practically vaulted over the cafeteria table and swept me into a hug.

"This is *insane!* I can't believe it! You're the greatest, Mackenzie! You get that, right? The freaking greatest!"

Except he didn't say "freaking" as he swung me around.

"Let's meet around six-thirty so we can check out your new wardrobe before the show."

"Sounds good to me. Jane, you in?"

She just waved her hand distractedly. "Yeah. Sure. Great. I have to concentrate now."

Jane liked to work her brain into mush before rewarding herself with an evening off—a habit Corey and I kept trying to break with no success.

"How'd you swing this, Mackenzie?" Corey was glowing with excitement. "Backstage passes? That's some serious shit."

"They were in my huge pile of letters. You wouldn't believe the invitations I've been getting. Stuff like going on *The Tyra Banks Show*."

Jane jerked her head up. "Is Tyra the one who talked about smiling with your eyes?"

"It's smize," Corey said knowledgeably. "Are you going to do any of it?"

"Me? On *Tyra*? She would devour me whole." I pointed at my face. "Don't be fooled by the cosmetics. This is temporary until the press get off my back. It took me almost an hour to do this, since I flinched every time I tried to use eyeliner. So don't get used to it, buddy."

Corey was grinning when I noticed a pair of freshman girls walking over . . . to our table.

"Do you mind if we sit with you?" The girl who spoke had long black hair and an outfit that looked casually expensive. She wouldn't have seemed out of place on a teen magazine cover. They were both so stylish that they looked more like the other juniors in our class than freshmen.

"No, that's fine," I replied. What else could I say? "Don't you want to sit at the Notable table so you can lead the elite in a few years?" I looked over at Chelsea. She was watching, and her open mouth made her look like a fish. A few seats away, Patrick sat looking adorable. My eyes wandered over to the distant table where I'd spotted Logan sitting with Spencer. He met my gaze and raised an eyebrow. I couldn't help smiling as it hit me for the first time what I had done: I'd out-Notabled the Notables.

Cool.

The girls were nice once I got past their "Disney princesses" looks. Melanie was a dead ringer for Pocahontas and Rachel looked like mermaid-turned-human Ariel. Maybe Corey had a point about my awkwardness opening doors, because the five of us complained about teachers, crappy cafeteria food, and homework until it began feeling comfortable. It wasn't supposed to feel good. It was supposed to be tense and nerve-racking and force me to deal with my panic-related gag reflex over being the center of attention. Melanie and Rachel just seemed too . . . harmless.

My mission in life had been to go unnoticed, something I'd failed at now that *everyone* knew me. People who couldn't pick me out of a lineup a week ago were telling reporters all about me. And part of me, the stupid part, actually thought it was kind of cool. Don't get me wrong, I still wished it hadn't happened, but the whole popularity thing had its advantages. Maybe I was spending too much time listening to Corey.

Or maybe I'd just spent too many years on the outside watching Chelsea rule the school. Now I could wield a little power. For the first time television shows about mean high school girls squabbling for control actually made sense. I'd always wondered what would compel the girls to act viciously, but now I got it. Popularity is fun. Or at the very least hanging out with Melanie and Rachel was pretty cool. Since I had no desire to shave my head (à la Britney Spears) or do drugs (à la Lindsay Lohan) or crash a car (à la Shia LaBeouf), I thought I was handling the fame pretty well.

Everything was changing: my wardrobe, my social status, my evening plans—everything. I had no idea how it had happened, but my well-structured, organized, conventional, invisible life had completely flipped. I could imagine myself sitting on a therapist's couch trying to explain. "Well, I was fine, Doc (minus a few abandonment issues) until I became famous. Oh, you saw the music video too? Great."

Nothing felt real anymore. I was still the same girl, attending the same high school, eating with the same friends, but none of it felt like it had a week ago. None of it. And I had no idea what I wanted to do about that.

Chapter 19

I didn't know what to expect. Shocking, right? All sarcasm aside, I couldn't imagine going backstage at a rock concert. Good thing I wasn't attending alone.

Of course, I wasn't too happy when Corey and Jane pulled up at my house, took one look at me, and ordered me to change.

"What," I grumbled, "is wrong with what I wore to school?"

Corey pushed me to my room. "Nothing, for school. This is a concert, Mackenzie."

"Thanks for stating the obvious but I don't see . . ."

Jane rolled her eyes. "Just do it, Kenzie. It's the only way to shut him up."

She was right. So I sat on my bed while Corey rifled through my greatly expanded closet and made appreciative sounds from inside.

"My god. You own a Valentino gown? That's ridiculous!"

"You're telling me," I said. "I'm not going to wear anything that fancy, um . . . ever."

He spun around. "If you don't wear this gorgeous dress, I'll kill you. Then I'll make sure you're buried in it."

I laughed. "So what are you forcing me to wear tonight?"

A pair of dark denim jeans were tossed in my face, followed by a sexy shirt.

"You're kidding with this one." I pointed to the plunging neckline. "There's no way I can pull this off."

Jane examined the top critically. "I like it."

Corey held up a pair of wedge heels. "You're not going to look like a high school girl in these."

I eyed him nervously. "I *am* a high schooler. What's wrong with looking my age?"

Corey flashed me a smile. "Most people think you're in middle school, sweetie."

"No, they don't!" I turned to Jane for confirmation. "Right?"

"Well, actually," she began.

"Oh, hell."

"It's the big doe-eyed thing you've got going on," she explained. "Sort of like . . . Bambi."

"I look like a deer!"

Jane paused. "Yeah, in a good way. Hey, can I borrow your shoes?" She pointed to my new Kate Spade flats.

I wriggled into my new outfit. "Sure. Can we just go now?"

But Corey had spotted the makeup MAC had sent over.

"Oh, hell," I repeated, as Corey attacked my face.

When Corey *finally* declared us concert ready, I was sporting some seriously smoky eyes. I looked vampy—but not in an I-will-suck-your-blood kind of way. More in an I-could-lure-you-to-the-bad-side kind of way. Corey was definitely skilled.

My mom did a double take when I entered the kitchen.

"Mom, do you want to order me to change this"—I gestured at my cleavage—"ensemble?"

My mom gave me the once-over and smiled. "Oh, that's a cute one! I didn't notice it earlier. Can I borrow it sometime?"

The sad thing is, I bet my mom would look way hotter in

my new clothes than I did. She's gorgeous and gets hit on at the restaurant all the time.

"Yeah," I said. "Feel free to raid my closet whenever."

That's the way we've always been with each other. Sometimes it almost feels like we're both parents keeping the family together.

"Have a good time, honey." She tucked a strand of hair behind my ear. "I know we haven't really talked about this much." She nodded at my outfit. She'd been so exhausted after work, and with the additional strain of the press, the two of us hadn't been able to discuss how my life was changing. My mom has always been great at carving out time for Dylan and me. Ever since my dad left, the two of us have snuggled on the couch with big mugs of hot chocolate and analyzed every little part of our lives. She's taken on the roles of mother / best friend / therapist. But the older I got, the busier I became . . . and the more I couldn't share. It wasn't anyone's fault, really—just the way it worked out.

"You know you don't have to do anything that feels wrong."

I guess it must be hard to see your little girl grow up. And become an instant Internet sensation.

"I know." I tugged the hem of the top up, not that it made a difference. "Well, except for this. Corey'll throw a fit if I change now. I'll be back after the show," I promised. "My homework's done and my cell phone is charged. I'll be fine."

She nodded and I slipped out of the house and into Corey's car, fighting a mixture of excitement and nerves. Still, it was a huge relief to see that the paparazzi had lost interest in house calls. There'd only been a handful of reporters at school that day too. My updated wardrobe got some buzz, but my fame seemed to have petered out. And soon, very soon, I'd just be one more girl in a sea of loud ReadySet fans.

I figured that my backstage passes would be the last celebrity freebie, and I was way more excited about the concert than about any stupid dresses (even ones created by Valentino). I was determined to make the most of it. So I tried to play it cool when Corey, Jane, and I were led backstage by a harried-looking techie who didn't appreciate having another duty added to her list.

Okay, I have always thought it's stupid the way people act differently around celebrities. I've never understood girls who do stuff like scream "ROBERT! OHMIGOD, ROBERT, I LOVE YOU!" at *Twilight* movie premieres—especially since they nearly faint if Robert Pattinson smiles back. Come on: he's a guy who claims to "sparkle" in a movie.

Lame.

Given that, I thought meeting the band would be no big deal. Well, a huge deal for *me,* of course, but I'd just play it cool. It turns out . . . not so much.

The assistant / tech woman rapped on a door and, after receiving a hollered response, shoved us inside and left.

The room looked like a tasteful backdrop for a photo shoot, all cream-colored walls and comfy-looking leather couches. Half-finished water bottles and beer cans littered a small wooden table next to a huge bowl of M&M's.

"Oh, hey." Timothy Goff nodded at us from the couch where he watched his bandmates compete on a Wii. "Glad you could make it."

I wobbled forward on my red wedge heels. Timothy Goff hadn't become a rock sensation just because of his music. He was gorgeous. Way more attractive than Robert Pattinson, in my personal opinion. His hair was sandy brown, his eyes a clear shade of blue, and his mouth was made for smiling. A little scar cutting through his right eyebrow kept him from being storybook handsome and added a bit of danger to the mix.

"Hey," I replied, none too steadily. "I'm Mackenzie. Er, Mackenzie Wellesley. Um . . . these are my friends Jane and Corey."

"I'm Tim," he replied.

I fought back the bizarre urge to giggle, scream, or gush something stupid like "I know!"

"Dominic's the one losing horribly to Chris." He introduced them since neither had looked up from the screen. They all looked young enough to be Notables at Smith High School. I couldn't imagine what it'd be like touring the country in a rock band at the age of seventeen. Although it sounded like it'd make for one hell of a college admission essay.

"Any of you up for Wii tennis?"

I couldn't believe it. *Timothy Goff* had introduced himself to us as Tim. As if we could just say, "Hi, Tim!" or "How's it going, Tim?" *Timothy Goff* was casually inviting us to play Wii. *TIMOTHY GOFF!*

I completely blanked. Words failed me. I just stood there gaping while "Tim" acted like it was perfectly normal for people to become speechless in his presence. It probably was too.

"I'm in."

Much to everyone's surprise, Jane moved to the couch, picked up a controller, and began to battle Dominic. Corey and I traded one startled look before we scooted over to watch the competition.

I'm not sure exactly how the tension vanished from the room, but one moment I was standing awkwardly by the couch and the next everyone was yelling, cheering, or swearing while Jane showed off her impressive backhand. And while, yes, Tim was the first real celebrity I'd ever met, he was so laid-back it felt almost . . . comfortable. Well, after the initial shock.

"I meant to ask," he said as Chris challenged Jane to a game, "what you thought of the music video."

Jane's forehand smash distracted me into a normal response. "It's great: artsy but not pretentious. I'd love it if it didn't include *me*."

He grinned, and suddenly I was worried that my legs wouldn't support me—that I'd be one of his swooning female fans. "I know the press can be a bit much . . . but when I saw the video, I just couldn't resist."

In that moment he could've filmed me doing anything and I would've forgiven him. I was that pathetically starstruck.

"Well." I tried to pull myself together. "It's one of your best songs. Deep down I might even be flattered." I paused to consider. "Eventually."

"She listened to *Dialects of the Unemployed* about a million times when the CD came out," Corey informed Tim. "*And* she created Rollerblade routines for each track. Trust me, she's flattered."

I elbowed Corey in the stomach. "I was trying to play it cool!"

"You Rollerblade?"

"Yeah," I said, wishing I could say something cooler, like I was a skilled ukulele player . . . anything else. "I know it hasn't been cool since the eighties. And let's be honest: the eighties isn't a good decade for inspiration."

"I don't know . . . my skintight leather pants are in."

There was a painful moment when Corey and I just stared at him in horror before Tim burst out laughing. "I'm joking."

"Oh, thank God, I doubt even you could pull that off," Corey said as he surveyed Tim's physique. It might have been my imagination, but I thought I sensed tension that had nothing to do with awkwardness. Corey quickly shook himself out of whatever he'd just been thinking and smiled. "Plus someone might throw red paint at you for wearing leather."

"Wouldn't be the weirdest thing I've had thrown at me," Tim admitted. "Usually it's bras from my, uh, overly devoted female fans. Still, once I was in the middle of 'Better Off Broken' when someone chucked a cucumber at me. It missed, but not by much."

"Then there was the 'Marry Me, Timothy' sign that knocked over the microphone stand," Dominic added. "That was memorable."

"And remember when the watermelon exploded? Mainly it's just water bottles and underwear though," Chris commented, although most of his attention was devoted to the Wii. Jane scored another point. "Damn. You're really good at this."

Jane smiled with satisfaction as if she were complimented every day by a drummer in a rock band. "Thanks. You should see me play Robot Unicorn Attack."

Jane proudly references her ability to play random computer games. Most people find it geeky. I find it endearing.

It shouldn't have worked: three boring high school students (and my brush with fame aside, I was still plenty boring) should not have meshed so well with a trio of rock stars even if we were all pretty close in age. I'd initially expected a quick meeting before we were kicked out of the room. Instead, Dominic was telling Jane that he'd kick her butt at Wii bowling later, as if it were obvious we'd all hang out after the show. Tim even programmed our numbers into his cell phone in case we weren't able to find them in the postconcert insanity. That's right: one of my favorite rock bands had my cell phone number.

And the real show hadn't even begun.

Chapter 20

ReadySet knows how to put on a seriously great concert. Corey, Jane, and I were rocking out in the wings to a beat that was pumping fast and hot. Even the air felt like it sizzled, and we weren't among the throngs. No shoving crowds, no elbows thrust into stomachs, or claustrophobia for us. Just me, my two best friends, and a freaking awesome band who grinned at us between songs . . . although maybe they were just laughing at our stupid dance moves. Either way, I loved it all.

I'd just taken a sip of water when Tim started talking into the mic.

"Hey, Portland, how's it going?"

The cheers that erupted made it clear everyone was having a great time.

Tim was sweaty from all the singing and the oppressive heat from the stage lights, but he still looked like a Greek god—if they wore jeans and plaid shirts and played guitars.

"So we just released our CD *Good to Go* last month."

He had to pause for all the hollering to die down.

"Thanks. And we just made a music video for 'Going Down' that um, *features* Mackenzie Wellesley. You've all seen it, right?"

The answering set of cheers and hooting had my every

muscle tightening. I was dreaming. Tim couldn't be about to make fun of me *onstage*. He had seemed so nice just a few minutes ago!

"Yeah, it's a funny video. But I was just hanging out with her backstage, and I have to say, I don't think the press has done her justice."

I closed my eyes. Oh, god, he was going to say, "She's even more socially awkward than YouTube let on. This girl is a total freak!" And then I'd have to curl up in a little ball and die. Maybe I'd get lucky and a stage light would fall on my head.

"She's not awkward at all, actually. She's awesome."

My head snapped up at that. "What?" I said to an equally stunned Jane and Corey. "Did he just say that I'm *awesome?*"

I jumped at the quick bite of pain in my arm. "Ouch!" I glared at Corey, who'd pinched me. Hard.

"Definitely not dreaming."

"So we'd like Mackenzie to come out onstage and join us for her song." He smiled and somehow looked even more like Apollo.

"Oh no! No. No," I muttered frantically. "This isn't happening."

I looked past him at the sea of faces . . . and panicked. I couldn't stroll out onstage in front of everyone! Not with all those people sizing me up and just *staring*. The applause grew steadily from the audience—and I was screwed.

I wasn't given a choice. Corey grabbed my arm while I stood rooted to the spot mouthing, "What? No! Wait, WHAT?" and he shoved me past the curtains.

The audience laughed as I wobbled the first few steps in the heels that had officially begun to pinch and hurt. I really wished that my friends were more supportively silent and less throw-her-to-the-lions. My whole body was trembling, and I could feel my legs quiver like an airplane in serious turbulence. I did my best to focus just on Tim's face, the glinting clear blue eyes, and not all the people behind him.

Dominic pounded out a rhythm as I walked over, something slow and just a little bit sexy. It distracted me enough to look over and catch an amused, cocky smile that did nothing to slow my pulse. He made me smile when he winked reassuringly.

"One, two, three," Tim counted out, and the band burst into life.

I had absolutely no idea what I should do.

Right next to me, Tim was singing, "You fell like a girl in a looking glass," and I realized that I did feel like Alice in Wonderland. I was in this whole new world, and I kept shifting from geeky to famous then back to loser status before shooting up once more to popularity. And the people in my life? Yeah, I had plenty of White Rabbits like my brother running around. Only instead of screeching, "I'm late! I'm late!" he said stuff like, "It's on YouTube! It's on YouTube!" And just when I started to think: *hmm, maybe I'm getting a handle on this situation,* I'd get quite literally thrust into the spotlight once more.

I stood there. Onstage. Motionless. In the back of my head I was screaming, *Dance, Mackenzie! Sway. Do something!* But I couldn't even manage the simplest of movements. Seriously. Tim was crooning to me, the audience was shouting out encouragement, and all the attention made me blush. I was still standing there like an idiot when Corey rescued me—which was only fair, since it was his fault in the first place. He ran out and swirled me into his arms. I've never been more grateful to see a familiar face.

Corey and I had taken a free Argentine tango class with Jane and had quit two months later because the instructor was a creeper who joked about dating teenage girls. I never thought the lessons would actually come in handy. Corey had only convinced me to go by promising it'd be a good extracurricular to add to my college applications.

I never thought I'd *tango* at a concert. Corey led me into a series of slick dance moves as the song played behind us. My body automatically responded to his movements, and I could hear cheering as the audience ate it up. Corey's heartbeat was erratic, but instead of panicking, he led me into a smooth dip. I was staring into Corey's eyes and sharing his infectious smile while several thousands of people watched on. Then suddenly the world straightened and I was spun out of his arms and into Tim's hold.

There I was, plastered against a certified rock star while he sang *my* song, as if there were only the two of us in the world. And when he tilted the microphone toward me, I joined right in. Okay, I'm never going to be on *American Idol,* but I don't have a bad singing voice. Jane once said it was too sultry, but that was years ago and I think she was jealous because she could never hit a note to save her life.

I saw Tim's eyes widen in surprise, then focus more intensely while he tightened his hold on me. My surroundings seemed indistinct and blurry around the edges. Those stage lights are no joke. I was practically blinded and could feel the sweat dripping down my back in a not-so-pleasant way. I was actually glad Corey had prodded me into wearing a top that showed more skin, since I was already so boiling hot I expected steam to roll off me in waves.

Still I focused on the song, giving it everything I had, when we reached the lines:

> You said, there was no harm in wondering.
> You said, it'd just be a peek,
> And you said, don't be a mother hen.
> You said, you could land on your feet.
> But we both know now,
> You had to learn somehow.

Alice, dear, things in mirrors are not as they seem.
Stop risking it all on one of your lunatic schemes.

It sounded good. Damn good. I don't have any idea how
he does it, but Tim makes even fairy-tale allusions edgy and
vaguely dark. The line about risking it all on lunatic
schemes? Yeah, it made me hesitate, because the song was
mine in more ways than one. I was risking my life. My perfectly ordered, ruthlessly organized life was at stake. And for
reasons I couldn't explain, I kept endangering it. *I* had
showed up to school in designer jeans, *I* had gone backstage
at a ReadySet concert, and *I* started to sing onstage. Sure, I'd
been pushed, prodded, and poked along the way: but I had
done it all myself.

I probably deserved another one of Jane's "Oh, Kenzie"s,
too.

For a moment, I couldn't decide what was scarier: that I
was—once again—putting myself in the line of media attention or that I didn't seem to care.

Either way, I'd definitely fallen down the rabbit hole.

Chapter 21

If you're hoping for ReadySet gossip, you're going to be disappointed. After having my privacy violated, I can see why celebrities hate the paparazzi. Famous people might understand it's a by-product of their occupations, but that doesn't make it any less intrusive or annoying.

So while Tim, Dominic, and Chris didn't sit around twirling their purity rings after the concert, the media made them out to be far more intense. They seemed content to kick back with Corey, Jane, and me after they'd showered and pulled on clean clothes from their trailer. The three of us didn't drink. Corey couldn't as our designated driver, and Jane and I were perfectly content to sip our Cokes. It was no big deal when we declined some offered beer. It did, however, bring up the subject of ages.

"Just how old are you guys?" Tim asked speculatively.

"Corey's eighteen, I'm seventeen, and Jane's sixteen—but we're all high school juniors."

"That's quite a spread to be in the same grade," Dominic commented.

"I was held back a year." Corey said it casually, as if it weren't a continual source of annoyance for him. "My parents read a study about boys doing better academically if they're held back in kindergarten." He shrugged. "It's not so bad. Of course, I'm stuck with these two." He gestured at Jane and me. "But it could be worse."

"What about you?" Chris asked Jane, and I could tell she was flattered that he'd taken the time to ask her a follow-up question. Of course, Jane is flattered if you so much as say you were impressed by her Wii skills. She's a light touch.

"I'm just a little young for a junior. But no one remembers that at school, since Kenzie and I have been in the same classes together since, what, second grade?"

I nodded. "Yeah, ever since Smith Elementary School."

She groaned, and I couldn't help grinning. Jane's experiences in elementary school had been no better than mine. Neither of us waxed nostalgic about the "simpler times."

"Don't remind me!"

That instantly caught everyone's attention.

"What happened?" Chris wanted to know.

Jane didn't look like she knew how to answer, so I cut in to help her out. "Jane's last name is Smith—as in Jane Smith. And since our town is *obsessed* with naming things after this *other* Smith family, she got a lot of dumb jokes over it. Kids teased her about every part of her name. That's how we became friends, actually."

"I was about to cry," Jane interjected. Now that I had broken the awkwardness she was fine with steering the story. "Some boys were bugging me at recess. They kept saying, 'You, Jane. Me, Tarzan.'" She grinned. "It really bothered me as a kid. Anyway, Kenzie whirled on them with this death ray glare and snapped, 'She's Jane, you're stupid.'"

Tim sent me one of his grins that ought to come with a warning sign: May Cause Heart Failure in Ordinary Girls.

"That was brave of you."

"Yeah, w-well," I stuttered, "I've been a wimp ever since."

Corey snorted. "Right. That's why you stared down Alex

Thompson when he shoved you in the cafeteria: to prove you are spineless." The sarcasm dripped off his tongue. "Here I thought you were standing up for yourself."

He had me there—and that fact felt oddly good. I *had* been sticking up for myself in the cafeteria and against a jerk who easily had a good eighty pounds of muscle on me.

But I didn't want it mentioned in front of ReadySet.

"Someone giving you guys trouble?" Tim's voice was casual, but his eyes never left Corey's.

"Just a little dweeb hazing," I said quickly. "Nothing too serious. Thanks, by the way, for what you said tonight. You know, about me being . . . erm, awesome."

Dominic gave me an appreciative once-over. "You sounded pretty good up there."

Chris nodded. "Any interest in performing?"

I nearly choked on my Coke. "Me? No. Oh, no. I'm more backstage than center stage."

"What about you?" Tim asked Jane.

"I sing," she replied easily with a grin sneaking up her face. "Until people start threatening to shove a gag down my throat."

"You can sing really loudly," Corey said, nudging her companionably with his foot. "Just not on key. You're still the champion of Wii Bowling though."

We didn't leave until after 1:30 a.m. when all the boys (Dominic grudgingly) agreed Jane was the Queen of the Wii. If it hadn't been a school night we would have hung out longer. I tried to remember the last time I'd had that much fun with anyone besides Jane and Corey. Running from the paparazzi, hiding in Victoria's Secret, and ice skating with Logan came to mind—but that was just because I was so exhausted from the concert. I nearly fell asleep in Corey's car, and I could tell by the lazy way Jane flipped through one of her ever-present textbooks that she was also ready to collapse.

So I didn't get the chance to dwell on my moment in the spotlight or to wonder what school would be like the next day. I just went into my room, slid into bed, and slept like the dead.

I woke up late. *Really* late. I thought groggily that I must have slept through my alarm clock as I raced around my room collecting textbooks, scattered papers, and homework while I pulled on my jeans.

I barged into the kitchen looking, to be honest, like hell. I'd forgotten to take off my makeup from the night before and now resembled a ghoul. My panicked frenzy had added a thin film of sweat to my pale face and tired, black-lined eyes. My mom didn't comment on it though. She just sat at the breakfast table while I tried to grab a few raspberry Pop-Tarts to eat on the run.

"Oh, good," she said calmly. "You're up. Now, sit down and I'll make you a real breakfast. We need to talk."

"I can't, Mom!" I said, feeling less like Alice in Wonderland and more like the White Rabbit. "I'm late!"

"I know that, sweetie. You're going to be a little later. Now, sit."

There's no arguing with my mom when she knows what she wants. I sat.

"So how was the concert?" she asked as she pulled out eggs from the refrigerator.

I rubbed my eyes, smearing around more of the leftover mascara. "It was great, Mom." And then because she was making real food for me, I elaborated. "We got to meet the band, and then Jane beat everyone on the Wii. I had a lot of fun." Which was weird since celebrities are supposed to be like Notables on crack, not like . . . well, regular people.

"That sounds nice, honey."

I eyed her suspiciously. My mom likes words of endearment but rarely does she use "sweetie" and "honey" back to back.

"Is there, um, something I should know?" I asked her.

"I was about to ask you the same question." She placed some toast onto a plate. "You should open the paper, hun."

Uh-oh. From "honey" to "hun." Never a good sign.

I flipped over the daily paper and gawked. My picture looked back at me; my face was lined with concentration as I studied my textbook. One of my classmates must have been able to sell one of the shots that they had snapped during class. It was unnerving to see myself so unguarded.

But it was the newspaper headline that really got to me. It screamed: **The Exciting New Romance Between Mackenzie Wellesley and Timothy Goff!** Below that was a series of pictures, the first of which had me plastered against Tim as we sang into his mic. I instantly dove into the article.

> Seventeen-year old Mackenzie Wellesley may have gone from lame to fame in less than a week because of a certain YouTube video, but she's had no trouble adjusting to life in the fast lane . . . or becoming an item with the hottest musician on the charts. Last night at the Rose Garden in Portland, Mackenzie showed her flare for performance in a choreographed dance routine and a stunning vocal display. Despite being previously considered camera shy, this young ingénue appears ready to step into the spotlight with her new boyfriend. But has the attention already gone to her head? A close source who prefers to remain anonymous says, "Mackenzie is heading down a dangerous path. She's only interested in Timothy Goff as a way to climb the social ladder. She'll trade him in the way she's been going through designer outfits."
>
> Ms. Wellesley certainly seems to have captured the interest of Mr. Goff. Just two days ago

she was quoted saying, "What love life?" but this photograph paints a very different picture. The same inside source went on to say, "I think Mackenzie's obvious boy-chasing tactics make her a very poor example for others. She's only going to hurt Timothy Goff—and many other boys in the process. Her parents should have taught her the value of a little self-respect."

The product of a broken home, Ms. Wellesley might find it best to reconnect with her father before the real reason that teen rock sensation Timothy Goff describes her as "awesome" is revealed. Perhaps her sensational singing wasn't the only thing that got a standing ovation last night. Mr. Goff's publicist chose not to confirm or deny their relationship at this time.

"Mom." I could barely speak. "I didn't. You know I'm not some kind of—of boy-crazy, social-climbing slut." I rubbed my eyes again. "I can't believe this. I've never been kissed, but I still have to assure everyone I'm not a skank who hooks up with rock stars."

"Language, Mackenzie." My mom doesn't tolerate insults beyond a strict PG rating.

"Fine. You know that I'm not sexually promiscuous."

She smiled and I felt some of my stomach knots unravel. My mom has a knack for calming me down. "Yes, I do. Honey, like it or not people are going to gossip. They're going to lie and you need to ignore it. I raised a smart, independent young woman, and I don't want you to let this upset you. Now, eat your eggs."

I speared a mouthful. "Thanks, Mom."

She joined me at the breakfast table and looked knowingly into my eyes. It's almost spooky how well she can read me.

"I trust you with boys, Mackenzie. What we need to discuss is the last part of the article."

I looked at her blankly. "The concert? Mom, it was an impromptu thing that only happened because Corey shoved me onstage."

"Not that, although I wish I'd seen it. You've always had a lovely voice. You really shouldn't have hidden during all your middle school choir performances. . . ."

"Then what was it?" I interrupted before she pushed me to join a community choir.

"The part about your father."

I stiffened like I'd just been zapped with a taser. My mom and I don't discuss my dad. Ever. Nothing there for us to discuss. As far as Dylan and I are concerned, he doesn't exist. We all preferred it that way.

"What about it?"

"Honey, he . . . well, he called."

The eggs that had been so delicious just a second earlier sank nastily in my stomach and thickened into cement. "He—he called you. When?"

"This morning. That's why I turned off your alarm and let you sleep in." She ran her hand soothingly down my hair in a gesture that was comforting and sweet. The same as she had done twelve years and five months ago when he'd walked out on us. I felt nauseated.

"Oh yeah." I tried to say it coolly—like it was no big deal he'd contacted us beyond child care checks. "What'd he want?"

"He said"—my mom rose to clear the dishes, a nervous habit of hers that popped out when she was worried—"he wanted to talk to you."

I let that soak in. "What about Dylan?"

My mom looked at me blankly. "What about him?"

And I guess that said it all. Of course my dad didn't ask

about Dylan. He wouldn't have called if it weren't for my newfound fame. That's just the way he works.

I nodded. "So . . . that's it. He just called and said . . . what? After twelve years he wants to chat?"

My mom twisted tense fingers. "He's, um, concerned about the recent press."

"Oh, I get it." I couldn't keep the bitterness out now. "I can be a skank as long as he never reads about it in the paper."

"Language, Mackenzie!"

"Seriously, Mom? Saying 'sexually promiscuous' doesn't change anything!"

She stiffened, and I knew it was stupid for me to fight about her Language Policy.

"How we speak matters, Mackenzie. Now, I know you're upset." She reached out a hand to stroke my hair again. "And you don't have to say a word to him. You are under no obligation whatsoever, but you had the right to know he called."

I had to do something, so I poured myself a glass of orange juice and sat down in silence.

"Okay," I said at last. "I'm not calling him back. Sorry I snapped at you."

"Oh, honey." She wrapped her arms around me and I let her hang on. She needed the physical contact as much as I did. She tilted my chin up to look into her eyes. "I worry about you. Your job is to be a kid. I see how hard you try to make everything perfect, and I wish you didn't feel the need to do that." She rubbed my shoulders. "It's okay, on occasion, to take a mental health day. I won't love you any less if your AP test score isn't perfect."

I was pathetically close to tears.

"Mom," I said slowly. "Everything would be different if it weren't for me. If I hadn't tripped at that stupid ballet recital, then you wouldn't have found out dad was cheating. He still might be here right now. He might not have left us. . . ."

My mom's fingers dug painfully into my shoulders as they clenched.

"If you hadn't tripped at that ballet recital I might not have found out . . . then. I hope I'd have figured it out eventually. It wouldn't change who he is, sweetheart. I'm *glad* you fell when you did."

I stared at her in disbelief. "You are?"

"Yes!" She laughed. "It forced me to look at my marriage. And if I could go back in time, I still wouldn't change anything. I got you and Dylan out of that mess—and you guys are the very best things that've ever happened to me."

I felt the tears sliding down my face now, slowly but steadily, and I made no move to swipe them away.

"No regrets?"

"None." She ruffled my hair. "Why don't you take a shower while I raid your closet. Then I'll give you a ride to school."

I smiled at her. "Love you, Mom."

"Oh, sweetie," she said. "I love you right back."

Chapter 22

I made it to school in time for lunch. My mom had made me model a few more of my new outfits for her while she picked out a few dresses she thoughtfully offered to store in her closet for a while. It was fun doing our girl bonding stuff. Especially when my mom took out some of my new nail polish and insisted we give each other pedicures as well as manicures. I could tell our dad conversation was still playing in her mind, but she didn't mention it.

"Oh, honey!" she said, when I finally emerged from my room in my Forever 21 jeans and bebe top and we headed toward the car. "You look wonderful!"

"Thanks, for all of this, Mom. Talk included. Although I don't think you should ever turn off my alarm clock again."

"Deal." She slid smoothly into the driver's seat.

"So . . . did you have to miss work today for this?"

"Nope." She signaled at the light. "My shift on Friday doesn't start until three, remember?"

I hadn't, and it was a relief to hear. Maybe I shouldn't worry about her, but I can't help it. That's the way I'm built.

"Do you have any plans for tonight?"

"I have to tutor Logan, then probably catch up on the classes I missed."

She grinned. "I'd have left you at home but you'd panic over skipping a whole day."

I nodded. "I'm nervous about lecture notes as it is. Guess that makes me neurotic and obsessive."

"What it makes you," my mom said firmly, "is dedicated." She pulled up to the school. "Just let me know if your plans change."

"Will do." I headed straight for the cafeteria to find Corey and Jane.

What I didn't expect was to find my two best friends telling a larger group of freshmen girls about the ReadySet concert. Melanie and Rachel were there with some of their friends. Our table actually looked way more exciting than the Notables'. Something Chelsea Halloway probably didn't appreciate.

My entrance caused a reaction that rippled through the entire cafeteria.

"Mackenzie! We were just talking about the concert last night." Melanie scooted to make room for me. "There's a video of you singing on YouTube. It sounds terrific!"

Great. Another video of me on YouTube was just what I needed.

"Thanks," I said instead. I didn't think she was just sucking up because I was famous. Then again, what did I know about that stuff? Maybe all of them were hoping I could score them designer bags.

I didn't have to say anything else, because that's when something unprecedented happened in the Smith High School cafeteria.

Chelsea stood up—flanked by Fake, Bake, and Patrick—and crossed the room to stand before the Invisible table. It felt like a well-planned chess move: Queen to K2.

"Hey, Mackenzie!" she said, like we were best friends who shared everything from lip gloss to gossip.

"Uh, hi." I tried to encompass all four of them with this greeting. Patrick was looking at me intensely, like he was trying to memorize my every feature so I'd be burned into his memory. My heart sped up and my cheeks flushed even as I told my inner romantic that Patrick wasn't realizing how perfect we'd be together at THAT EXACT MOMENT!

"I have to head out soon." Chelsea waved her hand elegantly as if I'd asked her to stay and she had to regally decline. "But I just love your new outfit!"

"Totally adorable," added Fake in a voice that sounded completely, well, fake.

I barely resisted the urge to nervously tug at my top. Rule number one of combat: show no weakness.

"Thanks." I hoped people would stop complimenting me so that I could just enjoy some friendly conversation. "You guys look great too." I stopped myself before adding, "as usual."

"Oh." Chelsea giggled and tossed her long silky hair back. "That's sweet of you. So will we be seeing you at Spencer's party tonight? He mentioned something about inviting you."

I barely kept myself from staring at her openmouthed.

"Uh, I didn't hear anything about it."

"Well, you've been too busy with celebrities." She let out another one of her perfect little giggles that made my skin crawl. "Tonight at nine, okay?" She didn't wait for me to say anything in response. "Great! See you then."

Fake and Bake swirled out of the cafeteria with her and left me at a silent table with the boy I've been crushing on since, I don't know . . . FOREVER!

"Want to join us?" I asked Patrick awkwardly.

He brushed his soft-looking, dirty blond bangs out of his warm chocolate eyes and sat right down next to me.

"Of course," he murmured. I turned to Corey and Jane in an attempt to get my hormones under control.

"So." Corey broke the awkward silence that had descended. "Who thinks that was an open invitation or for Mackenzie only?"

I rolled my eyes. "Of course it wasn't just for me. It'd be too rude to invite only me in front of other people. You guys must be included." I turned to Patrick for confirmation. "Right?"

"Erm." He looked like I'd just asked him about India's biggest export (textiles). "Spencer throws big parties, so, uh . . . no one will notice."

Not exactly the warm invitation I'd expected. In fact it smacked of "Invisibles will be tolerated if they stay Invisible." But I guess it was enough to get Melanie, Rachel, and the other girls excited. They instantly began debating what outfit a social event like this required.

I looked at Jane and Corey. "You guys will go with me, right?"

Jane stared at me like I'd lost my mind. "Sure. I'll just take a jet to France while I'm at it! Going to a concert one night and a party the next won't get in the way of my studying or my job or anything." Jane's even stricter about stuff like that than I am.

Corey just shrugged. "Works for me."

Out of the three of us, Corey's always had the most freedom to do whatever he wants. It helps that his dad and mom both agreed to a laissez-faire child-raising policy. Until Corey breaks their trust, they'll let him and his sisters do their own things. They're pretty awesome that way. I was impressed when his parents let Corey crash at my house for a sleepover. Corey had shrugged when I mentioned it. Apparently when he told them he was gay they instantly ordered shirts online—even though Forest Grove isn't the safest place to wear something that says Straight Supporter of Gay Rights.

"If you're going, I'll be there," Patrick told me softly. And I stopped breathing. Because how romantic is that?!

"Then I guess I'll have to go."

Yes, I flirted! And I didn't even make an idiot out of myself!

Patrick was about to say something adorable to me (I could just tell) when someone behind me distracted him. "Oh. Hey, Logan."

Logan nodded pleasantly at Patrick before turning to Corey. "I saw your moves from the concert. Pretty impressive."

Corey grinned back. "That was nothing. You should see the three of us when we're hyped up on sugar and too many episodes of *Glee*."

He laughed and sat down next to Jane. "I didn't see you onstage."

"Corey wasn't quick enough to shove us both. I prefer to do my dancing in private."

"Mackenzie was great." Patrick blurted it out, completely breaking the flow of conversation. Logan raised an eyebrow as if he'd just noticed me.

"Yeah, Mack was all right." That was it—that was all he said to me before introducing himself to Melanie, Rachel, and the other freshman girls. And I was oddly grateful that he didn't make a big deal out of it. All of the Notable attention made me feel a bit gross. Maybe if I was Chelsea I'd love being the center of conversation . . . but that's so not the way I work. Mainly because if I'm the center that means my friends are on the periphery.

The freshman girls were instantly crushing on Logan, and I couldn't exactly blame them. He's just so effortless. I couldn't help but admire the way he got people talking and then leaned back to let the conversation take shape. If that was a skill his dyslexia forced him to hone, I'd say it was a fair trade-off.

"I've got to head out," Patrick said, interrupting a story about Melanie's crazy aunt. I looked at my watch. We still had over fifteen minutes left for lunch and I couldn't see why he needed to rush. Then again, maybe he had to discuss an assignment with a teacher.

"Uh, okay," I said stupidly. "See you later."

"I'm counting on it."

Then he was gone and I was left wondering if maybe, just maybe, those fantasies of mine might actually come true.

Chapter 23

"Well, that was interesting."

I can always count on Corey to say something just when I hope it'll pass without comment. Patrick might have left the table, but Logan was still *right there*. I shot Corey a warning look that he ignored.

"I mean, that guy hasn't deigned to sit with us *ever*." Disapproval dripped from Corey, and I saw him trade looks with Jane and then Logan. It all felt too conspiratorial for my liking. Especially since I didn't appear to be within the trust circle.

I shrugged. "It's been a week of firsts."

My cell phone went off, interrupting Corey's next retort.

"Saved by the phone," I grinned as I flipped it open. "Hello?"

"Hey, Mackenzie. It's Tim."

I drew a complete blank. I sat there and tried to think if I knew anyone by that name. If some "Tim" from school wanted to talk to me, why wouldn't he just walk over to the table? Unless this was some creepy stalker who had managed to get my cell phone number. Considering the way my Facebook in-box had exploded with friend requests, it wasn't such a crazy thought.

"Tim," I mouthed to Corey and Jane questioningly. And then it hit me. *Of course*, Timothy Goff: rock superstar. My life is insane.

"Hey, Tim." I jerked up in my seat. "How's it going?"

"I'm good. Listen, we've got the night off and . . . Well, we're heading back to LA tomorrow since . . . We're scheduled to be on *Ellen* before we lay down some tracks for our next CD. . . ." I heard him breathe in exasperation. "I'm going about this all wrong. I was just wondering . . . do you think Corey is free?"

I couldn't have been more surprised if Jane had hit me with a stun gun.

"Free?" I repeated.

"God, I shouldn't be doing it like this. It's pathetic. Next thing you know I'll be slipping Corey a paper asking how much he likes me with three boxes for him to check. Let's just pretend this didn't happen."

"Hold up," I said, trying to prevent information overload.

"I know I'm going too fast, but I thought since I'm leaving soon I should probably make my move now. But I'm way off base, right? He's probably dating someone. God, he has a girlfriend!"

"Um, s-single," I stuttered, still trying to process the fact that a rock star appeared to need my help with his love life. "Totally single."

"Oh." That shut him up for a second. "So do you think he might be interested . . ."

"I think 'interested' is an understatement." I grinned hugely at Corey as he and Jane hung on my every word.

"Really?" Tim sounded shocked, relieved, and pleased. "I thought that maybe he . . . but I wasn't sure." There was a pause as what I'd said soaked in. "Thanks, Mackenzie. I had a feeling about you from the moment we met."

I laughed. "You did? And what feeling was that?"

"That you're the girl next door who doesn't know how great she really is."

"Aw, I'm blushing," I said, amused to note that my cheeks felt ruddier than they had been when Patrick flirted with me. Maybe because with Tim I *knew* there was no hidden agenda. He's way more famous, talented, popular, and rich than I am. So when he says that I'm great, it makes me think that maybe he's got a point.

The five-minute warning bell sounded.

"Listen, I've got to go. Talk to you later, Tim."

I snapped the phone shut and turned to find everyone staring at me. Even Logan didn't look as unfazed. Then again, it's not every day you hear a certified nerd talking to a rock star about her very single best friend.

But I wasn't going to let Corey, or anyone else, find out what Tim had asked me. Corey deserved to hear it from Tim when he worked up the nerve to call.

"So, Mackenzie." Melanie broke the stunned silence. "Are you still going to the party?"

I thought back to what my mom had said over breakfast—the part about needing to be a kid every now and then.

"Yeah," I replied. Seized by an impulsive idea, I decided to go with it. I smiled broadly at Melanie, Rachel, and the two new freshmen, Isobel and Claire. "If Corey doesn't mind shuttling us to the party, you guys are more than welcome to get ready at my house."

Corey nodded his head in consent as I ripped out a piece of paper from my binder and scribbled down my cell number and address. I handed it to Melanie.

"I'm probably going to need you guys to save me from becoming fashion roadkill" I said jokingly, even though I was painfully aware that this was a plausible outcome. Then I grabbed my books. "Logan, I'll see you after class for tutoring."

"Meet you in the parking lot." That was all he said before a holler from Spencer had him melting into the crowd.

I caught a sigh from Isobel and barely resisted saying, "I know." Even though a little voice in my head kept hollering, *But he's a NOTABLE,* it didn't mean that I couldn't notice his physical attractiveness. So, yeah, I could understand where Isobel was coming from.

I had way too much going on to obsess over some boy. Actually, I had too much going on to obsess over *any* boy . . . except Patrick.

Jane tugged on my jacket before I could head off to AP Gov. "Kenzie, you're doing okay, right? We shouldn't worry about you or anything?"

My friends are the greatest.

"No worries," I assured her. "I've got everything under control."

I had to sprint from classroom to classroom to get the assignments I'd missed during my short mental health vacation. Sometimes being responsible sucks. I did feel a bit guilty about making Logan wait for me by his car . . . until I saw Chelsea was keeping him company. He probably appreciated the opportunity to stare at her, ahem, *assets* without me around.

They instantly cut off their conversation when they noticed my approach.

"Sorry I'm late," I said, feeling like an intrusive third wheel.

Chelsea turned to me, and I waited for her to say something awful. Something like, "That's okay, we didn't miss you." Girls like Chelsea can get away with saying stuff like that—but she didn't. Instead her frown morphed into an overeager smile.

"Hey, Mackenzie!" She actually gave me a *hug!* It was too quick for me to back away, so I just stood there. "We need to talk about the party tonight! You want to get ready for it with me?"

Yeah, I so hadn't seen that one coming.

"I—um, I already made plans for that," I said gently on the off chance Chelsea had never been turned down before. "I'm sorry."

"Oh, that's okay." She waved a hand as if she'd expected that answer all along. "I just thought you might need some company. Anyhow"—she shot Logan an expressive look that baffled the hell out of me—"I'll see you both later." She opened her car door and slid in, but not before calling out, "Good luck with the studying!"

I waited until she'd driven away. "Well, that was weird."

Logan just shrugged. "No stranger than you on YouTube. Now parties and celebrities . . . I'm surprised you're still tutoring me."

I soaked in his words. He was right: I could try to make some money by capitalizing on my fame. But that wasn't me.

"I don't think I'll quit my day job," I told him as I climbed into his car.

"You could though," he replied, so casually I wondered if he wanted me to stop being his tutor—if this was his way of giving me a subtle hint. "That new video with you singing is getting a lot of hits."

"That's because of Tim, not me. I could never be a singer. Not a real one who tours and performs live. If Corey hadn't pushed me I never would've gone onstage. Jane and I are better off with our textbooks."

"If you say so." Logan just shrugged. "Why are you going to the party tonight?"

I tried to push away the dull ache that was coming from my very tired, sleep-deprived brain. "Look, I don't know why I'm going. I could say it's to prove something, or because I want to go, or because this may be the one time I'm invited to a party and I don't want to wonder what I missed. But the truth is: I don't know. I'm winging it." After opening my backpack, I jerked out my AP US book. "So let's concentrate on the stuff I do understand. Now, the Articles of Confederation . . ."

Chapter 24

We'd only been studying for about an hour when my cell phone started ringing to the tune of "I Need a Hero." Loudly.

Logan raised his eyebrows. "Timothy Goff?"

I shook my head and answered smoothly. "Hey, Corey." Then I jerked the phone away from my ear as his excited hollers pierced the air.

"Mackenzie! You'll never believe who just . . . I don't believe it! Oh, my God, I might just hyperventilate and die out of sheer amazement right now. You'll never guess who just called me."

"Tim." I said the name so matter-of-factly it shut him up. "So where are the two of you going tonight?"

"Out to dinner in Portland. I don't know where yet. He's got a meeting with his producer or something until eight, so we're doing a really late dinner and dessert. We *really* have to get ready together. I can't be freaking out like this on my date. And since Jane has decided she needs to memorize every mathematical formula in the known universe *tonight,* I need you."

I couldn't help laughing, "I'm so glad I can be your second choice."

"Me too!" He was so happy I doubt he caught my light edge of sarcasm. "I'll see you later!"

I closed the cell phone and grinned, knowing that Corey would pace his room for at least fifteen minutes before his heart rate began to drop. Corey was going on his first date, I was going to my first party (and possibly a date with Patrick), and Jane was . . . Jane was focusing on schoolwork for the night—which was boring but seemed to be what she wanted.

It was hard to believe one YouTube video could destroy my life and then somehow make everything perfect.

"So that phone call today was about Corey."

I'd nearly forgotten that Logan was there. There was so much excitement to take in, I felt like a sponge in a hurricane.

"Yeah, Corey and Tim are going out on a date." I shook my head in happy disbelief. "It's crazy, but if anyone can pull off a long-distance relationship with a rock star, it's Corey. Of course it's just a date but"—I looked down at my hand where my fingers were already crossed—"it could happen."

"And you're fine with that?"

"Um, no! My best friend has a date with someone nice, talented, and hot. I'm more than 'fine' with it. I'm thrilled!"

"Right, but don't you wish you had the date?"

"Do I want to date someone who meets the aforementioned criteria? Absolutely. But that doesn't change how I feel for Corey. You know, Jane and I always thought he'd be the first one of us to date. We never figured it'd be with a rock star, but . . . we were still right."

Logan seemed to consider all of this. "It was nice of you to invite the freshman girls."

I had no idea what he was talking about. "Huh?"

"To your house—for whatever girls do before a party. I thought you might ditch them for Chelsea."

I did my best not to scoff. "Okay, first of all: I'd never do that. The girls are nice. And I can't blow off the ritualistic primping, or else I'll be the only one there in sneakers and jeans." I gestured to my significantly trendier outfit. "My watchword is still *blend*."

He grinned. "Poor Mack has to get dressed up for the ball."

I glared but without any real heat. "You mock, but you've never worn heels."

He raised an eyebrow. "Well, that's quite an assumption." I gaped at him and his smile quirked. "But you're right, I haven't worn them."

"Well," I fumbled. His obvious amusement made his blue eyes seem even more vibrant. Clearly I needed more sleep if I was unable to come up with anything intelligent to say to Logan.

"Heels, uh, hurt. A lot. They're fun for about five minutes, but after that . . . not so much." Great, I was babbling. Just when I thought Logan no longer had the power to reduce me to incoherence.

"In Europe, around the 1400s, these insane platform shoes became popular. Women actually needed servants and canes to help them walk, which must have sucked. Anyhow. What were we talking about?"

"Chelsea and the freshmen girls." Logan leaned back in his chair, and my muscles start to loosen as I mimicked the pose.

"Oh. Right. I like the freshman girls. Well, I don't really know them, but they seem nice. One of the new girls at lunch, Isobel, I think? She seems quiet, but I saw her talking to Jane . . . so that's good. And Corey's going to come over, so it'll be great. It just wouldn't have been"—I searched for the right word—"casual with Chelsea. So it's not like it was some huge sacrifice for me not to flake out."

"Girls have so much drama."

"In my objective opinion, boys are way more confusing."

"Objective, huh?"

"Oh, yes," I said. "An impartial observation."

He laughed, but then his tone grew a touch more serious. "What in particular has you confused?"

Okay, I admit it, I was supertempted to yell: YOU! Why are you so damn confusing!? You seem smart and nice, but then I see you with Chelsea Halloway and it's obvious you're still not over her. Which makes no sense since *she* broke up with *you* for someone more popular—that ought to give you a hint as to how she operates! But when she came over, back when I was still Invisible, you just basked in the glow of her attention. Why do you keep switching from a nice guy to a Notable and then back again so I have NO FREAKING IDEA WHICH PERSON YOU REALLY ARE? *Why's* that, *huh, Logan!?*

I wisely kept my mouth shut.

"No specifics. Just general confusion. Speaking of generals, during the American Revolution . . ."

And I distracted him with history.

It was weird having Logan take me home when we both knew I'd see him later at an official Notable party. And yet, there he was dropping me off so I could swap designer outfits. Now Chelsea was acting friendly and strangers were sitting at my lunch table. It was hard to believe my life could be so dramatically different in one week.

"I'll, uh, see you tonight."

Well, I guess it's good to know that I'm still awkward.

Logan nodded and looked like he was about to say something big, something important, because he took a deep breath and got as far as "Listen . . ." when Corey leaned heavily on his horn in greeting.

"Never mind," he said. "See you later."

And then he was gone.

I swear if Corey hadn't been temporarily exempted from rational behavior due to severe first-date nerves, I would have killed him. And I sincerely doubt I would have regretted the murder.

Chapter 25

"**I** am freaking out here, Mackenzie! I am FREAKING OUT!"

That much was painfully obvious. Corey was doing some hard-core pacing around my room while he pawed nervously at his hair.

"Maybe I should cancel. This was a bad idea. I mean, what's a guy like Timothy Goff going to see in someone like me?"

I snorted. "Oh, I don't know . . . maybe a sweet, intelligent, wonderful guy who just happens to be INSANELY HOT." I patted his butt once, an affectionate gesture I've done for years, just to watch him jump in surprise. "Have I mentioned recently that I want you to father my children?"

He laughed. "We agreed that's a last resort." The inside joke was already loosening him up.

"It's going to be great." I pointed to my closet. "Here. Distract yourself by ordering me around. This will be the very last time I let you dress me up like your own personal Barbie doll."

The doorbell rang, and I left him digging through the shoes.

"Coming!" I hollered. But Dylan beat me to the door.

"Uh . . . hi." Melanie stood at the door with a duffle bag

and a confused expression. She double-checked the address I'd given her. "Is this Mackenzie's house?"

Dylan just stared at her while I pushed open the door and pretended not to notice the spreading of his Wellesley blush.

"Hey, Melanie. Glad you could make it!" I pushed Dylan aside so she could step into the hallway. "This is my brother, Dylan. Dylan, Melanie."

"Yeah, hi." I swear, Dylan's voice dropped a solid octave. "I think we met at a soccer game last year."

Which is when it hit me that Dylan's blush might not just be a hormonal reaction to a supercute freshman girl but from opening the door to this specific girl.

"Oh, right." It was impossible to tell if Melanie remembered him or was faking it. "It's good to see you again." She turned to me. "Thanks for inviting me over."

I grinned. "You won't be thanking me after Corey gets his hands on you. He's going to be psyched to talk fashion with someone with style."

Melanie laughed, a smooth, comfortable sound that was the opposite of Chelsea's giggle. "Sounds dangerous."

I pointed up the stairs. "First door on the right."

Dylan only managed to untangle his vocal cords when my bedroom door closed behind her. "Why didn't you tell me you invited Melanie Morris over here?!"

I raised my eyebrows. "I don't report to you, little brother. Mom's fine with me going to a party tonight. So you're just going to have to deal with it."

I started to breeze past him when he grabbed my arm. "You're going to a party tonight?"

"That's what I said."

"I should go with you."

I stared at him in disbelief. "Right. I should totally bring my little brother to my first high school party. Great idea."

He flushed. "Come on, Mackenzie. I'm not the embarrassing one in the family."

"Yeah. Still not going."

"Please." I knew it pained him to say it. "Please, can I go with you?"

Teasing him was way more fun when he didn't give me his puppy dog eyes. The brat knew it was hard for me to say no when he looked at me that way.

"No way. Mom would never give you permission."

He smiled. "Want to bet? If I tell her I'm concerned about you, she'll cave in a heartbeat."

I sighed. "Dylan, I'm not going to—"

But he cut me off before I could finish. "I *am* worried about you, Mackenzie. It's a party, and you don't have a good social track record. You need someone watching your back."

I looked at him intently. He might be irritating, but he was still my brother—and he never lied about the important things.

"If I say yes, you'll owe me big-time."

A smile spread warmly across his face. "Nah, we'll be even."

"Mackenzie! Get your cute butt up here!"

I rolled my eyes at Corey's not-so-subtle order.

"Coming!" I shouted. Then I stuck one finger into Dylan's chest. "Don't let me down."

I should've worried about Corey instead. Giving him carte blanche to access my new wardrobe was a very bad idea. When I finally entered my room, I found Corey and Melanie sighing over my clothes. They had transformed my room from neat into looking like a clothing factory had blown up and spewed its contents everywhere.

"About freaking time!" Corey huffed. "Okay, so we created three looks for you."

Melanie and I traded glances, and it struck me just how easily she'd slid into my life. I still wished Jane were going with us, even if she insisted on taking a textbook, but since she couldn't make it—well, I was glad Melanie could.

"What are you waiting for?" Corey demanded. "Try them on! Now!" Then he focused his attention on Melanie. "Let's see. . . . I'm thinking we should keep your look very simple."

"Hey!' I protested. "Why can't we keep *my* look simple?"

"Shut up and change," Corey said with obvious amusement. "You don't have the bone structure Melanie does."

"Thanks . . . I guess." Melanie didn't seem sure how to respond. "Mackenzie, do you mind if I spend the night at your house? I was going to stay with Isobel, but she panicked and backed out. I know it's inconvenient but . . ."

"It's fine," I finished. "Really. It'll be great. Corey, can you pick us up after your date?"

"I can play chauffeur, but it'll be late when I bring you back."

Melanie's eyes sparkled with excitement, and she managed to look even more wholesomely gorgeous. "Sounds good to me."

"Great. Oh, and Dylan wants to come."

"That's cool," Corey said. "Now, do I have to jam you into that dress or will you put it on yourself like a big girl?"

I wanted to protest, but instead I kept my head high and prepared for my first high school party.

But no dress, no makeup crew, no mass of supportive friends could have ever prepared me for what was to come.

Chapter 26

Iwas glad Dylan didn't comment on my outfit. He opened his mouth, probably to tell me to change, but closed it quickly. I'm not sure if it was my warning glare or his first look at Melanie that shut him up. My money is on Melanie, since I've never inspired fear in my brother and she looked, as Corey put it, like a wholesome rocker princess. I was also glad my mom had a late shift at the restaurant, because I'm not sure how she'd have felt about my, ahem, attire.

The dress was short, red, plunging, and screamed *SEX!* At least, that's what I thought when Corey pointed to it on the bed. Melanie agreed that it was perfect for the party. They assured me that I looked more like a very pricey and discreet call girl than a hooker. I hoped that last part was a joke. Even with the two of them insisting that I looked great and shouldn't change a thing, I nearly walked back into my room and pulled on my jeans. As it was, I only agreed to leave after Jane gave her opinion via Skype. She said I looked stunning and that she wanted to hear all about the party later. I felt a flash of envy because I should've been like Jane: curled up with a textbook and some hot chocolate, wearing flannel pajama pants and an old T-shirt. That's what I would've been doing if I hadn't become famous.

Melanie and Corey each grabbed one of my arms and escorted me, forcibly, from my room, down the stairs, through the hall, out the door, and into Corey's car—while Dylan trailed silently behind. I noticed that Dylan had changed and rumpled his hair in a way I would have described as sexy if he weren't my little brother. Unless I imagined it, Melanie's grip on me tightened when she saw him. I'd have to give that some thought when my stomach didn't feel like a knot of writhing snakes.

Corey cranked up the radio and I sang along mindlessly until Melanie said, "Wow, you really *can* sing!"

I was spared a response as Corey rolled to a stop. "We're here. All abort."

That's when I caught a good look at Spencer's house. I knew his family was rich, but it was one thing to know it and another to see the opulence firsthand. The house was a converted Victorian that looked big, white, and classic. There were balconies, columns, and what looked distinctly like a gazebo. And there were teenagers everywhere. Music was blaring from the house as laughter spilled out into the air.

"Are you sure . . ." I began.

"YES!" Melanie, Corey, and Dylan yelled simultaneously.

I slithered out of the car and walked over to the lowered driver's side window.

"Good luck on your date."

"Yeah." Corey smiled confidently, but I knew he was still freaked out.

I leaned closer. "You're the best guy I know and the reason I'm here." I grinned. "You're kind of like my fairy godmother."

"You won't turn into a pumpkin at midnight, will you?"

"No!" I laughed. "Besides you're the one meeting Prince Charming." I reached through the window and squeezed his arm. "And no one deserves a happily-ever-after more than you."

"Come on, Mackenzie!" Melanie rubbed her arms. "I'm cold."

"Okay." I stepped away from Corey and into the unknown. "See you later, Corey."

"Count on it." Then he stopped idling in the street and left for his adventure.

I didn't have time to mull over the way I'd splintered off from my two best friends. Melanie grabbed my arm and propelled me into Spencer's house the same way she had dragged me out of mine.

"Let's go!"

"Bossy, aren't you," Dylan commented.

"Yes, I am. Especially when hungry or cold." Melanie moved through the open door and around a group of mindlessly giggling girls. "Much better."

I wasn't so sure I agreed.

The house was packed with people, colors, sounds, and movement. The music almost drowned out my brain as it whirred into sensory overload. I was about to make up some lame excuse to bail, even if it meant freezing in my short dress, when I saw Logan.

He was leaning comfortably against a wall and talking with Spencer, who was obviously checking out a girl in skinny jeans and a tank top.

I tugged on Melanie's arm and pointed. "She's wearing pants! See! Why didn't Corey let me wear something like that?"

Melanie smiled up at me. "She probably doesn't have a dress like *that* in her closet begging for a night out."

"Yeah, but *she* won't catch pneumonia if she goes outside."

"We'll heat up soon enough in here. This place is a furnace."

She wasn't exaggerating: heat rolled off bodies in waves. "Let's see if we know anyone here."

Those words had just left Melanie's mouth when Logan looked up for the first time and his eyes connected with mine.

"Found someone," I muttered, forcing myself to walk over as if we were meeting for a study session.

"Hey." I tried to look confident, but I felt stupid. I stood there in my short, fire hydrant red dress thinking, *Gee, thanks, Corey. Way to talk me into this ridiculous outfit and then bail.* In that moment, I knew Corey, Jane, and Melanie had all been horribly wrong. I couldn't pull off a backless halter dress—especially one that dipped low in the front. I probably made the girls on *Jersey Shore* look classy in comparison.

Logan did a double take, and I could have cheerfully slugged Corey in the gut. I probably looked like a kid playing dress up. Suddenly everything felt like too much: the makeup, the dress, the earrings—all of it. I just wanted to pull on a baggy sweatshirt and hunker down with a good book.

"Um . . . hey," he replied. The house was full of people, and every square inch of counter space was crammed with alcohol, chips, and cheap plastic cups. There was a foot of distance between us, but it still felt too close to me. I was tempted to reach into my purse, pull out my cell phone, and demand that Corey pick me up *stat*. I'd give him an earful too. Then I'd point out in no uncertain terms that real life is not like a stupid chick flick.

"You look . . ." Logan trailed off when Spencer draped an arm over my shoulder. Apparently, I had captured his interest over Skinny Jeans.

He grinned at Logan. "Aren't you going to introduce us?"

He didn't recognize me. We'd gone to the same school for years and Spencer still couldn't place me. I was safe in my disguise as the vixen in red.

On impulse, I leaned into Spencer's arm and looked straight into his face.

"Mackenzie Wellesley." I didn't hide my amusement and grinned at them both. "Rarely called Mack."

Spencer's smile widened as he gave me the once-over.

"Who would have guessed," he commented smoothly. "Nice dress."

"Thanks. It's new."

Logan stepped forward, and much to my surprise Spencer disengaged his arm. It was like watching something on the Nature Channel: wolves being territorial as they rushed to assume alpha dog status, which was uncomfortable on so many levels.

"Um, this is Melanie . . ." I rushed into introductions and nearly blanched when I saw the Evil Trio swoop down on us. "And this is, uh, Dylan."

"Yeah. I haven't seen you since camp. How's it going?"

It took me by surprise when they instantly began talking about sports. I'd forgotten that Dylan and Logan knew each other.

"Mackenzie!" Chelsea's voice still held that friendly tone she'd slathered on earlier. "We're so glad you could make it!"

She assessed the situation in one quick, sweeping look from beneath her expertly darkened lashes. I tensed as her gaze lanced into Melanie and Dylan.

"And you brought your little brother and a friend with you. How sweet. . . ."

But it was obvious she didn't think it was sweet. Her tone made it very clear that she thought it was weird that I'd bring my middle school brother to a party. She had a point, I guess. As Fake and Bake tittered, the Wellesley blush rose on Dylan and me.

"Actually, Chelsea, he's with me." Melanie's smile was simultaneously innocent and smug. She tucked her arm into Dylan's as his mouth spread into a cocky grin.

"Bossy older women can't resist me."

I laughed as Melanie jabbed him in the stomach.

"We're going to dance," she said. "Catch up with you later, Mackenzie."

"See!" Dylan tossed over his shoulder. "Bossy."

Then they disappeared into the mass of swaying bodies—leaving me surrounded by Notables. Great.

"So . . ." I said uncomfortably. "Great party."

Spencer moved closer, and I caught him trying to look down my dress, which was ridiculous because guys don't do that kind of thing with me. They just *don't*.

"Want to take a tour?" he asked.

I had a feeling that beneath Spencer's smug exterior was a really nice guy, and as I was thinking, *Maybe the two of us could become friends* . . . my eyes locked on Logan. It was stupid to treat him like a life raft, but he knew what he was doing, while I was trying to keep my head above water.

"That's a great idea!" Chelsea declared. "Steffani and Ashley were about to get a drink." She moved closer to Logan, and her dress, a sparkly little black number, swayed seductively. "I need to borrow you for a minute."

My fingers tightened on the little clutch that Corey and Melanie insisted complemented my dress perfectly. Someone jostled into me and I lurched unsteadily on my heels. I had to grab Spencer's arm before I did a face-plant.

"A tour sounds great," I told him. "Although I might have to keep grabbing you for balance." I smiled self-deprecatingly. "I haven't mastered these shoes yet."

I hadn't been wrong about the heels. They were definitely going to kill me.

Spencer only grinned. "I never have a problem with a pretty girl grabbing me."

I laughed. "You get many girls with that line?"

"Tons."

"Must be the delivery." I didn't let go of his arm and had to restrain myself from holding on tighter when I noticed everyone's eyes glued on us.

I did my best to sound casual as though I flirted with Spencer all the time. "See you guys around."

And then we left. Steffani and Ashley trailed behind so that Chelsea and Logan could have privacy. I couldn't resist looking back just once. They were holding hands and moving toward the door—Smith High School's most popular students were getting back together again.

I don't know why, but it felt like someone sucker punched me in the stomach.

Chapter 27

"So . . . is it fun being rich?"

Okay, I didn't mean to ask that, but when you're being led around an ornate house with a fancy chandelier above the staircase it's hard to resist asking.

"It has its advantages." Spencer gestured at his parents' generously stocked bar as Fake and Bake ditched us to cheer on their boyfriends who were presently chugging cheap beer.

"I bet."

"So do you want to see the bedrooms?"

He asked it so suggestively I couldn't restrain my instinctive laughter.

"You're all show, aren't you?" I asked, knowing he'd never confirm it. "You live on insinuation and game play."

"Now you've gone and hurt my feelings." But his easy grin told me I was dead-on. Then the smile faded. "There are some games even I don't play. I hope Logan knows what he's doing this time."

"This time?" I repeated, noting the edge in Spencer's voice. I'd never seen him serious before. Something about Logan and Chelsea had to be getting his back up.

He shrugged, but there was tension in the movement. "Some guys fall for the same tricks no matter how obvious the ploy." He tried to brush off the mood. "It's the male curse to be forever bewitched by women," he said philosophically. "Speaking of which . . ." Spencer nodded his head as Patrick strode toward us.

Okay, I admit I entertained a brief fantasy that Patrick would kiss me until I couldn't think—like I was in some Taylor Swift music video and any second the lovably awkward girl (me) would triumph with the help of true love.

I wish the real world worked like that.

Instead, Patrick stood in front of us, looking like he had something to say and no idea how to go about it. After a long pause, I took my hand off of Spencer's arm—which meant I had to worry that I'd lose my tentative hold on balance.

"I'll catch you later," Spencer said at last with a suggestive wink. Then he went over to a large clump of girls where I thought I saw a flash of gray skinny jeans.

"I've been looking for you."

Why did I have to turn into a puddle at five simple words? It was just so sweet. Suddenly, I thought, *Maybe Corey and Melanie were right about this dress.*

"Uh, really?"

Yes, that's my oh-so brilliant response when a supercute boy says he's been looking for me. Shoot me, now.

"Yeah. Why don't we go somewhere quiet to talk." And before I could screw up the moment, he took my hand and led me to the front door—just like I'd imagined so many times before.

Only when I imagined it, I wasn't wearing heels that cut off my circulation. Plus I pictured something more along the lines of strolling together instead of being dragged. And in those daydreams I didn't keep banging into people so that I had to apologize with every step.

Still, it was great. Really.

I could see why he decided to change our venue. The air was refreshingly chilly after the sweltering heat of the house crammed past capacity. We could speak out here without fighting to be heard over music. Not that we were alone. Tons of kids enjoyed the landscaping that must have cost Spencer's parents a small fortune. There was a fountain. I kid you not, a legit fountain that glowed and gurgled beautifully. It all felt so romantic. The front porch railing had white twisty spindles and was perfect for a girl to put her weight on instead of taking off her heels. So I leaned on it as I looked at Patrick.

Some people are made for moonlight. It brought out the darkness in his brown eyes. Even without a jacket I began to feel warmer.

"Hi," I said simply. Everything was perfect. Even the whiff of weed that lingered in the air was perfect. "What's on your mind?"

"You."

He moved closer and my heart began to beat seriously fast. All I could think was, *It's going to happen! Patrick's going to kiss me! Any second now . . .*

"Wh-what about me?"

Why couldn't I just shut up and let him do it?

"That I'm in love with you."

I jerked away from him, breaking the spell of the moon-light, as I latched onto the railing to keep myself steady. My legs were wobbling.

"You're *what?!*" I said in disbelief . . . and maybe in a bit of horror. It was as if he'd told me, "I'm part alligator" or "I'm an undercover narcotics agent."

"I said, I'm in love with you," he repeated defensively.

I should have kept my mouth shut. Just nodded and cooed, "Oh? Why don't you show me?" Then I should've kissed him, but I just couldn't do it.

"No." I shook my head and prayed that any second I would wake up and he wouldn't be looking daggers at me. "No, you're not."

"What are you talking about? I think I know how I feel, Mackenzie!"

Oh yeah, no one can kill a romantic moment like me.

"You, just—you *can't* love me because . . . you don't even know me yet!"

And that's what was missing, I realized as he looked at me with stony coolness. Patrick had never expressed any interest up until a week ago. One lunch conversation and now he supposedly loved me?

Doubtful.

There was a momentary pause while Patrick soaked this in. Then his expression slowly softened, and I thought, *Maybe he gets it now. Maybe he sees that to love someone you have to accept them—quirks included.* I hoped he'd say, "Then let's fix that. Let's get to know each other." Then he'd gently shake my hand as if we were being formally introduced. "I'm Patrick and I'm ready to tell you anything, but first I'd like to hear about you."

I'd be a goner. I'd be freaking putty in his hands.

Instead he looked soulfully into my eyes. "I know you, Mackenzie."

Too bad, he had to say *that*.

"That's a logical fallacy. It's called 'begging the question.' You didn't actually challenge my premise that you don't know me. Instead, you just reasserted that you do." I tried to smile, but I felt sick. "That's how I think—all the time. Still love me?"

I took his icy silence as one hell of a retraction. "I didn't think so."

It hurt. Maybe it shouldn't have, since I was doing the pulling back, but it stung like a jellyfish. I guess that's what happens when you discover that you've had a gigantic crush on a boy who doesn't really exist . . . for years.

"I'm sorry," I said, and I meant it. I was sorry—for both of us. "I wish I were the girl you're looking for. But I'm just . . . not."

Patrick didn't just shrug and say, "Well, we can always be friends." Instead his anger flowed. "That's not it. You think you can do better than me, don't you?" The disgust in his voice would have made me step back if I hadn't already been trapped by the porch.

"What? No!"

"You think now that you're famous, you're too good for someone in high school." The way he eyed my dress made me feel exposed. "Or maybe I'm just not rich enough. Is that why you've been throwing yourself at Logan and Spencer?"

A hard slap across my face would have felt less painful.

"Wow." That's all I could say for a second because really, what else was there? "From love to gold digger in under thirty seconds. That's . . . wow. I guess if you had *really* loved me, you would've called me a slut."

I stood up straighter and released the railing. Time to put all the weight on my own two feet.

"If you think I pursue guys based on their bank accounts, then you don't know me at all." I studied him carefully. "That's more *your* style, right? You only started pouring on the charm after Tim said I was cool. You would've dumped me if I couldn't get your photo in the papers." My stomach clenched viciously. "And I was stupid enough to buy into it. I think you should leave now."

"You're going to regret this, Mackenzie." His voice was steady now. Cold and steady.

"Maybe not today, maybe not tomorrow. But soon and for the rest of my life." I quoted *Casablanca* but gave the line way more sarcasm than Humphrey Bogart had.

"What?" His stiffness wavered into confusion.

"Nothing . . . famous movie line. Forget it."

"You, Mackenzie," he said slowly, "have a thesaurus where your heart should be."

And with that he disappeared into the house.

"Encyclopedia," I corrected as I stared out into the night. It was beautiful and lonesome at the same time, with small lights illuminating the pathway from the fountain to the gazebo. "I have an encyclopedia where my heart should be."

That's what I muttered when I saw *exactly* where Logan and Chelsea had gone. They were standing in the center of the gazebo, and if I hadn't been looking at the structure, willing myself not to cry over Patrick, I never would have seen Chelsea reach up, take Logan's face in her hands, and kiss him.

So the off again was definitely on again.

And I knew then that Patrick was very wrong about my heart, because if it had actually been an encyclopedia I could have watched it all with perfect composure. Instead, I turned resolutely and marched back into the party.

I figured that alcohol was a heartache and teenage rebellion cliché for a reason. It was time for me to give it a try.

Which, as far as plans go, might have been my worst one yet.

Chapter 28

I drafted Spencer right off.

Considering that he was the only person I knew beyond a causal "hey, how's it going?" in the hallways, that might not be too surprising.

And it seemed to me that it's a good idea to explore new territory with a guide who's familiar with the route—kind of like diving with a buddy.

Anyhow, I grabbed his arm, but this time it was to steer him away from a group of girls and toward the makeshift bar.

"Not that I don't like your aggressive tactics, but . . ." He paused when he saw the way my eyes focused on the alcohol. "What's going on?"

I smiled, and for the first time since I'd come to that stupid party, I started to relax. "You are going to pour me a drink."

His grin widened. "Am I, now?"

"Yep." I leaned forward and pulled a clean red plastic cup from a stack. "What do you recommend?"

"That depends. What do you like?"

I shrugged. "I have no idea, and I doubt I'll enjoy any of it."

"But you still want to drink?"

I handed him the cup. "Fill 'er up."

"Okay, so we can get you some girly drink that tastes like fruit, or"—he poured liquid into the cup—"you can take this shot of tequila and chase it with some lime."

"Faulty dilemma," I muttered.

"What?"

"Faulty dilemma fallacy. You only gave two options, and . . . just hand it over."

In a few practiced moves, Spencer had salt on my hand and a slice of lime oozing on the countertop.

"Okay, it's simple. Salt. Shot. Lime. Got it?"

I ran through it a few times in my head. *Salt, shot, lime. Salt, shot, lime. Oh, my god, have I lost my mind?! This is so NOT me!*

"Got it."

"Okay. Go."

We were starting to generate a small crowd. I guess people wanted to see strait-laced Mackenzie Wellesley take her first shot. Talk about peer pressure, I was surrounded by strangers who were all saying stuff like, "You've got this!" and "You can do it!"

I licked the salt in my palm, and tossed back the tequila like I'd seen in the movies.

I very nearly choked.

It felt like I'd been blasted by a furnace. A strange fire cruised down my throat, followed closely by the taste of something sharp—almost acidic. Hastily I sucked on the lime while everyone around me cheered. When I looked up at Spencer, the warmth had seeped to my stomach and pooled there, glowing while the tang of the lime juice coated my mouth.

"I did it!" Even as I held up the empty cup I couldn't believe it. I don't know what I expected: divine intervention, a parent storming in, or maybe a concerned friend whisking me away. But I never thought I'd have the guts to do a shot of tequila.

"Did you see that?!" I demanded to Spencer. "I did it!"

"Yeah, downed it like a champ. Want another one?"

The warmth felt really good, especially after Patrick had flash-frozen me. And maybe it was my imagination, but I already felt less tense.

"I'm in!" I decided. Another cheer rose as I smiled at everyone. "Who wants to join me?"

Half an hour later I was in a very happy place. Spencer poured the drinks until a crash from the kitchen forced him to leave his post. Another hockey player named Kevin was more than happy to fill in for him. I felt like I was floating— only connected to my body through a tenuous thread. It would have disconcerted me if it hadn't been for the fact that I rather enjoyed the sensation.

"This is great!" I told Kevin and his girlfriend, Annie, happily as I sucked on my lime. "You guys are so cool! Isn't it crazy that we go to the same school and we've never really talked?"

They laughed and agreed in the way that people who are tipsy support people who are drunk.

I turned to Annie. "You are really pretty. I bet it'd be fun to be you. Kevin, don't you think it'd be fun to be Annie?"

Lady Gaga came pounding through the speakers.

"We have to dance!" I declared. "It's 'Poker Face.' You have to dance!" I didn't give them time to protest. Laughing, the three of us joined the masses on the makeshift dance floor that was formerly a living room. My whole body felt loose, whether from the alcohol or the music I couldn't be sure, and I never wanted my body to stop absorbing every beat.

"Melanie!" I hollered when I saw her talking to Dylan in a corner away from the action. I raced over. "You have to dance with me! You should meet Kevin and Annie too."

"Sure," she said agreeably, but her eyebrows bunched together as she examined me. "Mackenzie, are you okay?"

"I'm great! Well, except for the encyclopedia."

Dylan followed us to the dance floor, and Melanie turned to him in alarm. "Did you understand that?"

He shook his head and struggled to hold me in place. "Mackenzie, have you taken anything?"

"Salt, shot, lime. Can you believe it!? I don't know what I expected, but it feels really warm. Heat is just radiating from me—like I'm *nuclear* or something. Like I'm a *nuclear bomb!* I'm the bomb! Has anyone considered alcohol as an energy source?" I concentrated on getting my words out correctly. "Do I look like a bobblehead? Because I can't stop nodding. I wonder if dashboard hula girls feel like this."

Dylan started pulling me toward the front door.

"Why is everyone being dragged tonight?" I asked no one in particular. "What's wrong with walking? I like walking. It's nice. Rollerblading is better, but you can't do that here."

"Dylan, what are we going to do with her?" Melanie asked him urgently. "She's trashed. We can't let your mom see her like this."

I smiled sleepily at Melanie as my energy drained out. I put an arm around Dylan's shoulder.

"Mom will be okay, but do I have to go back? I'll just sleep on Dylan." I let my head rest against his. "You're a really great brother. I don't tell you that enough. Oh, and Dad should have asked about you today."

I felt Dylan stiffen. "Dad called?"

"Yeah. Guess I had to become famous to get us a phone call." He wrapped an arm around my waist to keep me upright. "He shouldn't have left you," I whispered, snuggling closer. "You're the best."

"What happened to her?"

My head jerked up at the sound of Logan's voice. "Oh, hey! Great party. I think the world is spinning now." I dimly noticed Spencer and Chelsea right next to him. "Hey, buddy. Salt, shot, lime," I repeated. "Still got it!"

Logan turned on Spencer. "How many shots did she have?"

"About two and a half when I left. I was going to cut her off, Logan. I swear!"

Logan turned up my face so I could look into his eyes. "Okay, Mack. Did you drink after Spencer left?"

"Sure," I said brightly, getting my second wind. Maybe because the touch of his fingers on my face made me feel like I'd just downed another shot. "With Kevin and Annie."

"Shit!" was Dylan's way of summing up the situation.

I nudged him with my elbow.

"Language!" I said in my best imitation of our mom.

"Okay, we need to sober her up. How are you guys getting home?"

"Corey was going to pick us up later," Melanie told him nervously. "After his date. But I don't think she's going to be upright that long."

Logan nodded. "Okay. Are the two of you sober?" He waited for Dylan's affirmative before continuing. "Good. Then you can stay here and man my post while I drive her back."

"Of course you will," Chelsea snarled. "You're such an idiot!" Then she flounced off.

"Uh-oh. Trouble in paradise." I looked up at Spencer, who was staring at me with a mixture of concern and guilt. "It really is paradise. You're house is *ridiculous*. It's even got a fountain!" I poked Dylan. "Did you see the fountain? Maybe we should all go see the fountain."

But no one appeared to be listening to me anymore. Logan was pulling car keys from his jacket and handing them to Dylan.

"Don't give these back unless you're sure. There are more in the cabinet by the bar. You got it?"

"I've got it."

"Okay. Spencer, you're officially down one designated driver. Find a replacement for me fast. Let's get her to the car."

But before Logan could drape my free arm over his shoulder, Dylan said in a voice that was deadly serious. "This is my sister, man. Hurt her and I'll hurt you. We clear on that?"

It was sweet of him to warn off a high school boy who could trash him. Then again, Dylan would put up one hell of a fight.

"We're clear."

"Hey!" I protested as Logan took hold of me. "I'm right here! I'm fine. That was really great of you, Dylan, but I can take care of myself." I bunched my hands into fists. "See!"

"Yeah, you're ferocious."

I turned to Melanie. "You know what I mean, right? They're acting like I'm a damsel in distress and I'm *not!*"

I admit that last part sounded pretty whiney.

"No, you're just a damsel." She opened the passenger's door of Logan's car.

"Wow, that was quick." It hit me then that I was leaving the party. "Wait! Just give me a second, I can snap out of this. Melanie. I didn't mean for this to happen. I'm so sorry I've ruined our first sleepover!"

She brushed my hair back. "It's fine, Mackenzie. Just feel better, okay?"

And with that, my seat belt was clicked into place and I sped away from my first high school party smelling like a bar floor and feeling worse . . . with Logan.

Yeah, I didn't see that one coming.

Chapter 29

"God, I'm stupid," I told Logan as I swayed in my seat. The world didn't want to stop spinning.

"No, you're not." Logan drummed his fingers on the steering wheel. "Usually."

"You're wrong. I'm stupid. I'm really stupid. I'm just good at hiding it." I craned my head to look at him. "Did you know that?"

"Nope. Must have fooled me."

I sat up straighter. "Really? I did? Because you're..." I considered for a moment. "Tough. You've got this look when you stare *really* hard." I mimicked his expression, "It's like you've got X-ray eyes!"

"X-ray eyes," he repeated, and I thought I heard amusement in his voice.

"Yeah! It's like you know what everyone is thinking. Although you can be pretty dumb too, no offense." I pressed my nose against the window and enjoyed the coolness. "When will the world stop spinning?"

"Soon. So I can be dumb?"

"Oh, yeah. But just with girls, I think. Otherwise you're way smart. God, I'm dumb."

"You've mentioned that already."

"Okay. I don't want to be repetitive. Why did I drink so

much? That was not smart." I struggled against my seat belt to face Logan. "And I'm always very responsible. Mackenzie Wellesley never does stuff like this. She knows better than to do tequila shots at a party. Bad decision."

"Ease up on yourself, Mack. So what do you mean, I'm dumb with girls?"

"Well, first, you like Chelsea Halloway. That's pretty dumb."

"I do." I couldn't tell if he said it as a question or a statement.

"Either that or you like her boobs." I chuckled. "Maybe I should shut up now."

"Oh, no, please. Enlighten me."

"Well, someday you guys will have Notable babies. They'll probably have superior immune systems, so that's a plus." I could feel the intensity of Logan's stare. "Of course the kids might become calculating, cutthroat, and cruel . . . so there's that." I leaned back against the seat as the world tilted again. "Calculating, cutthroat, and cruel," I repeated. "Well, I can still appreciate a good alliteration. That makes me smart, right?"

"Right."

"I just need to work on my social skills. Although people seemed to like me tonight." I tugged on his sleeve, enjoying the feel of plain cotton between my fingers. "Did'ya see that?"

"Yeah." His fingers tightened on the wheel. "I noticed."

I leaned toward him to whisper confidentially, "I think it's the dress."

He only studied me for a second while he idled at a red light, but it was long enough to make my pulse pound. "It's one hell of a dress, Mack."

"Thanks. My bra is cute too. See?" I tugged my halter strap so that a small corner of my bra was visible. I thought the car jerked, but that could have just been me.

"Jesus! Don't do that!"

I struggled to keep my eyes open. "Okay, this is bad news bears."

"No kidding."

"I can't believe I'm drunk . . . in your car. Tomorrow Mackenzie is going to feel *really* stupid." My stomach grumbled loudly. "You're not supposed to drink on an empty stomach, are you? I guess that's also bad news bears."

"*Of course* you didn't eat anything first. Perfect." He ran a frustrated hand through his hair. "Hell, you're going to my house, Mack."

"Ex-cuse me?" I said with self-righteous indignation. "You can't do that!"

"Oh yeah? Why's that, Mack?"

"Because of Chelsea!"

"And what," he inquired, "does Chelsea have to do with this?"

At the moment, I wasn't entirely sure. "She'll, uh . . . find out?"

"And . . ."

I didn't have anything past that.

"Okay," I said. "Until the world stops spinning. It will stop, right? Because I don't like this anymore."

"You'll be fine. You just won't want alcohol for a while."

I tried to snuggle against the car door. "But the warmth was nice! It almost made up for Patrick saying I'm a Skanky McSlut." I sighed. "Language."

"Why'd he say that?"

Was it just my imagination or was there a thread of anger in his voice?

"'Well, first he said he was in love with me."

"Well, that makes perfect sense, then."

I laughed quietly and shut my eyes. The world kept swaying.

"He thinks I said no because of you . . . and Spencer."

"What about us?"

I tried to smile, but my face didn't seem to be cooperating. "Even *I* got that part. Climbing the social ladder. You guys are hot, rich Notables. Maybe if I were into the popular scene, it wouldn't sound as crazy." I yawned. "I didn't tell him it was strike one."

"Stay awake, Mack. Almost there. Is that a strike against me or Patrick?"

"You, of course. Strike one: you're a Notable. Strike two: Chelsea. And strike three: you can be nice."

Logan pulled into his driveway. "Wait a second. I was eliminated because I'm too *nice*. What kind of bullshit reason is that?"

I tried to think it through, but my brain was awfully foggy. "Well, you're a Notable and you're never clumsy and you never look bad. Ever. It's not fair. Plus, even without Chelsea and Notable babies, everyone would wonder, 'What's he doing with *her*?' And then you'd say, 'Hmm, good question,' and you'd dump me. That wouldn't be nice."

"So you don't like that I'm popular and can walk without tripping." He said it slowly to convey my sheer stupidity. "It never occurred to you that I might not do the dumping?"

"No," I said honestly. "You like Chelsea. Want to hear something crazy?"

"Sure."

"I want to hate her. I *really* want to hate her because she makes me feel so *lame*. But she's right: I am lame." I threw up my hands in disgust. "Do you know how pathetic I was before YouTube? I couldn't say no to anyone. 'Hey, Mackenzie, can you look over this essay?' 'Sure, no problem.' 'Great! We'll pretend you don't exist starting . . . now.' " I sighed. "I had a crush on Patrick for four years. FOUR YEARS. And it took me until now to realize the guy I like *doesn't exist*." I fumbled for my seat belt. "I don't feel so good."

Logan got me out of his car and facing the bushes in

record time, which is where my body tried to dump all the salt, tequila, and lime.

"I'm sorry," I said before a fresh wave of nausea doubled me over again. I still felt detached from my body, like it was some other girl spilling her guts. Someone else hurling up her bad decision into the bushes—some less intelligent girl.

"It's okay, Mack." He held back my hair. "You're going to be fine."

My legs were wobbly from exhaustion, and all I wanted was to sleep until the world righted itself again.

"You're really nice."

"Yeah," said Logan. "You mentioned that."

"I still don't feel good." I rested my head against his jacket and tried to absorb the warmth.

"We just need to get you hydrated. Get some electrolytes in you." He halfcarried me to the door. "Some Gatorade, water . . . maybe some food. You'll be fine. Just be quiet, my parents are sleeping."

He unlocked and opened the door while I leaned against his house. Then he pulled me into the kitchen that had become so warmly familiar. I sat on one of the bar stools at the counter and watched him fill a glass of water. He handed it to me before he opened the refrigerator to examine its contents.

I took a sip. "Why'd you date her?"

"A few reasons. Drink."

"Beyond her looks," I added before I obediently focused on the water.

"Let's save this conversation for another time." He found the Gatorade, uncapped a bottle, and handed it to me. "Finish the water and then drink this."

"No," I said forcefully. "Tomorrow I'll feel guilty about prying. Tell me now." I looked suspiciously at the Gatorade. "If you want me to drink blue stuff, you owe me."

He laughed. "I owe you. Right." He sat down next to me though. "Okay. Well, I met Chelsea my first day of middle school. She walked right up to me and introduced herself. One second I was memorizing my locker combination and the next this gorgeous girl is talking to me. Drink."

I took another gulp.

"Chelsea always goes for what she wants, and she's not stupid. She might not be a merit scholar, but she knows how to make a situation work for her. Drink the Gatorade."

He got up to refill my water while I tentatively sipped the bright blue liquid in front of me. I didn't feel any better, but I didn't mention it.

"So why'd the two of you break up? It sounds like you had something." I pressed my forehead against the cool granite surface of his countertop.

"Not enough common ground, I guess. Chelsea likes to be in the center of everything. So we started going to parties together, and at first she was cool with me being on drunk duty and helping out the designated driver. Then she got sick of me spending all my time with people who were puking. I don't blame her. She was bored, annoyed, and lonely—and I didn't know how to fix any of that. So when she met Jake she promptly broke up with me." He looked contemplative for a second. "They seemed good together, so I'm surprised they didn't try to do the whole long-distance thing. Then again, Chelsea likes to have options."

"Was it a bad breakup?"

"Could've been worse. Of course, it could've been a lot better too. It's not exactly fun to hear that your girlfriend has been seeing someone else—the day after the seventh-grade dance." He shrugged and placed the water refill behind the Gatorade. "The more you drink now the better you'll feel tomorrow."

"Okay. The world is still spinning." I shut my eyes tightly before I opened them again. "I don't know why you're telling me all this."

"You asked . . . and now I get to ask you questions."

I made an expansive gesture that nearly knocked over my water. "I'm an open book."

"I'm dyslexic."

I laughed. "Ask away, then."

"Why did you really say no to Patrick tonight?"

"A bunch of reasons."

"Such as . . ."

"I kept writing his lines."

Logan gave me an exasperated look. "What does that mean?"

"In my head. I kept coming up with all these things for him to do or say or think. It was like . . . It was like if I could just believe hard enough he'd be what I was looking for. And I just, well, I want . . ." I drifted off as my head went fuzzy.

"Yes . . ." he prompted.

"More," I decided. "I don't want to write his lines! I want to be surprised and challenged and . . . *pushed* to be more than just Mackenzie Wellesley, Queen of Awkward. And I never want to be a placeholder. Patrick would've dumped me as soon as the popularity wore off. I didn't want to see it, but that doesn't make it any less true. Not that I would expect forever, we're in *high school,* but when he said he loved me, I could see the end like it was in high def. I'd be on the cafeteria floor, just like when Alex Thompson shoved me, and Patrick would stand over me and say, 'We're over, Mackenzie.' Then while I stuttered he'd finish me off. Something like, 'If you bought that load of crap, you must not be as smart as people think.' " I took another gulp. "Sorry, what was the question again?"

"You just answered it."

"Okay. That's good." I felt my stomach churn. "I think I'm going to be sick again."

Logan pulled me to the bathroom. He kept saying stuff

like, "You're going to be fine," as all the Gatorade turned his toilet blue. And when I sank against the wall between the toilet and the sink, he retrieved the water from the kitchen.

"You need to stay hydrated," he told me when I only used it to rinse my mouth before spitting it out. "You're going to have a wicked hangover tomorrow."

I shrugged. "It was worth it."

"I doubt it."

"No, really," I insisted. "I thought it would smell bad and taste worse." I wrinkled my nose. "I still don't like the way it smells . . . but the warmth is great. And now I know what it's like." My voice dropped to a confidential whisper. "That's always the worst: the not knowing. Because then you're stuck with a hundred questions no one can answer."

"Well, tomorrow you'll know all about hangovers."

I couldn't help grinning. "You're funny."

"You're a mess." He hauled me to my feet. "And I need to use your cell phone."

"Why do you need that? Wait! Should I be drunk-dialing? That's part of the experience, isn't it?" I launched myself at the clutch that was still sitting on the kitchen counter. "This is so exciting. Okay, who do I call . . . or should I text?"

In one deft move, Logan had my cell phone. "You are not calling anyone right now. You are going to drink more Gatorade while I tell your brother that you're crashing here for the night. Now, *drink*."

"This looks way more exciting in the movies."

"That's Hollywood for you. Hey, Dylan—no, she's fine." I pried off my shoes and giggled as they clattered to the floor. "She's still drunk and puking, but she's going to be fine. I'm going to have her crash here. Why don't you tell your mom she had a surprise sleepover or something." There was a long pause, then, "Okay. Yeah."

"Logan," I hissed. "*Psst!* Logan!"

He looked up and irritation shone through. "What?"

"Tell Dylan he's the best. Dylan, you're the best!" I called in the general direction of the cell phone.

"She says you're the best," he repeated, probably just to shut me up. "Okay. I'll tell her. Yeah. Thanks, man."

"Well," I said when he snapped it closed, "what'd he say?"

"That you should warn him the next time you want to destroy your liver. He's a good kid."

"He's the best." I tucked the phone back in my clutch. "I—wow, dizzy." I relaxed my head against his shoulder. "Can I sleep now?"

Logan moved my arm so that it draped over his shoulder and held me firmly around the waist. You'd think since I was drunk, had just thrown up, and was crazy sleep deprived, I wouldn't have felt anything at the touch. But I did. I just didn't have the energy to puzzle out what exactly I was feeling.

Logan grabbed a salad bowl before he led me out of the kitchen.

"Where are we going?" I mumbled near the hollow of his neck. "I don't want to move anymore. I just want to sleep."

"That's why we're going to bed."

I think at that point I was so exhausted he could have said, "That's why I intend to ravish you until morning," and I wouldn't have blinked.

Alcohol and me . . . not such a good combination.

Chapter 30

Logan Beckett did not try to take advantage of me. He loaned me a pair of sweatpants and a shirt and left his bedroom until I finished changing. He even stepped out again when I noticed my sleeping shirt was on backward. Although maybe he shouldn't have done that, since I took advantage of his absence. I crawled right into his bed and was nearly comatose when he knocked on the door to check on my progress.

"Come in," I mumbled. "Oh, hi. You have a very nice bed. I like it."

"So glad you approve. Now get out and I'll show you the guest room."

I clutched his pillow even tighter. "No way."

He sighed and placed the salad bowl next to the bed. "Fine. If you feel queasy, use this." He prowled around his room until he located a water bottle and placed it next to the bowl. "You should keep drinking. I'll see you in the morning."

"What?" I demanded. "Where are you going?"

"To the guest room."

"But," I slurred, "you can't do that. You have to stay here and make sure I don't die."

"I really doubt that's going to happen."

"It feels like it could." It did. I felt like I'd come down with something awful, like scurvy or malaria. I patted the bed next to me until he hesitantly sat down. "It'll be like a sleep-over with Corey."

"Yeah. Only I'm not gay."

"But see, it's still fine since you don't like me like that. And you're not going to kiss me. You probably could. It might even be nice. But you won't." I pulled him so he was lying down on top of the covers. He landed close enough to make kissing possible. "Tell me a secret."

"Do you ever shut up and sleep?"

"Nope. And I'm bossy. Tell me a secret."

"Besides the dyslexia?"

I scoffed into my pillow. "I bet lots of people know about that."

"You'd lose that bet. I don't publicize my 'learning difference.' "

I nudged him with my shoulder. "Still doesn't count. Tell me a secret."

He laughed, and then he suddenly became serious. "I—" He paused. "I don't understand you at all."

"That doesn't count either."

"Okay. That day at Starbucks when you looked at Patrick like, I don't know, like he'd just scored a hat trick . . ."

"A what?" I interrupted.

"Three goals in a game. Anyhow, I didn't like it."

"Because you wanted to wear the hat trick?"

Logan smiled, and I wanted to brush aside his bangs so that I could see if his eyes were more blue or gray. Of course to tell that, I'd also have to stop seeing double.

"Not quite." There was humor in his voice when he leaned closer and whispered, "It's not even a secret. You're the only one who hasn't figured it out."

I must have passed out. The next time I opened my eyes I was alone and very confused. Waking up in a strange bed and wearing someone else's clothes was not something I made a habit of doing. I sat up slowly. My head was pounding as I stared blearily around the room I'd been too exhausted to check out the night before.

It was clean. There were no huge piles of dirty clothes lying around like in Dylan's room. And there were no sexy pinup posters of Megan Fox on the door either. Instead, one wall had a huge map of the world with red and yellow pins sticking out of it like porcupine quills. Posters of intense waves, caught midcurl, lined the walls. There was a dartboard with a lot of holes around it where someone had seriously missed the mark. He had a small fish tank on his desk where an angelfish happily bobbed around. At least, it seemed pretty happy to me. Of course my head was swimming more than the fish.

I stood up to get a closer look at the drawings tacked above his desk. My feet sang with pain, and I nearly crumpled. I let out a low whimper and held my head in my hands. Oh yeah, I was regretting those high-heel shoes. Stupid patriarchal culture with stupid ideas of beauty—stupid me for going along with it.

The reminder of my heels triggered a series of memories. Walking into the party with Melanie and Dylan. Hanging out with Spencer. Officially killing the one chance I had at a high school boyfriend with Patrick. Watching Logan and Chelsea kiss in the gazebo.

I felt queasy and blamed it on my hangover. How could I have been so stupid? Who says, "Sorry, you're mistaken," when a guy puts everything on the line? No wonder Patrick had been such a jerk afterward. If he had actually been in love with me I would have crushed him like a clunker in a used car lot without any warning.

But my mental slideshow wasn't finished. I rubbed my head and muttered, "salt, shot, lime" in disgust. I vaguely remembered dancing with Kevin and . . . Amy? I must have been seriously plastered.

Classy.

My first party, and I need my little brother to help clean me up. A little fact Dylan would probably remind me of for the rest of my life—particularly when looking for a favor.

I forced myself to stand up and walk over to the fish as the night became seriously jumbled. Something about Chelsea . . . and a car ride with Logan. Had I thrown up? I was pretty sure I had. But the big question was *where*? Did I puke in the car?! I rubbed my eyes and kept walking toward the desk. There was a strip of corkboard on the wall, and all the pictures looked like Logan artwork to me. I leaned closer to get a good look. It was a whole series of drawings that looked like a detailed comic strip. In the very first one a dorky-looking girl (me?) stood on a lunch table and declared, "It's time for a revolution! I have the right to be seen!"

Which was kind of nice, actually,

Only in the next panel, Chelsea was shooting me a disgusted look and thinking, "I see you. Ever hear of makeup?"

Not so cool.

I looked down at the sweatpants and plain shirt that bagged around me and started to panic. How *exactly* had I come to be wearing this particular outfit? I thought I had put it on myself. I rubbed my eyes again and fervently wished that was the way things had gone down.

"So . . . you've met Dog."

The startled pounding of my heart matched pace with the thudding in my head. I whirled around to face Logan, who was leaning against the doorjamb, as if girls woke up in his bedroom all the time.

"Wh-what?" I stuttered.

"My fish."

"You have a fish named dog." I massaged my forehead. "Am I still drunk?"

He laughed. "Dog is Hebrew for fish. And since I'm allergic"—he shrugged—"it's the closest to having a dog as I'm ever going to get."

I nodded and then wished I hadn't. My head felt like it would split open any second.

"How are you feeling?" Logan grinned as I eyed him in obvious discomfort.

"Just dandy."

"Let's get you breakfast and some Advil," he said, pushing me toward the kitchen.

My stomach twisted at the thought of food. "Maybe two Advil and hold the food?"

"Wasn't it a week ago that you declared in this very room that you knew your limits?"

"Logan," I groaned. "Do me a favor? Shut up."

A chuckle from behind us had me spinning around. His parents had quietly entered the kitchen and heard every word.

"I—I'm sorry," I apologized quickly. For what, I'm not exactly sure. Maybe for telling their son to shut up, for standing hungover in their kitchen, for throwing up in their bathroom, or for spending the night in their son's bedroom— maybe for all of the above.

"Oh, we tell him to shut up all the time," said Logan's mom. She turned to me. "Are you feeling all right, Mackenzie?"

"Oh, sure. I'll be fine." My head wanted to crack wide open.

Logan's father poured out a huge glass of orange juice and handed it to me.

"Why don't you sit down and we'll fix you the Beckett family hangover cure." He winked. "It's doctor approved."

I sank onto one of the counter stools and tried not to be jealous of Logan for having two completely awesome parents. The teamwork between the pair was obvious. They moved around the kitchen, chopping up peppers and grating cheese without ever getting in each other's way. I wondered if my parents had ever had that together—if my dad had laughed and told my mom to stop being such a backseat cooker. Probably best not to think about it.

I sipped the orange juice, thanked Logan for the Advil, and tossed it back while the omelet sizzled and a slice of bread was popped into the toaster.

"Do you need help with anything?" I asked.

"No, I think we've got it. Why don't you tell us about the party last night?"

"Uh, well, I guess it was a good one." I used my orange juice as an excuse to stall and formulate my thoughts. "I don't really have anything to compare it to." I rubbed my forehead in self-disgust. "I can't believe this happened, and I'm really sorry for imposing. Getting drunk at parties— that's so not me."

"Well," Logan's father said, "do you go to parties?"

"No," Logan answered for me.

I glared at him and then sighed. "I really don't."

"Then I guess the experience was due to happen."

I stared at him. "But it shouldn't have! I was supposed to understand why it's such a coming-of-age cliché and wake up in my own bed. Not *this*." I gestured expansively.

Mrs. Beckett laughed. "Sounds like you got a little more than you bargained for." She handed me the toast. "Well, I'm glad you had people looking out for you." She turned to her son. "You made her drink water, right?"

He gave her a look that he'd probably perfected after a lifetime of answering the obvious. "Of course."

"Well, then. Eat this and you'll be feeling as good as new."

"Thanks." I encompassed all of them with my smile. "I really appreciate it."

"It's no problem." Mr. Beckett retrieved the salt and pepper shakers. "Logan, why don't you get the paper." It wasn't a question. All of us knew what the order meant: they wanted to say something . . . in private.

No sooner was Logan out of the room than Mrs. Beckett said, "You know, Mackenzie, we've been meaning to talk to you for a few days."

I nodded, because what else could I do?

"We know that your life has gotten a little . . . complicated recently. When we saw that YouTube clip, well"—her smile widened—"we thought it was pretty funny. Obviously, we're happy to teach you CPR so that . . ." Mr. Beckett nudged her, and she got back on topic, "but we never expected things to get so crazy for you."

"Neither did I," I told them honestly.

"We want you to know, we understand if tutoring is too much for you right now. Taking care of yourself needs to be your first priority."

I tried to process everything she was saying. "So . . . does that mean I'm fired?"

My heart plummeted at the thought, and I bit into my bread so they wouldn't see just how badly I wanted to keep my job. I hadn't even gotten the chance to try out any of my new ideas on Logan. We hadn't watched history movies or made fun of the ridiculous powdered wigs or . . . anything. And it was disturbing how much I'd actually been looking forward to hanging out with Logan.

"No, of course not." Logan's dad smiled at me. "But we understand if it's too much for you right now. We know that Logan isn't exactly the easiest person to teach."

"Because of his dyslexia, you mean." I don't know why I said it. Maybe because it seemed stupid to pretend it didn't exist.

"That can make things harder." Mrs. Beckett smiled. "But I was actually thinking more about his work ethic. He tends to procrastinate. That's why we were so surprised when he suggested getting a tutor—not that he was originally so keen on the idea."

I thought back to the brisk way that Logan hired me. "Yeah, I'd say he was less than keen. I might even say he was hostile."

"Well, I'm glad he told you about the dyslexia. It's not something he likes to talk about."

I nodded and tried to soak up all this new information. There was just so much coming out, and I hadn't even had a chance to absorb what had happened last night. Part of me wasn't sure I deserved the Dr. Becketts being this nice to me—not after I came back from a party only to hurl in their bathroom.

It was all so weird.

And before I could say anything, Logan had returned holding the newspaper and looking annoyed. The source of his irritation became instantly clear when he smacked the paper down in front of me. The headline said it all: *Wellesley Gets Wild!*

Just in case anyone was wondering what *kind* of wildness, there was a big picture of me in my dress, lime in hand, laughing up at Kevin. I hadn't noticed anyone taking photos at the party, but at that point I had been three shots deep and didn't notice much.

After noting the foolish smile and the half glaze to my eyes that had more to do with exhaustion than tequila, I read the article.

> Seventeen-year-old Mackenzie Wellesley may have only recently hit fame through her two wildly popular YouTube videos, but her notoriety shows no sign of waning. Instead, she has fu-

eled controversy with her recent behavior, which includes partying, drinking, and rumored drug use. Her love life appears to be even more muddled. Despite reports that she and Timothy Goff are "crazy about each other" and that "they talk all the time," Ms. Wellesley attended a high school party instead of seeing her alleged boyfriend, Timothy Goff, in nearby Portland. In fact, an intoxicated Ms. Wellesley left the party with an unknown boy. Given her meteoric rise to public attention, this type of poor judgment begs the question: can fame turn a good girl bad?

"Drug use!" I spluttered. "I've never used drugs in my life!" I held out an arm toward Logan's parents. "I swear! You can run a panel on me. It'll come back clean."

Logan's mom laid a gentle hand over mine. "We don't doubt it."

"I don't know," his dad said jokingly. "Looks like a junkie to me."

I turned to Logan. "You've got your dad's sense of humor."

"Ouch."

"I have to get home." I flipped the paper over so I couldn't keep looking at my stupid face. "I have to explain this to my mom."

"Of course." Mrs. Beckett agreed instantly. "Logan can take you back."

"Great." I turned back to him. "And, um, can I borrow your clothes? I'd rather not wear the dress."

"No problem," he said as we headed for the car.

But he was wrong. There were about to be several.

Chapter 31

Five minutes later Logan and I were alone in his car . . . and I was having a very fuzzy set of flashbacks.

"Pull over," I ordered when we reached the elementary school. I was relieved that he obeyed without saying a word. "I—I have to apologize. This is one big blanket apology for last night. I'm not entirely sure what I did or said, but I know I threw up and was generally annoying. And you really didn't need a drunk girl messing up your Friday night. So thanks for putting up with me. Now if you could somehow manage to forget everything, that'd be great."

"I don't know . . . your striptease was pretty memorable."

I choked. "My what!?"

"Kidding."

"So not funny. So very not funny."

"Look, nothing happened." Logan unclicked his seat belt and swiveled so he could look me straight in the eyes. "You cut loose for a night. If you ever want to do that again, you should arrange a designated driver beforehand."

"I know," I groaned. "And I shouldn't have gone home with you. That was stupid. The majority of rape victims know their assailants. Plus, given the amount of alcohol I consumed, I doubt I could've managed a decent defense. I'm lucky last night wasn't worse."

That realization sent cold spears down my spine. When I downed my first shot last night I was just thinking, *Patrick hates me and my life sucks. What do I have to lose?*

The answer to that was: a lot.

"Wait a second, it was not stupid to get in the car. You were drunk. You needed someone to make sure you drank water and didn't choke on your own vomit." I winced at the visual. "So a friend helped you out."

"Is that what you are?" I wondered aloud. "A friend."

"Sure. We talk, we've hung out, and we've got mutual friends. I know you're good for a loan, and I've helped you out of a scrape. Seems like we're friends to me."

I was about to agree. Really. I very nearly said, "Well, look at that. I've got a Notable friend." But, oh, no . . . I had to stomp all over it.

"So . . . what scrape did you help me out of?"

Logan instantly shut his mouth, which only made me more curious.

"Come on, Logan," I wheedled.

"It was no big deal," he said at last. "Spencer and I had a little chat with Alex after he shoved you in the cafeteria. So we made it clear he has to leave you alone. Problem solved."

I stared at him. "Are you insane?! Problem NOT solved! I handled it, okay. *I* told him to leave me alone. I don't need you warning people off for me. You think because you're, what, some big shot hockey captain you have the right to interfere?!"

"No, I was obligated to interfere. He knocked you to the ground, Mack, and he threatened to do it again. You needed help."

"I know exactly what he did." My voice was icy. "Like I said, I handled it. I can take care of myself. And you should've asked before you and your buddy decided to play white knight with *my life*."

His eyes became frosty. "It wasn't like that."

"Sure it was! What did you expect me to say? Thanks, Logan, for being my protector!" I scoffed. "I've managed to get along just fine without guys defending me from the big bad world."

"You're mixing me up with your dad, Mack. That's just stupid. Stop being pathetic and get over yourself."

I spluttered, "My dad has nothing to do with this. This is about lines and boundaries and personal space."

Logan snorted. "Right. So when you pried into my dyslexia and started asking about Chelsea, you were only interested in boundaries."

"I was drunk!"

"Not for the past week you haven't been. Not when you first made it your mission to figure me out."

And that's when it hit me—the epiphany really couldn't have come at a worse time: I had a massive crush on Logan Beckett.

He was right. Ever since we went ice skating I'd been trying to figure him out. Not because I wanted to pry into his personal life, I just thought he was interesting. Then he had started calling me Mack, and I liked it. That should have tipped me off instantly, because I *hate* being called Mack . . . or at least I *had* until he had started doing it. Maybe I even liked him a bit before that. Maybe it started at Starbucks when he said he liked my factoid.

I have to be the slowest teenage girl on the planet.

You'd think that this realization would mean something, right? Instead of fighting over something as small and insignificant as who warned off Alex Thompson, I would say something like, "*Look, Logan. This is just me being horribly stupid and insecure. I'm sorry. I'll become normal again in just a second. Do you think you might want to go out on a date with me when I don't have the hangover from hell?*"

That's exactly what I should have said.

But of course I didn't.

I'd like to point out that this realization had spectacularly poor timing and was also completely unwelcome. I had told myself even before our first tutoring session that this could not happen. I couldn't be like every other girl at Smith High School and have a crush on Logan Beckett. I had a million reasons for it too—not just the three I vaguely remembered giving Logan last night. It could never work. We would never work—because why would a guy (a Notable guy) want to date a loser like me when he could be with superconfident, übergorgeous Chelsea Halloway? He'd have to be crazy.

So I panicked. After the scene with Patrick the night before, I think I deserve some credit for not just bursting into tears like a kindergartener. I had a crush on Logan Beckett, and for the second time in less than twenty-four hours my heart was going to get stomped on.

"Maybe we shouldn't be doing this." I heard myself saying the words and yet I couldn't believe they came from me. I had lost control. My fight-or-flight reflexes had kicked in, and every cell in my body shrieked, *You're a stupid Invisible to him, remember? Get out of here before he realizes just how pathetic you are.*

"You don't want me prying, fine. Makes sense. I didn't fit into your world anyway. You're better off with a tutor who isn't awkward and *pathetic*. Maybe Chelsea can help you out. You two looked pretty cozy in the gazebo last night." The memory of it twisted my stomach into little knots. "You guys will be a much better fit."

"You were *spying on me*." Logan stared at me in disbelief, and I unbuckled my seat belt ready to make a hasty retreat.

"No!" I shouted. I don't even know when I switched into my "loud voice," but I was certainly making the most of it. "I wasn't spying! It's not *my* fault you were making out with her in public. Just a heads up, if you don't want people to see you shoving your tongue down someone's throat, try going somewhere with walls!"

"You were spying on me," he repeated as if I hadn't spoken at all.

"Don't flatter yourself. Or you know what? Go right ahead. I was spying on you. You got me. Secretly I'm deeply, madly, passionately in love with you. Oh baby, oh baby." I said the last bit in a flat monotone with a sharp edge of sarcasm. "Just what kind of an idiot do you take me for?"

Logan's jaw clenched. "Because only an idiot would be into a jock like me."

"Only an idiot would let herself be played by someone who's more interested in popularity than people."

I don't know where that came from. Maybe it was residual Patrick anger, but I was too mad, too scared, and way too hurt to think it through.

"I never played you, Mack." He said it quietly and with a fierce finality. "You used me to make a buck—and that's fine. You wanted the job to buy your precious MacBook. I get it. But no one forced you into anything. You could have said no to the tutoring, and you didn't have to sing with ReadySet. You also didn't have to shoot tequila at the party last night, or even show up for that matter. You chose to do all of it. So don't accuse me of playing you when you're the one making up the rules."

He snapped his seat belt back into place and pulled out. I watched the elementary school disappear as I absorbed his words in silence. I had no idea how the conversation and my blanket apology for the night before had gotten so royally screwed up.

"Mackenzie." My voice was hoarse when I said it, and I knew I had to get out of the car, away from Logan, and back into my normal pre-designer clothes before I turned into a pathetic moron who cries. I stiffened my spine and stared straight ahead while it felt like someone had put my heart into a juicer and was mashing it to a pulp. All I had left was my pride. "Mackenzie, not Mack."

"Of course." That was all he said. "Mackenzie, not Mack." And somehow that agreement felt like the hardest hit of all.

Chapter 32

Iran upstairs, opened the door to my room, and headed straight for my bed, hoping to pull the covers over my head like I'd done when the stupid video had first hit the Web and everything had changed. I wanted to go back to a simpler time. Back to when I had a crush on Logan Beckett but didn't know it. Back to before I made awful decisions that put me at risk. Back to when my biggest dilemma was whether to watch an episode of *Glee* or *The Office* as a study break treat.

I wanted desperately to go back to when I wasn't responsible for turning my life into crap. Because if there was one thing Logan was right about, it was that I had to fess up and take responsibility. Maybe with the initial YouTube video my fame was out of my control, but that didn't mean my actions hadn't shaped the following events. If I hadn't gotten so into it, hadn't worn the designer clothes, hadn't convinced myself that maybe I could pull off being some weak imitation of a Notable, none of this mess would have happened.

I needed a little alone time in my room so I could sort everything out. But even that was out of my reach. My bed was currently being occupied.

"Oh, hey. You're back," said Melanie as she pushed her long hair out of her eyes. "How are you feeling?"

I didn't know how to answer. *Well, I don't feel like puking because of tequila anymore. Now it's my own idiocy that makes me want to hurl.* Yeah, that wouldn't go over well.

I sat at the foot of my bed and hugged a pillow to my chest. It was oddly comforting. "Can I ask you something?" I said.

"Sure."

"Why did you want to sit with us? I mean, that video of me was all over YouTube, and the whole school was laughing at me. Eating lunch at my table could have been social suicide. So why'd you do it?"

Melanie sat up straighter. "Do you want the truth?"

"I think I can handle it."

"I watched the video and I thought, 'This girl is making an idiot out of herself with her CPR.' " I winced. "But then I thought, 'That's really cool of her.' Everyone knows Alex is a tool, but you were still hollering for a nurse and pounding on his chest." She shrugged. "So that's why I sat with you."

"Not because of the clothes or . . . any of the rest of it?"

Melanie laughed. "I don't need friends for clothes. The rest of it is cool but not worth sitting at the table if you guys were boring."

I may have alienated the boy I used to have a crush on *and* the boy I have a crush on, but somehow I had also made a really great friend.

"Let me ask you something," said Melanie. "Why did you think I was just doing it for the perks?"

She had me and we both knew it. I hugged the pillow even tighter.

"I don't know. Patrick was only interested in that."

Melanie gave me a skeptical look. "So you assumed that everyone was a wannabe? I don't think so. Come on, Mackenzie. Out with it."

"Look, it just made the most sense, okay!" I started rocking back and forth. "I'm geeky and I'm lame and I can't walk without tripping and when I'm nervous I spew out random facts. Even knowing all of that, I can't seem to change it. So, no, I don't understand why people would want to hang out with me."

"Mackenzie," Melanie said gently. "You're great. You're funny and just a little bit unpredictable. Plus I never have to worry that you'll make fun of me if I say the wrong thing. You guys might joke about it or tease me a little, but nothing vicious. That's why people like you. You might be intimidating in class, but if someone asked you for help, you'd be there."

"But that's just it: I never say no! I'm always just standing there waiting for people to walk out on me."

"I'm getting tired of this pity party," she said with a quick grin to take the sting out of her words. "Mackenzie, you've got a lot of stuff going for you. You've got looks, a great voice, and a ridiculously big brain, but if you don't believe that for yourself it doesn't matter what I think." She sighed and rubbed her eyes. "Get it?"

"Got it." And even though my life was still just as messy, our talk had me feeling a bit better.

"Good. Why don't you shower while I change?" She yawned. "Then I'm raiding your fridge. I'm starving."

I laughed. "Sure. Feel free to help yourself."

That's exactly what she did too. When I came downstairs wearing my baggy garage sale jeans and a boring brown shirt, she was munching on cereal in the kitchen with Dylan. Which I found pretty funny, since it was around eleven o'clock and he must have already eaten long ago. But there he was having another bowl of cereal with her. Someone was crushing—and hard.

"About time you got home," Dylan said to me. "I've been texting and calling you."

That must have been what woke me up in Logan's bed, but it had been muffled by my clutch and I'd been too disoriented to recognize it.

"Oh, sorry. I didn't realize," I wavered, not certain how to proceed. "So . . . how was the party after I left?"

"Great," said Melanie. Dylan just shrugged nonchalantly.

"It was pretty chill. We mainly helped Spencer handle the drunks. He was running understaffed what with Logan babysitting you."

I tried to remember that, as my little brother, Dylan got a free pass on a few cutting remarks. He'd been great last night when I had needed him, and it probably wasn't fun for him to watch his big sister get wasted at a party. So I would let the "babysitting" jibe slide.

"It was under control when Corey picked us up. He wants you to call him back right away."

I nodded and got myself a glass of water. Then I had a flashback to Logan ordering me to drink the Gatorade. I set the cup back down like it had scorched me.

"Sure, I'll do that in a second. What did, um, Mom have to say about . . . me?"

Dylan grinned. "You owe me big, Mackenzie, and I mean *big* for covering for you. I told her you had a friend spending the night and were probably just sleeping in. She didn't check before heading off to work, so as far as she knows you didn't get hammered and spend the night at Logan's." He gave me a shrewd look, the one reserved for when he thinks I'm going to lie and wants to catch me in the act. "Everything go okay over there?"

"Everything was fine."

I told myself it wasn't a lie. When I'd been at his house, everything between us had been great. We talked, he held my hair back when I puked, and he'd been so damn nice that I very nearly said we were friends in the car.

I didn't want to think about how badly I had screwed that up.

"I prayed to the porcelain gods," I said casually, as if the time I spent with my head in a toilet (and a bush) was just an amusing anecdote. "But I'm fine."

Dylan studied me a little longer and then turned his attention back to Melanie. I guess it was pretty big proof of his brotherly affection that he could focus on me for that long when Melanie was still in the room.

"You staying around for a while?" he asked as she rose to put her cereal bowl in the dishwasher. The slight tinge in his cheeks showed me that her answer mattered to him. But I don't think Melanie caught it.

"I should probably go pretty soon." She smiled at me. "I think Mackenzie could use the house to herself for a bit."

She was right. She was so right. As much as I liked Melanie, and I was starting to think of her as an extension to the Jane / Corey friendship unit, I needed my space. Maybe my life should have become simpler now that I was out of a job, but instead everything had grown increasingly complex. I needed to sort out my priorities . . . and check my bank account. I wanted to know how many hours I'd have to spend babysitting before the laptop would be mine.

So I gave her a hug. "I'm really glad you came, Melanie. Sorry I wasn't a good hostess. Next time I'll be better. I'll actually spend the night here too, I promise!"

She laughed. "No worries. Tell Corey I say 'hi.' " Then she scooped up the bag she'd brought with her last night.

"Are your parents picking you up?" Dylan asked.

"Nah." She said it casually, and I wondered if there was a story there. "I thought I'd walk. It's a nice day."

"I'll go with you." Dylan said it so matter-of-factly it wasn't quite an offer . . . more like a statement. "Mackenzie can have the house to herself that way."

Melanie looked surprised but recovered quickly.

"Okay," she agreed. "You can carry this, then." She thrust her bag at him. "We'll see you later, Mackenzie." She slipped her arm through Dylan's. "Now, tell me about all her most embarrassing moments."

"Tell her and die!" I called after them. I wasn't actually afraid he'd spill anything too confidential. Dylan's much better than I am at keeping his mouth shut.

As the two of them turned the corner, I couldn't help thinking that I could never have dumped my bag onto someone else. If Logan and I were walking to his house for a study session, I would have carried my backpack—all sixty pounds of textbooks—the entire way. It wouldn't have occurred to me to ask for his help because, hello, my body works just fine.

But it hit me as I watched Dylan carry a dinky bag that contained a dress, a pair of heels, and a small bag of toiletries that I didn't think Melanie was weak. I hadn't been tempted to roll my eyes. I hadn't thought, *Wow, there's another girl playing into the cultural expectation that women are fragile and need male assistance.* It just seemed kind of cute.

That's when I realized that for someone who prided herself on being open-minded about stuff like gay rights and gender equality, I had a serious case of tunnel vision.

Having a guy carry something or asking for help doesn't magically turn someone into a fragile damsel in distress. Just like wearing my low-cut red dress didn't give Patrick the right to call me a gold digger. I hated to admit it, but my mom was right: the terms skank and slut . . . they suck. A lot. Especially because my level of "sexual promiscuity" is not something that can be extrapolated from one outfit.

I'd been so sure that my quick flash of fame wouldn't change me, that under the lights and the designer jeans and the lip gloss I'd remain Mackenzie Wellesley. But I was wrong. As soon as I had stepped into that first pair of heels I had changed—and I wasn't sure it was possible to reverse it.

There was no rewind button on my life. I could donate everything to the Red Cross and I still couldn't be Invisible Mackenzie Wellesley.

Maybe that wasn't such a bad thing. It was easy to be proud of my low-budget wardrobe and to praise myself for being so unaffected by materialism . . . but it was such a lie. I enjoyed having new clothes. Receiving all of those packages of beautiful clothes had been overwhelming, sure, but I had loved it. Maybe it was weak of me to depend so much on clothing for bravery, but I had needed some seriously amazing outfits to perform onstage, to turn down Chelsea, and to go to my first high school party. The clothes might not make the girl, but it was much easier to feel good about myself in designer labels. It made me believe that maybe I wasn't quite as geeky and lame and socially awkward as I kept telling myself.

Logan was right: I did have the power to call the shots. I just hadn't mustered up the nerve to take a stand.

Disgusted with myself, I marched back into the kitchen, pulled out a yellow legal pad, and began to do something that had always worked for me before: I made a list.

Things Mackenzie Wellesley Needs to Get Over:

1. Low self-esteem. Seriously, what's up with this? I've got amazing friends who wouldn't waste their time with a loser. Time to ease up on myself.
2. The whole Notables / Invisibles hierarchy stuff. Patrick demonstrated last night that not only is this argument untrue and insulting, it also makes you sound like a jerk.
3. Any residual Dad issues. He left 12 years ago. Get over it already!
4. My awkwardness (see #1). A little babbling never killed anyone . . . I think.

5. Fear of rejection (see #3). Just because Dad walked out on us doesn't mean every guy is destined to treat me like dirt.
6. My whole money / college obsession. There will be a school that wants me. There will be a school that gives me enough financial aid. I don't have to overwork with AP classes and tutoring to prove myself.
7. Fear of the spotlight. The newspaper can write whatever it wants: my mom will still love me, my brother will still annoy me, and my friends will still laugh at / with me. Which is exactly how I want it.
8. Caring what other people think (see #7). I need to stop obsessing about what Chelsea / Patrick / Fake and Bake / anyone who reads the garbage in the papers believes about me.
9. Jumping to conclusions. For all I know, Chelsea and Logan were just sharing one last for-old-times kiss. Doubtful, but possible. And until I know something for sure, I shouldn't assume the worst.
10. Logan (?)

I tapped my pen against my lips as I considered the last item on my list. The rest suddenly seemed like child's play in comparison. It would probably be smart to cross out the question mark and just move on with my life. File him away in the growing folder of Boys Mackenzie Has Had a Crush On. I thought back to his murderous expression when I climbed out of the car that morning—definitely smarter to leave it at that. But as I stared at the name I remembered vaguely how he had (begrudgingly) forfeited his bed for me and had been there when I passed out.

He was the first guy since Corey to meet the real Mackenzie. The girl most people missed because of the babbling and the factoids and the awkwardness. Which meant that if he rejected me, I couldn't say he was just some stupid jock who wouldn't know a quality girl if she strolled up and started screaming, "ME! PICK ME!" Then again, if there was even the slightest chance he did like me and had only been sucking face with Chelsea because . . . well, for some reason *other* than that they were getting back together, avoiding him for the rest of the year could be my biggest mistake yet.

Shaking my head, I skipped a few spaces and started another list.

Things Mackenzie Wellesley Needs to Do:

1. Get control of this crazy YouTube stuff.
2. Trust my instincts.
3. Grab the life I want with both hands.

I was about to make #3 sound less cheesy when the phone rang. I was so preoccupied with my lists that I answered the phone on the second ring while I wondered what else deserved an entry on my list for life improvement.

"Hello?"

"Hello, is this Mackenzie Wellesley?" The businesslike tone threw me off.

"Uh, yeah."

"Great. This is Mary Connelly. I'm a producer on *The Ellen DeGeneres Show*. We want Ellen to interview you on Monday and then have you perform live with ReadySet. How does that sound?"

She spoke really quickly, like she was about to lose cell phone service any second. I could have sworn I heard someone call out "tall mocha Frappuccino" in the background.

"Wait. You want *me* to perform on the *Ellen* show?"

"That's why I'm calling."

I glanced down at my list. Get media control, trust instincts, and grab life. It looked like I was about to put myself to the test.

"I'll do it." My whole body went numb with shock, but I kept the phone cradled against my ear. "It's Ellen, so I'll do it. Oh, my God, I can't believe I'm actually going to do this."

"That's great, hon. Now we pay for airfare and lodging for you and your escort, and you'll receive some money for food. We need you, ready, at the studio first thing Monday morning."

"Sorry, my what?"

"You're under eighteen, right? All minors must travel with someone eighteen or older. And you need parental consent. I can e-mail you those forms right now. What's your address?"

I gave it to her while all of this information soaked in.

"Can I get your number? I'll call you back as soon as I confirm everything. I need to check on getting that permission first."

"You do that, hon. Check and call me right back. We thought we'd schedule Lady Gaga for Tuesday, but if you don't get back to me soon, she's taking your spot."

It was so weird to hear my name and Lady Gaga used in the same sentence.

"Understood." I jotted down the number she rattled off. "Thanks, Mary. For . . . wow. For the offer."

"No problem, hon. You just make sure it happens."

She disconnected, and I was alone in the house trying to formulate my first plan of attack.

Chapter 33

Maybe it was overly optimistic, but I had my bags packed by the time my mom came home for her lunch. Not that it had been easy for me, as packing was no longer a simple procedure. Instead I had scurried around my bedroom, trying to make snap decisions over which items in my designer closet actually reflected my personality . . . and which ones needed to find a new home—perhaps on eBay. I purposefully tucked my red dress in a drawer and slammed it shut. I wouldn't have to decide on it for a few days if everything went according to plan.

"Mackenzie?" my mom hollered up the stairs. "What are you doing home? Shouldn't you be tutoring right now?"

I set the suitcase aside and hurried down. "I've got the day off. Mom, you'll never guess who just called me! The *producer* of *The Ellen DeGeneres Show!* They want me to fly down to LA and as long as I have parental permission and you go with me, it's a done deal."

After talking with Mary, I realized just how badly I needed this trip. I had to get out of Oregon, even if it was just for a day, and it was about time I took control of the press.

"Hold on, honey." My mom held up her hand for silence. "We need to talk. I know I told you to be a teenager, but there are limits. You can't party every night, jet off to LA, and shirk your responsibilities here." She held up a copy of the newspaper. "And we need to talk about this—"

"Mom, it wasn't the way they made it sound," I interrupted. "I never did any drugs, I swear! I drank too much and I feel really bad about it. But Dylan and my friends made sure nothing happened to me. I'm really fine. And I promise I'll never drink again before I'm legal—maybe not even then."

She gave me one of her steely-eyed Mom looks. "Why didn't you *call* me last night? I would have picked you up. I'd much rather wake up to that than a call from the hospital."

"I'm sorry," I said, and I meant it. "I should have called. I wasn't nearly as unsafe as it sounds though. I got a ride from the designated driver, who was completely sober, I promise. So at the time I thought it was fine. I swear, if it happens again—which it won't—I'll call you."

"Good. Now tell me about this phone call."

"Okay, so the producer wants me there Monday morning, which means we need to fly out, like, *now*. Hotel and airfare are covered, and we even get a food stipend or something."

"I can't do it."

My mouth dropped open. "Mom, this is *Ellen* we're talking about here."

"I know who we're talking about, Mackenzie. I can't leave without any warning. I'd need to get someone to cover for me at work, and since Darlene came down with a nasty cold, I don't think it's going to happen. I'm sorry, honey."

I sank down into the sofa. All my plans had been ruined. No mom, no trip, no escape from my normal life so I could get some perspective. I don't know what I was about to say— "Don't worry about it, Mom. It's not a big deal. I'll be in my room unpacking if you need me." Whatever it was, my cell phone cut me off.

"I Need a Hero" blared into the silent kitchen.

I flipped it open. "Hey, Corey. How was your date?"

"Great!" His voice bubbled over like soup left on a very hot stove. "Best first date in the history of first dates."

"Oh, Corey, I'm so happy for you!" And a little bit jealous—a nasty voice in my head pointed out—but primarily happy.

"Yeah, he just called me with some great news! Tim said his agent called and they want *you* to join the band on *Ellen* with them. Did you hear about that?"

"Yeah, I got that call too."

"Okay, before you make arrangements, hear me out. Tim said there is room on the tour bus for both of us. We could ride down with them, fly out of LA Tuesday morning, and be back in school by Wednesday at the latest. Perfect, right?"

"You want us to ride to Los Angeles with a bunch of rock stars," I clarified, "for two days. Your parents would be cool with that?"

Corey laughed. "You must still be out of it from last night. We're talking about *my* parents, remember? I told them it was an opportunity for me to gain a whole new perspective on the entertainment industry. And then I mentioned that I was indispensable, since your mom would never agree to let you ride on the tour bus with three strange boys if I wasn't there too."

I let out a whistle as it sank in. "You're good. You could teach classes on how to get what you want."

"I'd rather focus on Speech and Debate. Now, we have to move *fast*. Tim, Dominic, and Chris want to be on the road within the next hour, so get permission, pack your bags, and let's get out of here!"

I looked at my mom warily as she sliced cheese for her turkey sandwich.

"Call you right back."

"But—"

"Call you right back," I repeated, and hung up.

"Mom, that was Corey."

Her expression was studiously blank. "I figured that out for myself. I take it he came up with alternative traveling arrangements."

I sat down at the table and folded my hands. "Would it be okay if the two of us made the trip in the . . ." My voice became softer and more hesitant. "ReadySet tour bus? Please?"

My mom stared at me. "I'm never telling you to act like a teenager again. Mackenzie, you can't shirk your responsibilities and go gallivanting off with some boy band you've never met. What about school? What about tutoring?"

"I've met them, Mom," I protested. "They're really nice, and I'd be going with Corey. I'll be fine. Plus, I got a break from my tutoring."

I didn't mention that this "break" might be permanent.

Her lips pursed and my heart sank. She was giving Mom Body Language that said, *I don't think so, missy.*

"You went to a party last night and a concert before that. You've had your fun. I don't think it's unreasonable for me to want you here for the rest of the weekend."

I nodded. "It's not unreasonable. This is a last-minute request, and I know that my timing couldn't be any worse. I got drunk at a party last night, and I understand if trusting me right now doesn't seem like the best idea. But Mom, it's me. You know you can trust me. I really need to do this interview. I need to prove to myself that I can handle this once and for all. How long have you been trying to get me out of my shell? Well, I'm ready to do it, Mom."

She considered that for a moment. "If you meet certain conditions . . . you can go."

I jumped out of my chair and wrapped her into a giant hug. "Just name your terms."

"Hold on. I want phone calls. Lots of phone calls from the road. You will pick up every time I call you, when I call you. No drinking. No drugs. No partying. I'm trusting you, Mackenzie." She said the last part slowly, emphasizing every word, so it would really sink in.

"Done and done." I ran into the computer room to print out the parental consent forms. "Just sign on the dotted line."

That's pretty much all it took. A signature and a few phone calls later, I was boarding a tour bus with my suitcase, my best friend, and my favorite rock band.

And I couldn't help thinking, *Hollywood, show me what you've got. I can take it.*

Chapter 34

The guys were great. I don't know if Tim got the others to clean up before we arrived, but the bus was totally presentable when Corey and I boarded with our stuff. No Playboy magazines or dirty underwear lying around. Which was a relief, actually, since with two new additions the bus was pretty cramped. Not that any of us seemed to mind. The minifridge was stocked with soft drinks so I could lean back against the supercomfy leather couch, pop open the top, and hang out with four very cool guys. And when Tim and Corey started holding hands it was such a sweet form of PDA that no one said anything in case it killed the moment.

"So, Mackenzie, I still haven't heard about the party." Corey's words instantly piqued everyone's interest.

I sipped on my Coke and tried to think of some way to get out of it. "I'm a bit fuzzy on certain parts myself."

Dominic laughed. "Drink too much?"

"Yep, tequila. Never again."

Tim grinned. "Blame it on the alcohol."

Everyone groaned at the Jamie Foxx song reference.

"Last night was . . . complicated. Patrick told me—I'm not making this up—that I'm only interested in guys for their money and popularity."

Corey tensed, and his eyes flashed with annoyance. "What an idiot!"

"And then I saw Logan making out with Chelsea." I didn't mean for that to come out. I was going to keep it to myself. What happens at night in a gazebo ought to stay private. Of course, they really should have found a better location for their make out session if they wanted it to be such a secret. That's how I justified blurting it out at the first opportunity.

"Who's Logan?" asked Tim.

Corey answered before I could. "He's a really great guy who Mackenzie *wants* to date, but she is too thickheaded to admit it."

"I don't . . . okay, yeah." I put my head in my hands. How was it that Corey could see everything so much sooner than me? Talk about unfair. "It gets worse."

Dominic, Chris, and Tim exchanged grins and leaned back in their seats as if they loved nothing more than watching an emotional train wreck.

"First I started drinking." Corey winced. "Yeah, I know. Bad idea. Anyhow Logan took me to his house since it was pretty obvious I needed to get out of there fast."

"I would've picked you up," he said with a frown. "You know I would've picked you up."

"I didn't want to ruin your night." I included Tim in my smile. "The two of you didn't need an idiot like me screwing up the date. Anyhow, Logan took me to his house."

Dominic got up to grab another can of soda. "His house. That's cozy."

"It didn't mean anything." That was the part that really sucked. "He was the designated driver before . . . not the point. So I puked and he told me all about Chelsea." I found myself searching for details that weren't altogether clear. "Something about how confident she is. He said she dumped him right after some big dance."

"What's the problem then?" asked Tim.

"That was ages ago, before she started flirting and he looked down her shirt in front of me and they made out in a gazebo."

"Okay, what else?" Corey said. "You're leaving stuff out. I can tell."

"He was great. Made me drink water. Loaned me clothes to sleep in. And, no, he didn't help me change," I said, knowing that Corey had been about to ask. "Everything was great. He told me a secret or something and then I fell asleep."

"What was the secret?" Chris jumped back into the conversation. Then looked defensive as everyone stared at him. "What? I want to know the secret."

"It wasn't much of a secret. Something about not liking the way I looked at Patrick this one time."

Corey's hand tightened reflexively to squeeze Tim's in excitement. "He said that!"

"Yeah, something along those lines. Then he said we were friends and I thought, *Okay, maybe not EXACTLY what I want, but it could be worse.* And things were fine between us until he let *a real secret* slip out. Apparently, he went behind my back and threatened Alex Thompson." I felt my indignation return in full force.

"Wait, who's Alex?" Tim wanted to know.

"The asshole who was pushing Mackenzie around."

"Oh." He soaked this in. "Then why do we care if Logan threatened him?"

"Because he didn't ask me for permission! It was stupid male macho garbage that I really don't need in my life."

"Wait a second," Corey interrupted. "Since when do people have to check in with you before helping you out? He wanted Alex to leave you alone and he made it happen."

"*I* made it happen!"

"So the real problem was that he stepped on your pride."

"Well." I had to think about that one. "Maybe . . ."

"Here's a question for you: what if it had been me?"

"What if what had been you?"

"What if I told you Alex kept shoving me around in the boys' locker room and kept making gay slurs directed at me. What would you do?"

My hands had curled into fists, and I could feel the anger pooling inside me. "Did he really do that to you, Corey? Did you report him to Principal Taylor?"

"Good ol' boy Taylor whose life revolves around our school athletics won't do anything that might jeopardize his star tackle." The bitterness was back in his voice.

"I'd—I'd, damn, I'd totally pick a fight with him." I looked down at my clenched hands. "I'd get pummeled, but it'd be worth it."

"Interesting, isn't it? You didn't need to ask for my permission first."

"That's completely different," I protested.

"I don't see how. You want to take a swing at him, and it has nothing to do with believing I'm weak. It has everything to do with the fact that I'm your best friend and he's blatantly homophobic. When you think a friend needs you, you don't always think clearly." He grinned at me. "We'd have to scrape you off the cafeteria floor."

"Hey!" I said defensively. "I'd do all right."

"My point is that you may not like his methods, but whatever Logan did worked. And as your best friend, I'm glad he did it. I wish I had thought to do it myself, actually."

"Corey, that's so not important right now. Is he leaving *you* alone?"

He grinned. "Look, I took care of it, so no need to attack him with a textbook, okay? After Taylor blew me off, I lodged a complaint with the guidance center. They hauled everyone in for a 'discussion.' " His smile was filled with humor. "My parents wore their rainbow What Part of Equality Don't You Understand? shirts. I'm really lucky to have so much support. Lots of people don't." His expression swiftly became serious. "I just hope he didn't go after you as a way to get at me."

I laughed. "No, I'm pretty sure he hates me plenty on my own. I wish you'd told me about it earlier."

His grin cocked back into place. "I didn't want you doing anything stupid. So . . . what happened after your hissy fit?"

"I do not have hissy fits," I said prissily. "I have heated arguments."

"Right. What happened next?"

It was strange trying so hard to recall what had been said only a few hours earlier. I blamed the tequila.

"I was trying to set boundaries, or something . . . it was, weird. Anyhow, I ended up quitting my job and royally pissing him off." I shrugged as if it didn't matter what Logan thought of me, even though, of course, it did. "I might have said something about him and Chelsea being perfect for each other. You sort of had to be there." I scanned the disbelieving faces of the boys in the tour bus with me. "What?"

"This is better than cable," Chris decided.

Dominic shook his head. "She's like an accident on the side of the road. I just can't seem to look away."

"I'm not that bad!" I insisted. I turned to Corey for confirmation. "Right?"

"You're worse. Why didn't you just stab a number two pencil through him while you were at it."

I stared at Corey in total confusion. I understand textbooks and I can make sense out of history lectures, but with real people . . . well, I wish they came with flashcards and translations.

"What are you talking about?"

"He's into you. Or he *was* anyway." Corey turned to the other three boys to get a consensus.

"Yeah."

"Sounds like the guy was into you."

"Definitely."

It just shows how strange my life had become that having a tribunal of rock stars discussing my love life felt normal to me.

"No way."

Corey shook his head. "Think about it."

So I did. I sat back in my plush leather seat while the guys talked amongst themselves and I thought about Logan Beckett. And this time I pretended that I was an impartial observer—a scientist looking to catalogue flirtatious behavior among high school male adolescents.

That impartiality didn't work too well when I remembered how he had deflected the conversation from me, sat down next to Jane, and taken the time to really listen to her. I mentally shrugged. For all I knew, maybe he was interested in Jane that way. Or maybe he was just a nice guy who had been born with social skills. None of that meant he liked me.

But as I replayed our almost-date at the mall that first day with the paparazzi chasing us, I thought Corey might have a point. The way he had grinned at me over kung pao chicken before telling me about his dyslexia could've meant anything. But combined with everything else . . .

"Oh, crap!"

Corey nodded. "My sentiments exactly."

They let me silently mull over how, exactly, I'd completely failed to notice that Logan, the most notable of Notables, had been interested in me as more than a tutor.

And now I had to figure out a way to make everything better.

Chapter 35

I called my mom about ten times from the road, which seemed a bit excessive to the guys, but I knew it would make her happy. Plus I thought when she got off work and sat down to go through her voice mail she'd appreciate the messages I'd left for her.

Messages like:

Me: Hey, Mom! It's me calling you again. We're just passing . . . Corey, where are we? Okay, well, Corey thinks we're near Ashland or Medford . . . or something. He's not too sure. But the bus driver knows exactly where we are, so everything's fine. Thanks again for letting me do this. I've got to go though since Tim's bugging me to try one of his new songs as a duet. Maybe you can hear the guitar in the background. That's him. Yeah, I know, Tim! On the phone here! Okay, I really have to go. Call you soon. Love you!

Click.

Corey and I both called Jane from the road too. She said she was glad we were having fun, that she'd be sure to see Ellen interview me, and that the two of us should try to get some homework done on the bus because otherwise we were never going to get caught up. That was exactly what we needed to hear to make us actually open the textbooks we'd brought along. Jane might be a bit on the staid, serious side, but she's the best person to go to when a reality check was needed. Even if she did throw in a few "Oh, Kenzie's."

So I took care of a large chunk of my homework, which would be superdifficult for any teenage girl who found herself on a tour bus with the very attractive members of a boy rock band. Talk about messing with your concentration. I worked for as long as I could and then dealt with Dylan. He called just to find out if "yes, I was fine" and "no, I would not ask Chris, Tim, or Dominic for a signed copy of their latest CD for him."

Little brothers. Even when they're concerned about your welfare, they can be awfully annoying.

But even with the phone calls and homework to distract me, most of the ride was spent hanging out and talking, which gave me more than enough time to really get to know the guys.

I bet you want to know everything.

Too bad.

You'll have to watch VH1 *Behind The Music,* just like everyone else.

I can tell you that we had a few jam sessions along Interstate 5—and that we sounded really good. I thought maybe that whole singing-onstage-with-Tim YouTube video clip had been some kind of fluke. I expected to join in on the vocals only for them to holler, "Stop! Stop! You're off-key! This is too painful!"

But instead, Tim kept saying stuff like, "Let's try having you come in about two beats earlier, so you actually start before I do. Okay, sounds good. Now what if you . . ."

It went on like that for well over three hours. By the end of it, the song sounded freaking awesome. It was like all the vocals layered over each other to create this really great texture. Kind of like baklava: all sweet and delicious, layered and smooth—and by the end of it my voice was so entwined in the song that I thought of it as mine too. It would still sound good without me . . . but I was totally the honey drizzle that kept the layers sticking.

That's right: the honey drizzle.

So when *Ellen*'s producer called again, asking if I'd sing with ReadySet, I instantly agreed. The song needed me—and that was a direct quote from Timothy Goff. In fact, Tim had already set up some time for us in a recording studio after the interview. I didn't let myself think about that. I had enough to worry about just being interviewed by Ellen. Old Mackenzie would have been freaking out, hyperventilating into a brown paper bag, and begging Tim to call whomever he needed to contact *to get me out of it!* But every time I felt my panic level rising to the danger zone I reminded myself that I was in control. I was making all the decisions. I even sort of enjoyed the sensation. I could feel the quick jumping of my pulse, and it made me feel so *alive*.

That's what had been missing from my life before. I'd been comfortable, I'd been invisible, and for the most part, I'd been content.

But I hadn't felt this alive—this wonderfully and terrifyingly vulnerable since, well, ever.

The closer the bus came to its destination the more wired I felt. It was kind of like having a ministroke. I'd laugh at a joke and be totally relaxed while munching on the food we'd grabbed from some greasy fast-food place and then I'd think, *In less than twelve hours, I'll be on the set of* Ellen! Every muscle, tissue, and fiber in my body would constrict and I'd wonder if I had just dreamed it all up. Any second I would wake up and I'd just be Logan's lame tutor, ReadySet wouldn't have heard of me, and I would never get invited to do a talk show. All of this made much more sense as the product of an overactive imagination or a very weird dream.

But when Dominic shook me awake after my second night

sleeping on the leather couch, it was all too real for me to have created the whole thing. Even after I had scarfed down a banana loaf with my mocha Frappuccino I had trouble believing that we'd just roll up to the studio lot, get buzzed inside, and then have interns hustle us off to prep rooms to be made camera ready.

I managed to grab Corey's hand before I could be abducted by a woman who kept barking things into her earpiece like, "We need makeup and wardrobe on standby! Greg, have the mics been checked? Get on that, please." She smiled as she led us through twisting hallways full of props, equipment, and people. "We're so excited about today's show. Did you have a nice drive?"

Before either of us could answer, we reached the makeup room. "Great. Okay, here you are. Sorry we don't have time to talk. Things are crazy right now." She pressed her earpiece. "Cynthia, I said we'd do that next week, honey. Uh-huh." She rolled her eyes expressively. "Okay, well, you need to make it work."

She cut off any reply Corey or I might have had with a quick, albeit distant smile. "Charlene here will have you looking great." She patted my shoulder quickly. "Break a leg, sweetie."

Then she swooped out the way she'd swirled in and demanded that Bryant give her an update stat.

"Think everyone in Hollywood uses pet names?" I muttered nervously to Corey as Charlene wheeled over a mountain of cosmetics.

"Of course they do, snookums. That's how they get out of remembering anyone's actual names."

Charlene chuckled, and the sound was rich, low, and soothing. "Michelle's always a little intense, but she keeps things running." In a movement that showed both grace and years of practice, Charlene flicked open several sets of eyeshadow. "Most everyone here is running on caffeine and determination. That includes me. Now, let's get a good look at you, sweetie."

She gave my face an intense study, as if my every pore needed close examination.

"You have flawless skin," she told me as she pulled out one of her brushes. "You don't need cover-up or anything." She shook her head. "You've probably never had acne a day in your life, have you."

I didn't know what to say to that. "Uh, yeah. That's never been a problem."

Charlene gave another one of her chuckles. "Some people have all the luck. Well, you're making it easier for me. Close your eyes, please."

It was weird to hear myself being described as lucky. I'd spent so many years thinking that everything about myself (with a few exceptions like my mom, brother, and friends) was the product of misfortune. I'd never considered myself lucky with my looks. It was all just too blah. Brown hair, brown eyes, and skin that turned the color of an overripe tomato when I blushed.

Charlene kept up a steady running commentary as she worked on me. "We'll have Michael fix your hair once I'm done. He'll know exactly how best to set off that dress of yours. It's gorgeous. Where'd you get it?"

I shrugged, which I realized was a mistake when she hissed and jerked her hand back before whatever she was applying smudged. I knew that I was in the right outfit. Last night, I hadn't felt so casual when I was pawing through the clothing I hastily packed in my suitcase in a desperate attempt to find something to wear. When I saw the dress, the rich blue one I'd held breathlessly in my bedroom that first day when the packages started coming, I knew that it had been waiting for this. It had been waiting for me to figure out that it was the simplicity in the dress, the stylish but discreet way it draped on curves, that made it me. While that red halter dress I'd worn to the party was fun and flashy, it just didn't suit me the way this did.

Maybe it's stupid, but picking out that dress on my own felt like a step—a big one. While I was glad Corey had nodded his approval after a critical examination, and the rest of the guys had wolf whistled, I would have worn it even if he'd said, "You know, Mackenzie, it's nice but I think we can do better." I knew it was right, and for the first time that was all that mattered.

"BCBG Max Azria." It still felt strange for me to label drop.

"Well, it looks amazing," Charlene continued. "Makes your skin look creamy and really pulls out the brown in your eyes."

I had no idea what she meant. I mean, my eyes are so obviously brown I doubt I need a dress to make them look browner. But it sounded like she approved, so I wisely kept my mouth shut.

"You know who you look like?" she said thoughtfully while applying another coat of something to my eyelids. I really wanted her to just be finished already. "Anne Hathaway. Doesn't she look like a young Anne Hathaway? Right after *The Princess Diaries* or something."

"Yeah, she does actually." I could hear the amusement in Corey's voice and was tempted to risk the annoyance of Charlene and sneak a peak at him. Then I remembered she was doing eyeliner and quickly shut my eyes again.

"She could even pull off a Keira Knightley look." Charlene moved to my mouth, and I felt her coat my lips with something that stung but in a good way. "She's stunning, but too thin in my opinion. She looks like she could use a week's worth of home-cooked meals," she clucked. "They say there's no such thing as too thin in Hollywood, but trust me, honey, it's not true. You don't go starving yourself, now. Blot."

"I won't," I promised as I followed her orders.

"Good." She carefully applied mascara for me. I had to keep reminding myself that I should trust the professional as the wand came closer and closer to my eye. It was hard for me not to flinch. "You're ready for Michael now, honey." She shut her makeup case with a satisfying snap. "Just be yourself and you'll be fine."

It was great advice, and I kept mentally repeating it to myself while Michael, Corey, and I chatted about the show and the celebrities whose hair had been in his hands. I actually turned Charlene's words into my own personal mantra. Be myself. Just be myself. To my own self, be true.

That was what I thought, punctuated by, *Oh, my God, I'm really going to do this!* on an endless loop as I stood in the wings waiting for my introduction, for the music to play, for my cue to be given.

Then it was showtime.

Chapter 36

Ellen DeGeneres played the YouTube video before my introduction—well, the last twenty seconds or so. Just enough for the audience to see my frantic expression and Alex's shocked one as I pumped away with the chest compressions. My screaming set of questions (AM I KILLING HIM RIGHT NOW?) blared out, much to the amusement of everyone in the room. So when I strolled onto the stage with jellyfish legs, it was to the sounds of applause and laughter from the studio audience.

I smiled at the audience, which was gyrating to one of ReadySet's megahits as I focused on placing one foot in front of the other. Suddenly, I was getting a friendly hug from Ellen, who is even prettier up close than on TV. Her short blond hair and blue eyes gleamed under the set lights. It made me wonder if she had someone like Charlene following her around everywhere backstage. I doubted it. She just seemed too low-key casual for that, especially since she was wearing basic jeans, sneakers, a white shirt, and a vest. It's not everyone who can pull off a vest, but Ellen made it look surprisingly good.

"Hi, Mackenzie," Ellen said, releasing me from the hug so we could both sink into the überplushy furniture.

"Hi. Thanks for having me on the show."

Good. Words were coming out of my mouth. That was a very good sign.

"Thanks for being here. So about that YouTube video . . ."

I laughed self-consciously. "Yeah. That was pretty embarrassing."

"It's hilarious. It really is one of the funniest things I have ever seen. When he started twitching and you just shoved him back into the pavement." She laughed. "You really had no idea he was fine?"

I shook my head. "I wish it had all been an act, but the video wasn't planned. I'm not a good actor. I could never convince anyone if it wasn't genuinely me, freaking out."

"Have you thought about taking any CPR classes?"

I grinned at her even though that question had been haunting me through the halls of Smith High School. Actually what I heard the most were catcalls of, "Hey, Mackenzie! Want to practice mouth-to-mouth?" but it was similar. It made me wonder whether Logan and Spencer had talked to anyone else at school for me. I made myself focus on the question again. My one moment on national television was not the time to obsess over some boy. Even Logan.

"No CPR plans at the moment, and after that experience I have definitely ruled out medicine as a possible career."

"So tell me about this video. Who did all the filming? It's remarkably steady."

"You know what? I honestly don't know. That's one mystery I haven't solved. I just came home and found my little brother, Dylan, freaking out."

Ellen grinned. "What did he say?"

"Well, he yelled about how I was all over the Internet. Then he mentioned shipping me off somewhere until the embarrassment died down. I think he wanted to disown me."

"Well, that was brotherly." Ellen's deadpan made everyone laugh.

"No, he was great. Not at first, maybe, but my family and

friends have really been great about all of this. It hasn't been easy on them either. When you hear that I became famous over YouTube, it sounds like my life has suddenly become all about rock stars and designer clothes. That's been part of it for sure, but it's been way more complicated. I'm talking *crowds* of people taking pictures and the paparazzi following me—and that's just the obvious stuff. There have been all sorts of crazy rumors going around."

"Rumors about what?"

"Sex . . . drugs . . . rock and roll."

"Speaking of rock and roll," Ellen segued, and the audience laughed, knowing exactly where she was going with her lead-in. "We heard you were awfully close with a certain rock star."

And then up on the screen behind her was a blown-up copy of Tim and me at the concert. Blown up 300 percent you could really see the dopey, awestruck expression on my face, which had more to do with singing onstage than being love-struck . . . but nobody else knew that.

"Uh, yeah," I managed. "That's Tim."

"Oh, you call him Tim. Do you call him anything else? Like, say, 'my boyfriend.' "

I couldn't help snorting with laughter. Which must have appeared oh-so attractive on television, but the whole thing was just ridiculous. Hearing Ellen guess about my love life (well, Tim's love life) tempted me to say, "No, Ellen, see he's dating my best friend Corey." Then Corey could wave lamely at the camera from his seat in the audience. But even though I knew Ellen would love that, I couldn't *out* my best friend and his new rock star boyfriend on national television.

So instead I said, "No, Ellen. Tim is just a friend. He's a really great guy, but there's nothing like that going on between us. He's actually involved with someone at the moment."

The audience let out a sigh, which probably included some

disappointment from his loyal female fan base. If only they knew.

"He's really great at giving relationship advice though—all the guys are, actually."

Maybe I should've just waited for Ellen to ask another question.

"Have you become close with the other members of the band?"

"Uh, Chris and Dominic? Sure. I rode down here on the tour bus with all of them."

"Sounds like you were surrounded by some very attractive young men."

I wasn't sure how to respond,

"Um, yeah. I guess I was. It wasn't a big deal though. The guys were great."

"Oh, I bet."

I tried to hold back another snort. "It wasn't like that. These guys are actually my friends, which happened surprisingly fast. I guess when you spend two days on the road, that happens, though."

"So you spent two days on the road with a group of rock stars. What did you have to talk about?"

"It was funny, actually. My friend Corey asked about my love life, so suddenly I had all the boys translating guy speak for me."

"Ah, guy speak. That's kind of like Pig Latin, isn't it?"

Ellen makes everything funnier. Although I guess she has to, since that's her job.

"Yeah, see, guy makes no sense to me. So they were all giving me dating advice. Which I greatly appreciated."

Ellen's eyes twinkled with mirth. "Really. Is your love life that confusing?"

"Oh, yeah."

"Tell us about it."

"Well, there are these guys and . . . I cannot believe I am sharing this on national television!"

"Can't stop now!"

But I probably should have.

"Well, I guess I was interested in both of them, only I didn't realize it. And both of them hardly knew I existed, so it didn't seem to matter what I thought. Until the videos hit YouTube, and they really started talking to me."

"Ooh," said Ellen. "I like the sound of this."

"Yeah, apparently when you're famous, people pay attention. Anyhow, I went to a party—where *I did not do drugs*. I was just trying not to geek out, because this was the first party I'd ever been invited to, when they walked over."

I could feel all eyes glued to me, and I knew the story would be all over school by the next day, but I didn't care. I was taking charge.

"Uh-oh."

"Right. So one of them took me outside, and I'm trying not to trip in my heels since I've never worn them before and they're already cutting off my circulation."

"Ouch," said Ellen feelingly. "That's why I wear sneakers."

"That would have felt significantly better. Anyhow, we're outside, and it's a beautiful night, and he's looking soulfully into my eyes." I turned toward her and opened mine a little wider to demonstrate. "Kind of like this. And I'm thrilled he even knows my name . . . when he tells me that he loves me."

I made a face so that everyone could tell I wasn't enamored with Patrick's declaration. The weird thing was, while I knew I should *definitely* be keeping my mouth shut, I thought it was fair game. Patrick had accused me of only being after the fame, and I was making him regret those words in a very real way. It was more than a little fun to watch karma kick into action.

"The nerve! Saying that he loves you. What an awful thing to do." Ellen couldn't keep her face straight.

"To be fair, my reaction was bad. Really bad. He said, 'I love you,' and all I could come up with as a response was, 'No, you don't.' "

The audience roared with appreciative laughter.

"Seriously. And while we were doing the whole, 'Yes, I do' 'No, you don't' back-and-forth thing, I saw the other guy making out with the most popular girl in school."

Everyone said "aw" sympathetically, which actually made me feel better about the whole thing. I had no idea that discussing my personal life on television would feel so . . . therapeutic.

"So that's why it was great having a whole panel of guys giving me advice."

"Apologizing here might work." Ellen turned toward a camera. "She didn't mean it, 'I love you' boy!"

"Well, actually I did."

"I'm confused. What was wrong with 'I love you' boy?"

"Nothing, really. It's just . . . okay, he's the type who'd buy someone roses for Valentine's Day. Which on the surface is great. Nothing wrong with roses. But even if you dropped some serious hints that what you *really* wanted was an artichoke with a big pink bow on it so that you could have a heart-ichoke, he'd still get the generic roses. And for me . . ."

"You want an artichoke." Ellen made it sound ridiculous but not in a bad way. Just like it was really funny.

"Yeah, I want an artichoke."

Put that way, my life made a lot more sense. Logan was an artichoke. He was multilayered and a bit prickly, but he was also edgy and fun and different. I should have recognized it before, but I guess I'd been too thrown off by his Notableness.

"Well, I bet you'll have no trouble getting them now. So

after this first video hit YouTube, you became a singer. You have a wonderful voice. Why don't you tell us about that."

"Well, Tim sent me an invitation to his Portland concert, and I took two of my friends backstage. So Corey and Jane"—I paused and waved at the camera with a sheepish grin. "Hi, Jane!"

Ellen waved too. "Hi, Jane."

"She's going to love that. Anyhow, the three of us went to the concert, and after I stopped mentally shrieking at being in their proximity, we got to know the guys. So when Tim invited me out onto the stage, my friend Corey—that's Corey." I pointed at him and, startled, he smiled at the camera that had swiveled around to face him. "Corey thought it'd be funny to make me go onstage. That scared the hell out of me, since I'm not overly confident about my dancing skills."

Which was totally the wrong thing to say in front of Ellen. She grinned.

"It's easy. Let's see what you've got."

Since she was out of her chair and dancing to the music that was instantly beating through the room, I couldn't exactly refuse. Especially since the audience was cheering for me. That's how I ended up dancing on *The Ellen DeGeneres Show* even after I promised myself I wouldn't.

It was thankfully short, and as we settled back into our seats she gave me a warm smile that was full of amusement.

"You were fine."

"Hah. Thanks. That's sweet of you to say. But when I was at the concert I completely froze, so Corey rushed on as a dance partner. Then Tim thought it'd be funny to get me to sing with him for a bit . . . and the rest is on YouTube."

"Well, you sound terrific. Do you have any singing plans?"

"You know, I really don't. I'm flattered that people like the clip, but I know I don't have the drive you need to make it in the industry. On the bus ride here the guys and I fooled around a bit—"

"Aha!"

"Musically!" I laughed. "We worked on a song together that I think we're going to play for you. And if no one throws tomatoes, then I'll record it in the studios with them—but that's going to be it. Then it's back to studying for AP tests and tutoring."

Although, I probably shouldn't have mentioned the tutoring, given the precarious way I'd left things with Logan.

"Well, we can't wait to hear it. But before we do, I've got something for you."

I sat up straighter. "You didn't have to. Really, Ellen, just being here is more than exciting enough."

"Well, we found something that every studious, awkward girl needs. Especially if she's going to stay in touch with her rock star boy 'friend.' "

She handed me a rectangular package that had some serious weight to it. I ripped off the wrapping paper in quick, economical movements to reveal something that quite frankly made my heart do a squeezing palpitation thing.

It was a laptop. A brand-new MacBook. I was instantly sure of that when I felt the squishy laptop case. Of course Ellen's face was branded across the cover, and it read Ellen-Book—but that just made it even cooler.

I didn't scream. That in itself is a minor miracle considering the way Ellen DeGeneres casually handed me the very thing I'd been obsessing over for months. I'd wasted so much time calculating: How many hours of tutoring would it take? What if I did some babysitting on the weekend? How many months of setting aside every dollar before a laptop would be mine? All of that work, and the computer was just handed to me with no strings attached.

I remembered Logan's accusation: that I'd just been using him for a laptop—and I knew that in the beginning he might have been right. I cared about doing the job, being responsible, earning my wages, but I didn't particularly care about him. And now, that had changed. If I did go back to the tu-toring he'd know that the laptop had nothing to do with it.

Because now the laptop was mine . . . and it had nothing to do with him.

I clutched at the computer in disbelief. "Oh, my God," I gasped. "Thank you so much! I love it!"

Ellen smiled broadly. "Glad you like it. The very talented band ReadySet will be here after this message. Don't go away."

And with that, the show stopped recording for a commercial break.

Chapter 37

Before I had time to breathe, Tim, Chris, and Dominic were set up onstage and ready to go. Right next to Tim was an empty mic waiting for me. Which was craziness, since what I had said to Ellen was completely true: I had a nice little voice. Emphasis on little. I was not going to be on *American Idol* anytime ever.

"Nervous?" Ellen asked, although I thought the answer was obvious.

"Uh, terrified really."

"You're going to be great."

I needed to hear her say that more than I wanted to admit.

"I really appreciate all of this," I told her, gesturing at my laptop. "It feels rather surreal, but . . . thanks." I ran a hand through my hair and hoped that I hadn't just accidentally destroyed the look Michael had painstakingly created. "It's just, I've never been in the spotlight before. I've never wanted it! I've always been the awkward girl people only notice when they need help with homework. And now I'm spilling my personal life for everyone in America and I'm going to sing with a famous rock group and . . . it's just insane!"

Ellen listened. I think that's why she's so good at her job. She really knows how to listen.

"You don't have to be anyone but yourself."

I stifled a groan. "I know! I mean, that's what people keep telling me. But it's not that easy, is it? Because what if myself is just boring?"

She shrugged. "Do you think you're boring?"

I laughed and looked back at the mic. "Not at the moment."

"Then I don't think you need to worry about it. You seem plenty interesting to me. You're going to be great."

"Ellen, we're starting in five, four, three, two . . ." one of the cameramen announced loudly.

"Hi, so we're back with Mackenzie Wellesley and ReadySet. You ready, Mackenzie?"

I smiled. "I think so."

And for the first time in the past two weeks, I felt sure. I had practiced on the bus with these guys for hours. If I had sucked, they would have let me know. So I took my position in the group before I gave Tim my nod.

The band burst into life, and I was in the heart of it. It was even better than it had been at the Rose Garden in Portland. For one thing, this time I knew exactly what Tim wanted— he'd drilled me on it long enough in the bus. I still felt the churning of adrenaline and panic, but I tamped it down. Some part of me kept saying, *This is your first and last major performance, Mackenzie! Make it good!*

I rocked out to the music. I kept my eyes on Corey in the audience and belted the song out like I was in my bedroom back home. The nice thing about singing is that when you do it, you're not expected to dance. So Tim and I hit the vocals with everything we had, and Corey would probably say I sang with "attitude" into the mic. It was like my own Sasha Fierce had jumped out and taken over. Except, I felt right somehow. More than that, I felt brave.

The whole thing was finished almost as quickly as it had begun. I was shooed offstage before Ellen conducted an interview with a real A-list star (I think it was Robert Pattinson promoting his latest movie). Not that I cared, because the second we were backstage I was engulfed in a huge group hug. Tim kept crowing, "Did you hear that! We were fricking awesome!"

Only he didn't say "fricking," and I didn't make any comments on his language.

"That," I said when I could finally speak, "was amazing!"

Tim whipped out his cell phone. "I'm going to see if we can get an earlier time slot at that recording studio. I want to drop this single fast." He flashed me his most charming smile. "You were dead-on. Damn, Mackenzie. You were freaking perfect. You can't go back to Oregon now. We need you for vocals."

Tim didn't say "freaking," either, but I was more distracted by the way Chris and Dominic were nodding their heads in agreement like synchronized bobbleheads.

I gave myself one moment to fantasize about how my life could be as a member of ReadySet. Spending my life on the road and in recording studios, going to events like the Grammys, and chatting at parties with people like Robert Pattinson about Ellen and other mutual friends. It sounded pretty damn cool. Except . . .

"I have to go back home, just like I had to come here. I had to prove to myself that I could face the press. But now"—I shrugged—"I'm ready to say good-bye to the music industry and fade from the public eye."

Tim's mouth dropped open. "You're kidding me! I thought that was just to build up the story! You can't *stop*. You had so much fun onstage!"

I pictured Jane and Melanie eating lunch together with the other new freshman girls in my absence. "I'll have fun at home too. I'll record the song, and if any of you are ever near Portland, you can always crash at my place. I'm seriously going to miss you guys." I wrapped my arms around Chris and then Dominic. "But as much as I hate it, I'm not finished with high school."

Tim couldn't accept that easily. He spent the rest of the day trying to convince me to change my mind or, in his words, "to stop being such an idiot." I didn't take offense. It actually felt good to be wanted as we laid down my vocals in the studio . . . even though the process seemed to take forever. We had to order in pizza because the time crunch was so intense, what with our flight back to Portland the next morning. We even had cots brought into the studio so that we could nap while technicians tinkered with equipment. Apparently that's how rock stars pull all-nighters. By the time my part of the track was finished, all of us were so exhausted we only had the energy to exchange sleepy good-byes. Tim made me promise to keep in touch even if I persisted in "ignoring the opportunity of a lifetime." And while I didn't think I was making a mistake, even in my sleep-deprived state, I knew I was going to miss them.

Dominic, Chris, and I went to hail a cab so that Tim and Corey could have some privacy with their good-bye. Judging by the gleam in Corey's eyes they'd definitely moved beyond handholding. Well, that and the fact that he spent the entire ride to the airport as well as the flight back to Portland discussing the likelihood of a long-distance relationship working out. I listened as he tried to convince himself it would be a snap. Then I had to make supportive cooing noises as he showed me all the text messages he and Tim had sent each other.

I really hoped I'd never been this annoying with my guy issues.

The whole thing was sickeningly cute. Especially since the closer we got to landing in Portland, the more nervous I became. What the hell had I been thinking telling that much about my personal life on *Ellen*? I'd just *had* to start babbling, only this time what came out was way worse than a random historical fact. "I love you boy" was going to want me to drop dead. He probably wasn't the only one either. I briefly considered starting a list of people who had reason to hate my guts.

Patrick. Alex. Chelsea. Logan.

I slowly realized that I had mentioned Logan on national television—worse, I had admitted to having a crush on him. I really hoped that whole making-out-with-Chelsea thing wasn't supposed to be a secret, because it was definitely going to come out now. Spencer would probably hate me too—if he didn't already.

It looked like I had a whole lot of groveling to do.

So I was lost in my thoughts when Corey's parents picked us up at the airport. Thankfully they were the only welcoming committee. Apparently, my very public interview had done what my hiding hadn't—made me a nonissue. Tim had told me last night that since I had made it clear the two of us weren't dating, I was officially a C-list star. At least one thing was going my way. I didn't have to say anything in the car, because Corey was speaking so quickly that I couldn't get a word in edgewise—which let me continue stewing over my life in peace.

My financial situation was different now. I hadn't even begun to process the coolness of laying down a track when Tim's agent handed me paperwork for the royalties on the song I was now being featured in. That's right: royalties.

I probably should have seen it coming, but to be honest I was really doing the whole recording thing as a favor. After all the work we put into perfecting the song on the bus, there was no way I could back out of recording it. But it honestly never occurred to me that I'd be getting paid. Even if, according to Tim, it was a pittance of what I could make if I stayed on.

That royalties thing had changed everything. Sure, it was

just one song, but as soon as that album dropped (and you know it's going to go platinum. This is *ReadySet* we're talking about!) I was going to receive checks in the mail. The whole thing was crazy, especially knowing that millions of people would snag it from iTunes. Even if I only got a nickel from every download . . . that was a lot of nickels.

And yeah, I wasn't going to suddenly buy my mom a nicer house, but paying for college without a mountain of student loans didn't seem quite so impossible. Not to mention I now had an awesome topic for an application essay.

All it took was humiliating myself on the Internet to make all my dreams come true.

Well, most of them.

Maybe some of those dreams, like having Patrick interested in me and getting my dad's attention, had been awful . . . but at least my family was still intact.

But some of my dreams, like expanding my social group beyond Corey and Jane, had worked shockingly well.

I'd been brave too. After years of hiding in the wings, I'd conquered the center stage. I'd even out-Notabled the Notables, and I still thought I was pretty much the same person. If I could handle all of that, I could probably even take on Chelsea Halloway . . . although I would still prefer not to.

Now I just had to see whether I could work my way through an apology with someone who might very possibly want me dead.

Chapter 38

Ionly made a couple stops between my home and the hockey rink. Corey's parents dropped me off and I lugged my stuff up to my room, called my mom so she wouldn't worry, and showered off the sweaty nastiness that came from being squeezed in a tiny plane between Corey and an obese armrest hog.

There was no way I could make it for any part of the school day. Okay, *technically* I could've gone to school to pick up more assignments, but that could wait for one more day. So keeping a close eye on the clock, I slipped into a casual outfit of jeans, flats, and a loose plaid shirt over a plain tee and a jacket. Nothing flashy. Nothing that screamed for attention—normal regular clothes that felt like me.

Once I was dressed, I grabbed my roomy messenger tote, an old pair of Dylan's hockey skates, and my iPod. I had to move fast in case I lost my nerve. I spent the whole plane ride going through "what-if" scenarios, but there was only one way to find out. So I put on my happiest, most chipper music and I tried to enjoy the walk. The weather was surprisingly nice for December in Forest Grove. There were still heavy clouds—Oregon weather practically requires it to be overcast—but there were icy patches of blue peeking out here and there. And there were twinkle lights hanging on the buildings and trees that would light up the puny downtown beautifully when night fell. The chill air felt good against my skin, making me appreciate the warmth of the bank even more when I walked in to make my first withdrawal after years of deposits.

It was weird having money in my pocket. I didn't even think to bring a wallet since I had never needed one before. I quickened my pace, ducked into a Blockbuster, and tried not to overthink my situation. *Just go with your instincts,* I told myself, *like a jungle cat or something.*

Shaking my head at the inane metaphor, I paused only to tuck my overthought-so-it-doesn't-really-count-as-an-impulse-buy purchase into my bag next to the skates. As I approached the rink I told myself I was doing the right thing. This was much better than an impersonal text message saying "Let's talk" or an awkward phone message of me going, "Uh, hey, Logan. It's me, Mackenzie. Um . . . so, this is awkward. Can we, um, get together and talk?"

Meeting up with him at the hockey rink wasn't *stalking,* I told myself. It wasn't my fault I had his schedule memorized. If he hadn't wanted me to know where he'd be, then he never should have hired me in the first place. It wasn't like now that I was no longer his tutor, his schedule flew right out of my head.

It'd be better for this particular confrontation *not* to take place at school. I stepped into the chill of the hockey rink, as cold radiated from the ice. I zipped up my jacket and felt a rush of adrenaline spike through my system.

Down girl, I told myself. *You handled being on* Ellen. *You can handle this.*

I settled down into the booth, only instead of pulling out textbooks so I could pretend to be working while I secretly watched the guys, I took out the skates and began lacing up.

I waited nervously for the practice to be over. I stood up when the coach blew his whistle and made my approach while everyone was paying attention to his words of advice or whatever it was he was saying.

I was standing right by the entrance to the ice when the guys started leaving. Most of them looked at me curiously but kept going right past me and into the locker room. I could hear the little voice in my head screaming, *MAYDAY! MAYDAY! ABORT MISSION! ABORT!!!*

Did I listen? No-o-o.

"Uh, hey, Patrick," I said, as he started to move past me. "How's it going?"

Stupid. Stupid.

He gave me a look that had about as much heat as the ice he'd just left. "Fine."

"Good."

He nodded and left, leaving me oddly pleased that we'd managed one short, polite conversation.

Maybe he didn't completely hate me. That was something.

Spencer tossed a friendly smile my way when he noticed me standing there. He was locked in conversation with Logan and the coach, and as I watched he elbowed Logan and jerked his head ever so slightly in my direction.

I watched Logan as his eyes scanned the area Spencer had indicated before they settled on me. There was a long pause and I couldn't move. Logan was fifteen feet away listening to the coach and looking right through me. Spencer muttered something that I couldn't catch, but Logan's disinterested shrug needed no translation.

I fought the urge to flee by reminding myself that I couldn't run away every time I felt uncomfortable, embarrassed, or hurt. Plus I really couldn't make a quick or graceful getaway in hockey skates. At best I could waddle back to the booth and try to exchange the skates for sneakers before Logan could reach me—but then I'd only look like a coward. So I stiffened my back and, clutching my messenger bag for good luck, I stepped onto thin ice—metaphorically and literally.

The coach, a pudgy balding man in a Windbreaker, laid a thick hand on Logan's shoulder and said something about watching the defensive line before skating away. I moved slowly onto the ice toward the boys. It felt like a horrible dream where every time you're about to cross the finish line it jumps back another twenty feet. Cautiously I adjusted to having ice under me and was able to glide over to them.

"Uh, hey," I said, and turned to Spencer first because looking at him was easier than seeing the complete disinterest radiating off of Logan. "Sorry about . . . you know, getting trashed at your party. Not my finest moment."

He laughed. "Next time we'll have you stick to Coke."

Which made me feel a flutter of hope because he'd just said, "Next time." As in, I could come back even though I had thoroughly humiliated myself the first time. Maybe I wasn't completely in the doghouse after all. I looked at Logan to see what he made of this whole "next time" thing, but he just seemed bored.

So I was in the doghouse after all.

"Sounds good," I managed.

"We'll only put a little rum in it." His smile was quick and filled with humor. "I've got to head out. I'll see you later, man." He called that last part over his shoulder to Logan as he moved with the confident speed of long practice over to the exit.

That left the place empty except for Logan and me. Which wasn't intimidating or scary at all. Oh, wait—yes, it was.

"So . . ." I began awkwardly. "We should talk."

"Okay. Talk."

He really wasn't going to make it easy for me. Determined to be as casual as he was about all of this, I started skating laps, and it didn't surprise me when he matched my pace with minimal effort.

"I owe you an apology. It was really nice of you to help me

out at the party. You were under no obligation and I appreciate it."

He shrugged and still looked bored. "That it?"

"No." I stifled back a wave of annoyance. "I'm sorry I
yelled at you over the Alex thing. I'm used to handling things
myself. I actually prefer it that way, but it was nice of you to
tell him to back off even if I'm not crazy about the way you
handled it."

"Okay."

I shook my head in disbelief and wondered why I'd even
wasted my time and energy on a guy like Logan Beckett.
Here I was, doing the right thing and trying to clear the air,
while he looked like I was explaining the life cycle of a cen-
tipede. Any second and I'd bore him into a coma.

"You know what? That's it. That's all the apology you're
going to get. Take it or leave it." Indignation felt a hell of a
lot better than the queasy nerves I'd had in my stomach. I
dug in my pockets and came out with a fifty-dollar bill.

"Here." I handed it to him with anger pulsing through me.
He took the bill instinctively and then thoughtlessly crumpled it up in his fist as his hand clenched. "Now we're even."

"Not even close," he retorted. "Why are you doing this,
Mackenzie? Dylan told me you fled town to go on *Ellen*. Do
you need more fodder for the media? Is that why you spied
on me in the first place? Or are you here for something else?"
His eyes flashed with anger, and for just a second he looked
as raw as I felt. Then it was gone.

"I'm just doing this to clear the air," I said, but I couldn't
help wondering if that was true. It was the reason I'd given
myself to see him, but part of me, the stupid part, had hoped
that everything would work out between us. That I could go
back to being his tutor and Chelsea would dump him again
and the two of us would get together. Stupid. Very stupid.

"And I wasn't spying on you!" My voice raised an octave.
"How many times do I have to tell you that! I was just out-

side and I happened to see the two of you making out, okay? Not a big deal. I mean: I get it. The two of you have a history, and history repeats itself. And it's none of my business that you were kissing her anyway. I won't mention it again."

I decided not to tell him that I had inadvertently discussed it on *Ellen* already. He'd find out soon enough. And if he did watch my interview, he'd get to see just how much I liked him. I never should have blurted out those details on television. But it was too late to take it back now. Too late to point out that he would be better off with someone smart and sweet and—okay—awkward than with Chelsea. Someone who could make him laugh. Someone like, oh, I dunno, *me!*

"I wasn't," he said shortly.

"What are you talking about?" I demanded. "I was right there. I saw the two of you kissing."

"No, you saw her kissing me. Big difference."

My heart gave a *ka-thump* that I tried very hard to ignore. "It didn't look like you were fending her off with a stick."

"No, I wasn't. She kissed me, and then I explained it wasn't going to happen again." He smiled icily. "Satisfied?"

"Oh," I said, feeling like an idiot. "Well, um. Good to know. Not that it's, you know, any of my business."

Oh, hell, I was seconds away from stuttering.

"Right. Look, let's just forget it. Doesn't matter." He turned smoothly on the ice and started for the exit.

"Hold up!" I nearly did a face-plant as I tried to follow him. "I—I got something for you."

I could see the surprise in his dark blue eyes as he turned around to face me.

"You got something. For me," he stated slowly.

"It was an impulse buy." I smiled and felt my heart do another one of those intense *ka-thumps* as I dug into my messenger bag and pulled it out. "You know, to help clear the air, I guess. Here."

I shoved it at him and watched as he slowly turned his present over and looked at me. "John Adams?"

"Yeah. HBO did this miniseries on him a while ago and I never saw it and I heard it was good." I shrugged nervously. "I understand if you don't want it. I just thought it'd be fun, you know, to watch it. Together."

I'm amazed I could speak. My mouth felt dry and my hands had gone all clammy.

The truth is, there's something way scarier than singing in public, or answering questions about your love life on national television, or being swarmed by the paparazzi. And that's telling the guy (or girl) you like that you like them. Personally, I'd take the *Ellen* show any day over this.

But that's why I had to do it.

"So." Logan looked from me to the DVD box set and then back to me. "You want to be my tutor again?"

"Well, yes and no." I took a deep breath of air that felt extra cold from the chill of the ice skating rink. I really hoped I wasn't making a mistake, and as I hesitated for one last second I remembered the secret Logan had told me. The one he'd probably thought I was too drunk to remember in the morning. About how I'd looked at Patrick that day at Starbucks . . . and how he hadn't liked it.

"I-thought-it-could-be-a-date." The words came out so fast they sort of blurred together. "Or not. That's fine too. And it wouldn't have to be a big deal. Just a movie and some popcorn. Or, you know . . ."

But neither one of us found out what I'd been about to babble because Logan tugged on my jacket until I slid across the ice and bumped into him. Only he didn't seem to mind. Not if the way his mouth instantly covered mine was any indication.

I'd like to say: wow.

If someone had asked me for the name of the second president of the United States (John Adams, of course) I wouldn't have been able to answer ... because when Logan Beckett kissed me, my brain shut down. All the thoughts in my head, the worries, the concerns, the stresses, became as quiet and still as the empty ice skating rink around us. All I could feel were his lips on mine. Oh, and my heart wasn't just doing that single *ka-thump* anymore. It was beating hot and fast.

And I was kissing Logan right back.

"So," I said when we came up for air, "I take it that's a yes to a date."

Pressed against each other that closely I could see every speck of gray in his eyes and I could watch the mouth that had just kissed me brainless spread into a grin. A smug, confident grin that I had never thought I'd have aimed at me. Then again, I had doubted Logan would ever see me as anything besides a geeky tutor. I guess that just goes to show how quickly things can change.

"That's a yes, Mack." He tucked a strand of my hair behind one ear. "You know," he said conversationally as he lightly brushed his lips against mine, "I think we found something you're not awkward at."

"Kissing?"

"Mmm-hmm."

My brain nearly shorted out when he used his fingers to angle my chin.

"Then I guess we should keep doing it."

And that's exactly what we did.

FOOD FOR THOUGHT

1. At the beginning of the novel, Mackenzie blames her mistimed elementary school ballet accident for her parents' divorce. She also feels like her dad ditched them, then replaced them for the ballet teacher and a new family. Have you ever blamed yourself for something that was beyond your control? If you thought you were being replaced, how would you handle it?

2. Everyone at Smith High School thinks of Mackenzie as the resident nerd because she does well in class and is willing to raise her hand when she knows the answer. Does this make her a geek? Is that such a bad thing to be? How does being an outsider come in handy for Mackenzie and her friends?

3. The Notables at Smith High School make popularity look easy and maintain a social hierarchy within the school. How does this change when Mackenzie becomes famous? Are they really as put together up close as Mackenzie first thought they were? Where do you see yourself fitting into your school's social scene? Do you think you would be happier somewhere else?

4. Mackenzie considers herself an Invisible, and therefore below the notice of Notables. How does this perception help when she begins tutoring Logan? How does it hold her back? How does Logan and Mackenzie's relationship change as she is thrust into the spotlight?

5. Chelsea Halloway has a talent for making Mackenzie feel small and insignificant . . . and Mackenzie doesn't know how to deal with it. How should she have tried to

stand up for herself? Was Mackenzie's technique of staying Invisible the smartest path for her to take?

6. When the video of Mackenzie knocking over Alex Thompson hits YouTube, her life gets turned upside down with the force of the insane media attention. Does the media go too far when they chase her and Logan into the mall? Why does the line blur between public and private when someone becomes famous? How would you handle being the center of national attention?

7. The YouTube video makes Mackenzie the center of attention, and even though she doesn't *want* the attention, it comes with some really great perks: great clothes, backstage concert tickets, and access to celebrities. What would you want most if you were to become famous? What aspect of being a celebrity would you hate? Would it make a difference what thrust you into the national spotlight, whether it was because of an accident or an unseen talent?

8. Mackenzie is very responsible when it comes to money, but it can also be a sensitive issue for her. How does her reaction to money differ from Logan's attitude to it? To Spencer's? Is it as simple as when you have money you aren't afraid of spending it? Is it possible to become too obsessed with saving money rather than spending it?

Check out Marni's next book,

FAUXMANCE,

in stores in October 2012.

Chapter 1

I looked like a skank.

I tugged down the green monstrosity wrapped tightly around my waist so that it brushed mid-thigh and I tried to remember why I put up with Jennifer Lawley as my best friend. This time, she had gone too far.

"I can't do this!"

It wasn't the first time I had tried mutiny, and given that I was now *wearing* the aforementioned green monstrosity instead of staring at it on a hanger, I guess she was justified in believing that I'd back down.

But never again.

She plumped up her already cheery red lips and rolled her eyes at me in the mirror.

"Come on, Holly. It's not so bad."

"Not so bad!" I sputtered. "We look like mutants! Worse than that! We look like slutty mutants whose clothing went through a woodchipper!"

"We look like Santa's helpers. Get into the spirit of things already. 'Tis the season, you know!"

Right, because nothing perks up a girl more than hearing Christmas carols twenty-four / seven and being forced to ask little children if they've been naughty or nice lately. And while I hadn't actually asked any kids about their naughty-to-nice ratio, it was only because I had yet to join the crowds in the Westside Pavilion to serve my time as "Santa's Little Helper." I still knew what was coming. Crying babies, and overprotective parents who snapped orders and bitched into their cell phones about their stupid yearly Christmas cards. And given the very short nature of our "Santa's Little Helpers" skirts, I had a feeling that Jen and I would be on the receiving end of more than a few crude suggestions about how we could help certain boys fully enjoy their Christmas season.

Let me tell you: you have to be desperate to agree to become an elf in Los Angeles. Or anywhere else, for that matter.

But that's exactly what I was: desperate. Maybe if I had an allowance, or a regular source of income, I wouldn't have been taking a Christmas cruise to the Mexican Riviera with my grandpa and (wince) my cousins with absolutely nothing appropriate to wear. But my grandpa believes I need to know the true value of money. I know it, all right. . . . It makes the difference between being mocked and accepted.

Under normal circumstances, Jen would tell me how lucky I am to have a grandpa who wants to celebrate his seventy-fifth birthday in paradise. She would be envious of me for trading in smoggy Los Angeles for sunny beaches and fruity drinks. Hell, under normal circumstances, I would be thrilled to go myself. If it weren't for my cousins. To be fair, Andrew and Jacob are okay. I mean, they're teenage boys who would be more than a little interested in noting the length of Jen's short skirt. But they're relatively harmless.

Alison and Claire, on the other hand, are like the Olsen twins on bitch steroids.

I don't think I'm exaggerating here.

Alison and Claire are an amalgamation of all the twenty-first-century social problems: they are self-entitled, material-istic jerks who enjoy online bullying, teasing, and general unpleasantness as hobbies. They also have a talent for detecting every crack in someone's self-esteem, which they then hammer away at until the tormented person breaks into a million shattered pieces.

And I'm lucky enough to share a gene pool with them.

Which is why I know from firsthand experience that if I show up for the cruise wearing the same jeans I've had for the last two years, they'll start calling me Annie again. As in Little Orphan Annie. Because ever since my parents died in a car accident, that's exactly what I've been—an orphan.

Real nice, right?

But it's not all bad. I mean, it's not like I ever knew my parents in any meaningful way. Apparently, I was a fussy baby, so at the nine-month mark they asked my grandpa to watch me for a weekend while they took a much needed mini-break.

And when my exhausted dad fell asleep at the wheel and crashed into a tree, what started as a two-day visit turned into a permanent living situation.

My grandpa was great about the whole thing. There were never any parental duties that he skipped out on. He supported me in becoming a Girl Scout, helped me sell boxes of cookies, and then hugged me tightly when I told him that none of the other girls liked me. He told me they just didn't appreciate my chutzpah the way he did. And even though he went to Synagogue every week, he never pressured me to have a Bat Mitzvah or go by Rachel, my Jewish-sounding middle name. Grandpa understood that after a brutal ten hours of labor on Christmas Day, his Jewish daughter and her Catholic-raised husband thought the prickly name Holly was appropriate.

If only they could see me now—dressed up like a tarty elf.

I tugged down my skirt once again.

"I mean it." I told Jen. "You said I only had to try on the costume and then I could back out. Well, I tried it on. I look like a holiday hooker. Can we go now? I need to start sending copies of my résumé out to department stores."

Jen tugged her own costume down, only she was adjusting the low-dipping green shirt so that it flashed a cheery bit of red bra under the cleavage.

"Like you have a résumé!"

She had a point.

"Then clearly we need to get out of here so that I can make one up and *then* I can start handing it out to department stores."

"The economy, as always, sucks. No one is hiring, Holly. It's a Christmas miracle that we found this job as it is. Now we are going to go out there and spread some holiday cheer!"

I didn't know how she could manage to say that last bit with a straight face.

"A Christmas miracle that has me sluttified and asking people how 'naughty' they've been?" I squawked. "If we were outside, we could get arrested for this!"

"It's not indecent exposure on an elf." She flicked back the red streak in her bangs. "Look, there are *kids* out there and they expect us to make them happy. Are you really going to disappoint the *children?*"

Jen knew I had a soft spot for kids, and if it got me out of the dressing room and into the mall where she could try out her flirting technique in her green elf skirt, then she was going to play the *you can't disappoint the children card* for all it was worth.

"Fine," I grumbled, "but you—"

"Owe you big-time," she finished for me. "Yeah, Holly, I know. Whatever. Now let's boldly go where many elves have gone before."

"Fine. Let's just get this thing over with then."

Jen grabbed my arm and thrust me out the door of the employee bathroom like she didn't trust me to actually leave.

She knows me way too well.

The outside world was an absolute madhouse. Shoppers in December should be forced to take a sedative before trying to purchase presents for loved ones. One particularly frazzled mother was yelling at her daughter, "No, I'm not going to buy you any plastic ponies, Krystal! And if I hear one more word about them, Christmas will be canceled!"

Jen and I were shoved and jostled by strangers who madly searched for just the right gift that said, "I love and appreciate you. Also, I'm sorry about that stupid thing I did last week. Forgive me?" With the pressure to be thoughtful, creative, generous, and sweet all tied into a present, it was a wonder that more people didn't off themselves during the holiday season. It's not so much that I really *minded* Christmas . . . just the way it eclipsed my birthday. My grandpa did his best, but I never had a real party since no parents wanted to schlep their kids around the day after Christmas when they could gaze bleary-eyed at the fake plastic tree sitting in the living room. But when grandpa told me his plans for this year—that in celebration of his mid-December birthday we were spending the holidays on a family cruise with my aunt and her picture-perfect nuclear family—I really wanted to ask if I could stay with Jen in LA instead.

Hence the need for new clothes and the job that forced me to spread holiday cheer. And act jolly. And all that other nonsense.

So I plastered a big ol' smile on my face as Jen and I walked up to the special area where Santa was evidently enjoying the last of his lunch break with a cup of eggnog in his hand.

It wasn't until we were right next to St. Nick that we realized eggnog wasn't the main ingredient in his drink.

Apparently I wasn't the only one having trouble getting into the holiday spirit.

Although he seemed to become significantly more chipper when he spotted Jen and me in our outfits. "C'mere!" he suggested. "Sit on Santa's lap!"

Then he cackled as if he had said something incredibly clever instead of creepily attempting to hit on a pair of high school girls.

Jen clutched my hideous green tunic sleeve. "Oh, my God!" she breathed in horror. "Not Santa!"

Jen was one of those kids who resolutely believed all through elementary school that the big man came down her chimney. She also wanted to give other children that same feeling of magic each year. I didn't care. I mean, I *like* kids, but it's not like they aren't going to figure out *eventually* that they sat on some weird guy's lap every year.

"Yep. It looks like good St. Nick has been a bit on the naughty side this year."

Santa lolled back in his huge chair, apparently oblivious to our whispered conversation.

"Should we report him?" I asked Jen. "Or better yet, can we leave now? The man reeks, and if he spews, we don't want to be the ones cleaning it up."

I might have been hired to prance around in this ridiculous outfit, but no one had said anything about vomit duties—I checked.

"Holly!" Jen practically growled my name. "We don't have time to search for someone! We can't let a pervy Santa near these kids! We have to *do* something now!"

"Okay. I'm not disagreeing with you, Jen. I'm just not sure how you expect us to fix it."

Santa chose that moment to ask me blearily, "So tell me, have you been *naughty* this year?"

Another happy round of cackles followed that witticism.

"Just stay here and try to cover for me," Jen said, marching over to the long line of kids who had been tugging on their parents' sleeves and asking if it was time *yet*. "Um, I'm sorry, folks, but Santa just got an urgent message from his toy shop, so he needs to head for the North Pole straight away. But he's really sorry for the inconvenience and he wishes you all a *Merr-ry Christmas*."

"But he's sitting right there!" an indignant mother snapped. "We've been waiting in this stupid line for over two hours and my son is going to see Santa!"

And that's when all hell broke loose.

The disgruntled parents, children in tow, charged past Jen and headed straight for the highly inebriated Santa, who wasn't so smashed he didn't recognize the danger in a stampede of determined parents.

"Holly!" Jen yelled. So I did the only thing I could think of—I stood right in front of pervy Santa and waved my arms in the universal signal for *Please don't crush me! Please!*

For a brief moment it looked like it might work too. The mob slowed, and I cleared my throat to make some inane promise of a replacement Santa right away, when Santa lived up to his pervy reputation by reaching out and copping a feel of my short, green-clad butt.

And that's why I slapped Santa across the face in front of a whole line of impressionable young children.

Hard.

One second I was seeing red and mentally cursing the stupid commercial holiday and its tacky decorations and repetitive music and the general *crappiness* of my situation and the next a little boy was yelling, "You can't hit Santa! You're a bad elf!" at me.

Then he charged.

The blow to my stomach hurt like hell and forced the wind out of me. I stepped away from the little maniac and promptly tripped over the stair of the Santa platform, crashing into St. Nick, who was the one who had started this whole nightmare. But everyone in line apparently seemed to think that I was trying to commit Santa-cide, so what started as a minor tussle turned into a full-on brawl, with Jen screeching for mall security while attempting to shove her way over to me. Santa, half a dozen enraged shoppers, and I were all rolling around the floor, scrambling, and struggling to breathe given the number of elbows we had received (on purpose and accidentally) right in the gut.

And things only got worse as I went crashing into the mall's fake Christmas tree, which tilted, then toppled over, causing dozens of shiny glass ornaments to shatter upon impact. Everyone—Santa, shoppers, Jen and I—all stopped moving and absorbed the wreckage we had created in a matter of minutes. I was still staring in horror when I felt a firm tug on my arm as mall security started dragging my skanky, elf-clad posterior away while Jen trailed behind us chattering the whole time.

"Well, good riddance! I never really wanted that job in the first place. Too many crazies." Her face brightened. "And now we get to enjoy the holiday without ruining it with work!"

I just glared at her. "I've got a security escort. I'm wearing a slutty elf costume and Santa just groped me. Now might not be the best time to tell me *it was all for nothing!*"

I knew murder was against the law and that killing Santa at Christmas was wrong. But I didn't remember any regulations against elf-icide.

Jen turned her puppy-dog eyes on me. "I'm sorry. Let's go to my house, get out of these stupid clothes and see if I've got something you can wear on the cruise. I'm really sorry, Holly. I'll make it up to you."

Except we both knew that she couldn't when I heard an all too familiar voice yelling out my name.

My grandpa. With my whole family—aunt, uncle, cousins—the lot of them staring at me as if . . . I had just gotten into a fight with Santa.

He shook his head, and I knew it wasn't because he was admiring my chutzpah this time. "We wanted to support you on your first day of work."

Well, that plan had definitely backfired.

It was only then that I noticed Alison and Claire both had their iPhones out and had obviously taken photos of the whole thing.

Alison grinned at me maliciously, flicking her eyes over my barely there skirt. "Ho. Ho. Ho."

'Tis the season, all right.

To make me want to crawl under a rock and die of mortification.

And don't miss Jane's story

INVISIBLE,

coming next year!

There is nothing surprising about my life.

Seriously. The list of things I haven't done far exceeds the coming-of-age things I have experienced. I've never been bad. No tagging graffiti on my high school walls, no toilet-papering my neighbor's house, no long make-out sessions with a boyfriend until the car windows become foggy. I practically come with a PG-13 rating stamped on my forehead. The one remarkable thing about my past sixteen years of life is the complete lack of things to remark upon. Probably because I've made being invisible an art form. I can hide in plain sight just by being too boring to notice. It helps that everything about me is average: from my murky blue eyes and chestnut-auburn hair to my pale, gangly body.

And I know that I've got it good: the all-American life that most people only see in Gap commercials. White picket fence, bagged lunches, loving parents, perfect older sister—the whole package. Even my name is a cliché: Jane Smith. It also comes with the standard "you Jane, me Tarzan" jokes, which thankfully stopped early on in middle school. Unfortunately, the only time I'm noticed in most of my classes is when a teacher says, "See how the date of this essay is double spaced beneath Jane Smith? Oh. We have a Jane Smith here, now, don't we? Isn't that funny! Don't try to turn this paper in, Jane!" I've gotten really good at faking smiles when teachers chuckle over the sheer coincidence that an example and a student share the same name.

Anyway, most of the time I am fine with my "average-ness," or whatever you want to call it. My mantra has always been, "Better ignored than ridiculed." When you attend Smith High School, in Forest Grove, Oregon—a stunningly mediocre school in a seriously lame town—you have to accept that things can go one of two ways: boring or brutal.

Just because I've managed to live drama free doesn't mean it's easy to escape scrutiny from the effortlessly cool crowd. Out of my friends I'm the only one who has maintained a low profile. That's how I've survived three years of high school without making a single enemy. I'm never harassed in the hallways, mocked in the gym locker room, or ridiculed to my face. Not everyone, including my best friends Kenzie, Corey, and Isobel, can say the same. But now that Corey is dating the lead singer from ReadySet and Kenzie is in a relationship with Logan, being invisible tends to be . . . lonely.

Anyhow, you would think that I'd avoid the madness, the three-ring media circus in the wake of the YouTube video. And in some ways, you would be right. For the most part I stayed in the shadows. But that's because the story, not the writer, gets attention. So even though I'm the girl who wrote an article for her school newspaper that nobody—not even the dedicated snoops at *People* magazine—saw coming, I remained Invisible.

Except . . . I did accidentally snag the attention of some celebrities. Turns out, people tend to get really upset when their innermost secrets are splashed all over the front page. When you outrage the rich, the powerful and the famous, they tend to come at you with everything in their arsenal. Not exactly a fair fight for a puny high school student. That's the part of journalism class that I wasn't warned about: it's a narrow line between byline and headline.

It's just too bad I didn't realize before I began writing how one story could fully blast my well-ordered, well-regulated, well-planned life to hell.